No Sacrifice Too Great

No Sacrifice Too Great

Volume 6 of the Cutler Family Chronicles

William C. Hammond

McBooks Press

Guilford, Connecticut

To Sheree Mayes Fenwick
A lady of grace and beauty
who brought light into darkness
and bestowed the ultimate gift
of renewed life

McBooks Press

An imprint of Globe Pequot, the trade division of
The Rowman & Littlefield Publishing Group, Inc.
4501 Forbes Blvd., Ste. 200
Lanham, MD 20706
www.rowman.com

Distributed by NATIONAL BOOK NETWORK

British Library Cataloguing in Publication Information available

Library of Congress Cataloging-in-Publication Data

Names: Hammond, William C., 1947– author.
Title: No sacrifice too great / William C. Hammond.
Description: Guilford, Connecticut : McBooks Press, [2022] | Series: The
   Cutler family chronicles ; volume 6 | Summary: "The sixth volume in the
   award-winning series profiling the American perspective in the Age of
   Sail. Chronicles the swashbuckling adventures of the Cutler family as
   the United States takes on Great Britain in the War of 1812"—Provided
   by publisher.
Identifiers: LCCN 2021021608 (print) | LCCN 2021021609 (ebook) | ISBN
   9781493058174 (cloth) | ISBN 9781493058181 (epub)
Subjects: GSAFD: Historical fiction.
Classification: LCC PS3608.A69586 N6 2022 (print) | LCC PS3608.A69586
   (ebook) | DDC 813/.6—dc23
LC record available at https://lccn.loc.gov/2021021608
LC ebook record available at https://lccn.loc.gov/2021021609

♾™ The paper used in this publication meets the minimum requirements of American National Standard for Information Sciences—Permanence of Paper for Printed Library Materials, ANSI/NISO Z39.48-1992.

Contents

Acknowledgments vii
Prologue ix

CHAPTER 1: 41°42'N 55°33'W. 1
CHAPTER 2: Boston, Massachusetts 19
CHAPTER 3: Lynnhaven Bay, Virginia 37
CHAPTER 4: Lake Ontario. 49
CHAPTER 5: Boston, Massachusetts 65
CHAPTER 6: Lake Erie. .75
CHAPTER 7: Thames River, Upper Canada 89
CHAPTER 8: Alexandria, Virginia 97
CHAPTER 9: Hingham, Massachusetts. 107
CHAPTER 10: Alexandria, Virginia. 125
CHAPTER 11: Plattsburgh, New York 145
CHAPTER 12: Hingham, Massachusetts 159
CHAPTER 13: North Point, Maryland 171
CHAPTER 14: Grand Terre, Louisiana 187
CHAPTER 15: New Orleans, Louisiana 199

Historical Footnotes 221

By the Eternal, they shall not sleep on our soil.
—GEN. ANDREW JACKSON, NEW ORLEANS, LOUISIANA,
DECEMBER 23, 1814

Acknowledgments

THE PUBLICATION OF THIS BOOK MARKS, TO DATE, TWENTY YEARS OF work on the Cutler Family Chronicles. When I set out to begin research for *A Matter of Honor* in 1999, my family suspected that I had taken leave of my senses, and that my resolve to write not one but six or more novels of historical fiction would lead to bitter disappointment if not outright disaster. Contrary to their understandable fears, however, the development of this series has been, in several important ways, a seminal event in my personal and professional development.

In any such literary endeavor, legions of people both known and previously unknown come to the fore to offer support, suggestions, and critiques. Certain of these people are near and dear to my heart—my beloved late wife, Victoria, first among them, followed closely by our three sons: Churchill, Brooks, and Harrison. Others have contributed with a suggestion here or a word of encouragement there. Such is the motivational elixir of all writers. Victoria is gone now, a victim of cancer in 2011, but her legacy lives on in this and in all volumes of the Chronicles.

It is, of course, impossible to acknowledge all those who have blessed my life with their involvement in my writing. I can only pray that they know who they are and that they are valued beyond words. That reality notwithstanding, there are a small number of individuals whose assistance in, and support of, this book's creation go far beyond any call to duty, friendship, or family loyalty. The gratitude I feel for the people listed below is immense.

Jess M. Brallier has been my friend, publishing colleague, and fellow author since we started working together at Little, Brown more than forty years ago. I continue to cherish his insights, wisdom, and counsel on a daily basis, which is why he has been a reader of my books from day one.

Mindy Conner of Winston-Salem, North Carolina, has served as my editor for many years. Not only is she the finest editor of my acquaintance, she is one of the finest people I have ever known.

My literary agent, Richard Curtis of Richard Curtis Associates, New York City. Over the years Richard and I have developed a meaningful and productive relationship, one I continue to value highly. It was Richard who forged the propitious business relationship with Globe Pequot/McBooks Press when events in the publishing industry necessitated that I find a new publisher for my books.

George D. Jepson, the editorial director of McBooks Press. When approached by Richard Curtis, George jumped at the opportunity to bring the Cutler Family Chronicles under the umbrella of his successful publishing program. His support of, and enthusiasm for, my writing means more to me than I can properly express.

Judy and Clyde Biddle, two dear and lifelong friends, offered me their lovely home in Pinehurst, North Carolina, as a writing venue in a village that is a writer's paradise. The first half of this novel was written in Pinehurst. Judy and Clyde's love and generosity have made this book possible.

Lastly, my love and gratitude go to my present wife, Sheree Fenwick. This book is dedicated to her. As the result of sharing similar stories of grief and recovery, Sheree and I have made a new life together. The second half of this book was written in her home in Puhoi, New Zealand. I thank Sheree, and I thank the members of her wonderful family—Sean, Holly, Chelsea, Luka, Chloe, and Esme—for similarly opening their hearts and homes to me. I love you all.

William C. Hammond III
Puhoi, New Zealand

Prologue

THE DEBACLE KNOWN TO HISTORY AS THE CHESAPEAKE AFFAIR HAD humiliated the nation and enflamed its citizens. That a Royal Navy frigate could fire with impunity into a U.S. Navy frigate was intolerable to an American public already fuming over Britain's transgressions at sea. The United States, after all, was at peace with Great Britain. What possible justification could there be for such an overt act of war? In home waters, by God!

No sooner had USS *Chesapeake* limped back to her home port in Norfolk, Virginia, than War Hawks in Congress were pounding the drums of retribution. Secretary of State James Madison dispatched hot words of protest to Whitehall in London while President Thomas Jefferson urged citizens of the seventeen states to remain calm. He, too, was incensed. But to his mind this was not the moment for the United States to pick a fight with Great Britain.

That was five years ago, in June 1807. Much had happened before that date, and much more would happen after it to fan the flames of war. At the crux of the matter, from the American perspective, was the impressment of American sailors by the Royal Navy and the right of free trade—even to France, Britain's ancient enemy. Added to that was Britain's flagrant support of the Shawnees and other Indian nations within the Illinois, Indiana, Michigan, and Mississippi territories. These Indians were stirring up trouble on the western frontier, and the British seemed only too happy to oblige them with weapons and whatever else they required to advance their common cause against the United States. In 1811 William Henry Harrison, governor of the Indiana Territory, had defeated the Indian leader Tecumseh at Tippecanoe and destroyed his base of operations, but that surprise raid had served only to strengthen Tecumseh's ties to the British.

The British, of course, had a somewhat different perspective. In their eyes they were in a fight for national survival, and therefore nothing was off-limits or sacrosanct. While Napoleon possessed the world's strongest army, Britain possessed the world's strongest navy, and the Lords of the Admiralty were determined to do whatever was necessary to maintain that status. The Royal Navy and its impressment gangs were thus given free rein to seize sailors wherever they could find them to bolster the 140,000 crewmen required to man Britain's five hundred active warships, eighty-three of which were cruising in North American waters in 1811. Shipboard life was often spartan and brutal in these vessels, inspiring many British tars to jump ship to the more amenable accommodations found in American warships and merchantmen. Three such deserters, all claiming to be American citizens, had run from a Royal Navy brig anchored in Lynnhaven Bay and taken refuge in USS *Chesapeake* at the Washington Navy Yard. When Capt. James Barron, under sail to the Mediterranean, refused to give them up, Captain Humphreys of HMS *Leopard*, acting on orders from his superior officer in Halifax, blasted the American frigate into compliance.

In addition to regaining men viewed as British citizens, and thus subject to service in His Majesty's navy, Britain sought to deprive France of the vast stores of food and supplies being conveyed to Europe in American holds. Only by blockading European ports could Britain effectively deny French soldiers the wherewithal to continue France's quest for global domination. Besides, was not France also threatening the United States with its infamous Berlin and Milan Decrees? Bloody well right it was, and where was the outrage in America over *those* abominations? So if the fledgling United States wanted to stick its nose in where it didn't belong and ignore international realities, that was jolly well too bad for them. Americans would suffer the consequences.

Americans did suffer. And not just at the hands of the British and the French. They suffered from rulings of their own government. In a futile attempt to punish those two countries for their manifold sins, President Jefferson, in one of his last acts in office, imposed an embargo on trade to and from *every* nation. Problem was, those nations didn't give a damn; their merchants carried on trade as usual. As a result, only Americans were hurt by the embargo, especially New England families such as the Cutlers of Hingham, Massachusetts, who depended on the carrying trade for their livelihood. In one of his first acts as the new president in 1809, James Madison repealed the embargo and replaced it with the Non-Intercourse Act, another sorry piece of legislation that sought to punish England or France, whichever country interfered the most with American trade and sailors' rights—which, of course, was Great Britain since Britannia ruled the waves. Britannia also accounted for the vast majority of exports from and imports into the United States, so once again the American public was made to suffer.

Jefferson and Madison were correct on one issue, however: The U.S. Army was woefully ill prepared to wage war even as war broke out. Precious few senior officers had battlefield experience, and the handful of soldiers under their command had received only token training. The U.S. Navy, however, was another matter. Although it was only eighteen years old in 1812 and boasted but three active frigates and a handful of smaller vessels, embedded in its five-thousand-man muster roll were officers and sailors as seasoned and competent as any in the Royal Navy. "Preble's Boys"—the captains, lieutenants, and midshipmen who had learned their trade while serving under Commo. Edward Preble in the Mediterranean during the war against Tripoli—were men of exceptional skill and daring. Several of the older ones had also served under Commo. Thomas Truxtun in the Quasi-War with France in the late 1790s.

Among Preble's Boys was young James Cutler, currently serving as second lieutenant in USS *Constitution*. Jamie's older brother, Will, was serving in a similar capacity under Capt. Oliver Hazard Perry in a ship to be determined. Their father, Richard Cutler, now retired, had served in the old Continental Navy and had commanded his own ship in the Barbary campaign in North Africa. The ways of the sea and the discipline it demands were deeply rooted in the Cutler family's heritage.

Loyal Americans though they were, the Cutlers, like most New England families, vehemently opposed war with Great Britain even though their ships and sailors were often the prey being hunted by Royal

Navy vessels. Their pedigree, after all, was English, and the Cutlers had English relatives living in England and on a family-owned sugar plantation on the island of Barbados in the West Indies. The family's focus remained on the China trade of the Far East. To them and others like them, the very thought of provoking another war with Great Britain was foolhardy and reckless to the extreme.

Their protests and warnings, however, were drowned out in Congress by the stirring oratory of such War Hawks as Henry Clay of Kentucky and John C. Calhoun of South Carolina, who insisted eloquently that America had the sacred duty to restore her national honor and uphold international law. To such men, too, war presented an ideal opportunity to deal once and for all with the Indian menace on America's western frontier. They also had their sights set on low-lying fruit in Canada—land and other riches ripe for the picking while the bulk of British land forces were occupied in Europe.

It was as though a mighty river fed by countless smaller streams was raging out of control and spilling into a whipped up, white-capped bay, and no one in Washington or elsewhere had the will or skill to check its flow. By the dawn of 1812 a mantle of inevitability was settling over the American nation. Seeing no practical way to buck the tides of history, on June 18, 1812, President James Madison signed a formal declaration of war against the United Kingdom of Great Britain and Ireland.

CHAPTER ONE

41°42'N 55°33'W

August 19, 1812

"DECK THERE!"

Midn. Richard Curtis, stationed at the base of the mainmast, looked up into great clouds of white canvas where the leeches of topsails shivered in the stiffening breeze. Perched 150 feet up on the topgallant yard, a quartermaster's mate on lookout duty was pointing off to starboard. The voice Curtis had heard, however, had come not from the lookout but from an able-rated sailor stationed halfway down the mast on the fighting top.

"Deck, aye!" Curtis called up through cupped hands. "What is it, Brace?"

"Ayres has spotted a ship ahead, sir," Brace called down. "She's hull down on a starboard tack."

"Bearing?"

"West-southwesterly, sir. She's ship-rigged and flying all plain sail to royals!"

"Is she keeping company?" Curtis asked significantly.

The question was relayed up to Ayres. Several moments later the reply was shouted down to Brace and on to Curtis. "Apparently not, sir."

"Very well, Brace. I shall inform Mr. Cutler."

The young midshipman quickstepped aft on the flush deck to where Jamie Cutler, the ship's current senior officer of the deck, stood afore the mizzenmast in front of two fellow commissioned officers, the sailing master, and three midshipmen. Behind them, two quartermaster's mates worked the great double wheel at the helm.

Curtis snapped the duty officer a crisp salute and made his report.

"Thank you, Mr. Curtis," Jamie said upon its conclusion. "You may return to station. Keep me informed."

"Aye, aye, sir."

For several moments Jamie stood in silent contemplation, mentally digesting what Curtis had told him. He chewed on his lower lip as he glanced up to the mizzen truck where a broad pennant flapped furiously in the northerly breeze under a pewter-gray sky. *Constitution* was on a southerly course on a larboard tack. Courses, topsails, topgallants, jibs, and spanker—a good number of the ship's three dozen sails—were propelling her along at twelve knots, close to her maximum hull speed. And out of sight to him and the others on deck sailed another ship following a more westerly course. That she was flying all plain sail to royals suggested that she was not a merchantman. That she was following such a course further suggested that she was making for Halifax, Nova Scotia, home port for the North American Station of the Royal Navy.

"Mr. Shippen!" Jamie suddenly cried out.

A midshipman stepped forward. "Sir!"

"Pass word for Mr. Adams," referring to the boatswain. "Mr. Stewart!"

A second midshipman stepped forward.

"Please give the captain my respects and inform him that his presence is requested on deck."

"Aye, aye, sir!" Stewart saluted and disappeared down the aft companionway ladder.

In short order a man of impressive build with wavy black hair and long sideburns on an otherwise clean-shaven face emerged from below onto the weather deck. He was clad in buff trousers, a loose-fitting white linen shirt, and a sea-blue undress uniform coat adorned with gold buttons, gold edging, and twin gold epaulets. In 1799, during the war with France in the Caribbean, he had served as first lieutenant under Capt. Silas Talbot in *Constitution*. Later, during the Barbary War, he had commanded the schooner USS *Enterprise* and, later still, the brig USS *Argus*, in which he played a pivotal role in the naval bombardment and subsequent seizure of the Tripolitan seaport of Derne. For services becoming a naval officer, two years earlier at age thirty-three, Isaac Hull had been appointed captain of *Constitution*, one of the four superfrigates that projected the latent power and prestige of the fledgling U.S. Navy onto the world stage.

"What do we have, Mr. Cutler?" Hull inquired as he adjusted the fit of his fore-and-aft cocked hat.

Jamie touched the front end of his hat. "Good afternoon, Captain. Seaman Ayres has sighted sails of consequence heading on a southwesterly course. According to Ayres she is sailing solo. On the assumption she is British and you wish to give chase, I have summoned the bosun."

"I see. I assume we remain on course?

"We do, sir. South by west."

"Very well." Hull swung his gaze to his first lieutenant, who up to this point had stood by in silence. "Any thoughts to share about this mystery ship, Mr. Morris?"

Charles Morris locked his blue-gray eyes on his captain. "I agree with Mr. Cutler that she's not likely one of Commodore Rodgers's squadron," he said, and Hull nodded. The twenty-eight-year-old officer from Connecticut was a man of few words, but when he did choose to speak, he normally had good cause. He, too, had served with distinction in the Caribbean against France and in the Mediterranean against the Barbary pirates. In the daring midnight raid in Tripoli harbor that had recaptured and then set fire to USS *Philadelphia*—thus preventing the 36-gun U.S. Navy frigate from being added to the Tripolitan naval fleet—Morris not only had volunteered to join Capt. Stephen Decatur in what had every trapping of a suicide mission, he was the first American to jump aboard the doomed warship and have at it with Arab sailors and Marines on guard duty. "If what Ayres says is true—and I have every confidence it is, given the measure of the man—we need not be concerned that we have again stumbled upon a British squadron."

"Let us hope not," Hull said with a wry smile.

There was reason for this gentle stab at mirth, although it had taken the passage of time to find even a tinge of humor in what had transpired. A month earlier, *Constitution* had unwittingly sailed into a viper's nest.

With orders to join USS *United States* and the squadron of Commo. John Rodgers, *Constitution* had departed Boston for the prearranged rendezvous area north of Bermuda. Not finding the American squadron there, Captain Hull had, on his own accord, sailed north to the mouth of the St. Lawrence River to harry British shipping at that critical crossroads of Canadian commerce. Along the way there they had sighted five ships that Hull and his officers took to be the ships of Rodgers's squadron. When upon closer inspection these ships turned out to be five British frigates, *Constitution* had quickly turned southward, only to become becalmed. It was only after a fifty-seven-hour chase featuring a judicious use of kedge anchors as proposed by Lieutenant Morris—coupled with the coming of darkness and what seemed to be a divinely inspired burst of wind—that "the pride of New England" had eluded disaster.

"Mr. Cutler? Further thoughts?" Captain Hull inquired of his second officer.

"I agree with Mr. Morris," the young man replied. He also had served under Commodore Preble in the Mediterranean in *Constitution* and had played a meaningful role in the midnight raid. That service not only gained him a promotion from midshipman to lieutenant, it put him among Preble's Boys, the American naval elite, and made him a man whose opinions deserved consideration. "If she's not ours, she must be British," he continued. "No other nation has men-of-war in these waters. The question I ask myself is why she is sailing solo. These days, that is not the norm for Royal Navy frigates."

"Your conclusion?"

"Well, sir, if indeed she is British, she's likely making for Halifax. Perhaps she is in distress or in need of repairs. If so, we can use that to our advantage."

"Just so, Mr. Cutler. My sentiments exactly."

Before them, having just arrived aft, the boatswain stood at attention. He was dressed in typical sailor's garb of loose-fitting duck trousers, white cotton shirt, black neckerchief, and a low-crowned black hat. His sole symbol of authority was the silver bosun's whistle hanging at his chest from a leather lanyard slung around his neck. He saluted the captain when Hull noticed him.

"Mr. Adams," Hull said to him, "we have sighted a ship that may be a British warship. Until we have confirmed her identity, we shall clap on all sail in pursuit. In the meantime, we must assume we are sailing into battle. Inform your mates and stand by to shorten sail. If I need that done, I shall need it done smartly. Understood?"

"Aye, aye, sir." The warrant officer saluted before turning on his heels.

Hull spoke next to Samuel Eames, the wizened old sailing master. Of the entire ship's complement, including the captain, he was the most seasoned and skilled sailor.

"Mr. Eames, we shall bring her up and lay her on a course west by north. We'll approach our quarry from the north. That will give us the weather gauge should we decide to come down on her."

"Aye, aye, sir."

Captain Hull turned to his second lieutenant. "You have the gun deck, Mr. Cutler. But first, if you please, light aloft and tell me what you see. I too have every confidence in Seaman Ayres. But another set of eyes up there won't hurt. And 'tis your pair of eyes that I require at the moment."

James Cutler touched his hat. "Understood, sir." As he began walking forward toward the mainmast, he heard Hull send a midshipman down two decks to the wardroom to summon Archibald Henderson, captain of Marines. Hull then ordered his first lieutenant to bring *Constitution* on a new course to bring the wind from her larboard quarter to her starboard beam, an evolution that demanded attention to braces, buntlines, sheets, and a host of other mechanisms dedicated to the ship's mile upon mile of standing and running rigging. As *Constitution*'s bow swung to starboard—in tune with the harsh shriek of bosun's whistles piping the captain's orders throughout the ship—three staysails sprouted between the mizzenmast and mainmast, and another three between the mainmast and foremast. With this additional press of sail, much of the ship's maximum 42,000 square feet of canvas was now pulling its weight.

At the base of the mainmast, James Cutler handed Midshipman Curtis his hat and stepped out onto the thick horizontal plank that defined the starboard mainmast chain-wale. Grabbing hold of the tar-encrusted shrouds, he climbed with determined and uninterrupted steps up the ratlines, using the frigate's slight heel to larboard to facilitate his climb. He kept his gaze up, never down, until he had pulled himself up through the lubber's hole and onto the semicircular platform at the maintop. Only then did he chance a glance down at the clusters of tiny heads craned up, watching and waiting. Without a word to Billy Brace he continued crawling upward to the horizontal cross-timbers that spread the narrower shrouds leading to the juncture of the topmast and topgallant mast.

Unlike his father, Jamie Cutler had never suffered from a fear of heights. As boys growing up on the South Shore of Massachusetts, he and Will had enjoyed going to Hingham Harbor and skylarking in the standing rigging of vessels in their family's merchant fleet, often vying against each other to be first to slap a hand on the mainmast truck. Will had usually won the contest; he was older, more skilled, and consumed by a bluster that many local residents found daunting. On one occasion, with their mother watching anxiously from the dock, Jamie's foot had slipped off a ratline. Although he had caught himself in time—and Will had double-timed over to him to make certain he had—Katherine Cutler had never again ventured to the harbor to watch her sons at play.

Jamie answered the salute of Seaman Ayres and then secured himself with hempen cords near the spreaders abaft the crosstrees. Up here, the breeze was stiffer and the effect of wind-whipped waves more pronounced. Still, the ship's 2,200-ton displacement kept such undulations to a minimum.

"Where away?" he asked when Ayres handed him a long glass. Coaxing back strands of chestnut-brown hair blown free from their queue, Jamie brought the glass to his eye and peered through it to where Ayres was pointing. And there she was, hull up, sailing slowly away from *Constitution* on a slant that revealed her stern and larboard side. As Jamie brought the ship into clearer focus, he immediately saw several distinguishing features that his father and other naval officers had impressed upon him from a tender age. What she was was obvious. Any lubber from Concord could identify the ship rig and sleek lines of a frigate. That she was British was equally obvious: A blue Royal Navy ensign fluttered defiantly from the truck of each of her three masts. Nonetheless, she was no ordinary British frigate. What was unique about her—and what gave away her provenance—was her low tumble home; her long, thin bow-sprit; and the narrow cut of her yards and sails. This ship might be flying the British jack, he mused, but she was not British-built.

"Sir?" Ayres inquired when Jamie returned the glass to him. "Can you make out her name?"

"Not at this distance," Jamie replied as he freed himself from the ropes. "But that's hardly necessary. Has she added sail?"

"None that I can see, sir," Ayres shouted over the thrum of wind. "To the contrary, she's taken in her royals."

"Very well. Keep a weather eye on her and report everything you see. And David," he added, using a first-name familiarity aloft that he would never have used on deck, "be careful up here. We can't afford to lose you. Got it?"

Their eyes locked for a moment. "Aye, sir, I have it." The look Ayres gave Jamie spoke volumes. All the crew knew Jamie Cutler as a man who looked after the welfare of his men. "And thank ye kindly for saying that, sir."

"Right, then."

Jamie seized hold of a taut hempen backstay leading down to the starboard side of the weather deck. Wrapping his legs around it, he descended hand under hand until he reached the chain-wale. From there he jumped down onto the deck and strode purposely aft past the inquisitive stares of sailors and idlers to the helm where he saluted Hull.

"She's *Guerrière*, Captain," he said, referring to a French fifth-rate that HMS *Blanche* had captured off the Faroe Islands six years earlier and pressed into service in the Royal Navy.

Hull narrowed his eyes. "You're certain of that, Lieutenant?"

"Quite certain, Captain. Her lines and sails give her away, and I had a glimpse of her last month. As you may recall, she took part in that chase."

"Yes, I do recall that, and I thank you for the reminder of it," Hull snorted. "Well, it didn't take long to establish her pedigree, did it? Is she showing us her heels?"

"Doesn't appear to be, sir. Surely she has seen us. But according to Ayres, she is not adding sail. In fact, she appears to be shortening it."

"Wants a fight, does she? Well, by God, she's come to the right place for that!" Staring dead ahead, Hull invested several moments in considering his choices. Then: "We shall clear for action, Mr. Morris. I shall have the royal yards sent down and the remaining yards slung with chains." The latter command was a precaution to prevent heavy spars from crashing onto the deck in battle should they be shattered by shot. "Mr. Cutler, you may advise the gun captains to loose the guns on both sides. Double-shot them with grape and ball. I aim to get in close, to within piston shot. Mr. Eames, steady as she goes."

"Steady as she goes," Eames calmly repeated the order to the two seamen at the double wheel.

"Shall we beat to quarters, sir?" Morris asked, seeking clarification.

"Yes, Mr. Morris, we shall," Hull replied.

"*We shall beat to quarters!*" Morris shouted out a moment later through a speaking trumpet. "*Clear for action!*" Young Marine drummers on the two upper decks instantly launched into a rigorous staccato tattoo.

As the screech of bosun's whistles broke out anew, Jamie strode as quickly as naval decorum allowed to the large, rectangular hatchway located amidships. Broad wooden steps led down to the gun deck, where a healthy portion of the ship's complement of 440 men was standing by twenty-six ten-foot, three-ton long guns, each gun painted a gleaming black and resting upon a truck painted blood red to match the paint on the deck. Within minutes, the inner-facing hard canvas walls of the captain's day cabin at the far end aft and its furnishings were removed and stowed below, along with everything else movable that might explode into a torrent of deadly wooden missiles if struck by enemy shot. As the walls were removed, four additional 24-pounder guns came into view, two to a side.

"Gun captains!" Jamie shouted from the base of the steps through a speaking trumpet, singling out the lieutenants commanding the gun batteries and the senior midshipmen and gunner's mates responsible for the proper service of each individual long gun. But in truth he was also addressing the wormers, rammers, spongers, and others within the twelve-man gun crews attached to each gun. "As you can hear, Captain Hull is ordering us to clear for action." After allowing a rollicking good cheer to erupt, he continued, "Loose the guns and remove tampions," referring to the wooden stopper at each gun's muzzle, "then double-shot each gun with ball and grape."

As the gun crews jumped to comply, other sailors pumped a thin film of water onto the deck and sprinkled sand across its forty-foot beam to afford better footing in spilt blood. Guns were released from their lashings and rolled inboard by their side-tackle. Powder monkeys, the eight- to ten-year-old boys assisting the gunners, appeared from the ship's magazine on the lowest deck carrying twenty-four-pound round shot. Other boys toted canisters of grapeshot: small cast-iron balls bound together by a canvas bag that, when fired from a cannon, had the lethal effect of a mammoth shotgun blast.

Above him, on the weather deck, Jamie heard the deep voice of Archibald Henderson, his commands echoed in tone and urgency by his Marine lieutenant, William Bush, and his sergeant, John Brady. Many in the fifty-four-man Marine guard contingent were ordered to duty at the twenty-four 32-pounder carronades: snub-nosed, smooth-bore anti-personnel weapons mounted on casters to permit better aim and maximum killing efficiency at close range. Twelve of these guns were positioned on the quarterdeck astern, six to a side. A similar array was posted at the bow, just behind two 24-pounder bow chasers. Henderson ordered his riflemen up the ratlines to the three fighting tops with rifles, grenades, and swivel guns. Still other Marines were being deployed behind the bedroll-stuffed netting that ran along the perimeter of the weather deck. The remaining few were placed on guard duty at the companionways on the weather and gun decks with orders to prevent anyone without proper authorization from going below to the relative safety of the berthing and orlop decks.

After inspecting each gun on the gun deck and its crew—offering encouragement, instruction, or reprimand where warranted—Jamie Cutler walked back up the stairs into the cleansing breeze of a late summer afternoon on the North Atlantic. A quick survey of the weather deck confirmed that *Constitution* was well prepared for battle. Marines were manning their stations awaiting further orders, as were sailors in the rigging and on deck. A glance up confirmed, to his surprise, that the fore course and main course had already been brailed up and were hanging in their gear, the topsails had been double-reefed, the topgallants were hanging loosely folded on yards lowered to their caps, and all six staysails and the flying jib had been taken in. A quick glance ahead indicated why *Constitution*'s sail plan had been so quickly reduced. She had closed fast on *Guerrière*—so fast it all but confirmed that the British captain was far more inclined to fight than flee, and that despite a glaring disparity in both manpower and firepower between the two ships.

Typical British disdain for American arms, Jamie thought. He was not surprised by such bravado and indeed was impressed by it. Never had he known a Royal Navy captain to shy away from an enemy, whatever the odds might be against him.

Suddenly Midshipman Curtis cried out in a voice fraught with excitement, "She's laying her main topsail to the mast!" Then, seconds later, "She's turning into the wind and presenting her broadside!"

His report was hardly necessary. The two ships were close enough for those on *Constitution*'s deck to clearly discern their adversary throwing down the gauntlet with her topsail and coming into the wind as close as she could lie to present her starboard battery to her enemy coming at her from behind, bow-on.

Jamie clambered back down the steps and picked up the speaking trumpet. "Steady, men. Steady. Run out your guns, both sides. Wait for my command!"

The deck instantly came alive with the grunts of men and the rumble of heavy guns being hauled out until the front of each truck bumped against the bulwark and the muzzle was fully extended out its port. Then dead silence pervaded the deck, broken only by the moan of wind high in the rigging and the faint gurgle of seawater running along the frigate's sides. Jamie drew out his watch and noted the time: nearly one bell into the first dogwatch.

Returning the timepiece to his waistcoat pocket, he again reviewed the math in his head. Although he did not know the enemy ship's exact armament, a fifth-rate in the Royal Navy traditionally carried thirty-eight guns but could, as did *Constitution*, carry additional ordnance at the discretion of her captain. Her long guns were likely 18-pounders, as opposed to *Constitution*'s 24-pounders, and she would have fewer of them given her shorter length. Her carronades would likely be of equal caliber but also fewer in number. So *Constitution* carried a considerably greater weight of broadside and a ship's complement nearly twice that of a ship of *Guerrière*'s size. Comforting thoughts, perhaps, but Lt. James Cutler understood better than most men on that gun deck that such comparisons could be misleading. *Guerrière* held one critical advantage over her adversary: Her officers, gun crews, sailors, and Marines had been on a war footing for two decades, and as a result were far more seasoned than *Constitution*'s untested crew.

Of a sudden, the angry thunder of cannon intruded upon the private thoughts of every man jack on *Constitution*. Instinctively, sailors, gunners, and powder monkeys braced for impact. But none was forthcoming.

"Fell well short!" someone shouted.

"She's wearing ship!" someone else shouted in warning. "She means to present her larboard battery!" Jamie pictured the British gun crews removing quoins from their guns to lift the barrels to maximum elevation. Then, close by, a single blast of cannon fire sent a quiver down the length of *Constitution*.

"Ours," Jamie said to no one in particular. "A bow chaser. A ranging shot, no doubt. Steady, men. Wait for my order."

One angry report followed another and another and another. The men below heard the unnerving whine of an eighteen-pound ball ripping through rigging and tearing canvas overhead.

Jamie felt *Constitution* swing off the wind to parallel *Guerrière*'s course just as Midn. Henry Bancroft's head appeared in the open hatchway above. "The captain's compliments, Mr. Cutler," he shouted down, "and you may fire the starboard battery as your guns bear!"

Jamie waved a hand in acknowledgment and strode to a gun port hinged open by two chains running from the top of the lid and through the hull. Peering out, he saw *Constitution* still closing on *Guerrière*, the result of Captain Hull ordering the main topgallant sail to be raised. *Constitution*'s bowsprit had pulled even with *Guerrière*'s stern, with less than a cable's length of somber-looking water separating the two. Now even with her larboard quarter. Now her beam. *Constitution*'s forward starboard guns and *Guerrière*'s aft larboard guns faced each other barrel to barrel.

Jamie stepped back to amidships and took up the speaking trumpet. Struggling to keep his tone casual, he silently counted to ten to allow the two ships to lie side to side.

"Steady, men. Steady," he coaxed through the trumpet. "Remember: every other gun aimed at her masts. Steady . . . steady . . . *Now*, by God! Unleash hell, boys! *Fire!*"

A great cheer went up as the gun captain at number 1 gun at the bow jerked hard on a bronze lanyard, sending a sizzle down to the main charge in the barrel and igniting the six-pound bag of powder. Grape and a twenty-four-pound ball streaked forward and the gun's carriage lurched backward until checked by its breeching ropes. Down the line, one gun after another discharged its payload in an angry swirl of orange flame and white sparks, until number 29 gun, farthest aft on the starboard side, went silent, adding its aftermath to the eye-stinging, throat-parching acrid smoke consuming the gun deck.

"Reload!" Jamie shouted, the order immediately taken up by every gun captain on the starboard battery. Fanning away clouds of reeking smoke with their hands, gun crews furiously sponged out lingering sparks from the barrels before reloading the guns and ramming home powder, ball, and grape. But with the reload came a sudden cacophonous explosion from *Guerrière*'s broadside. The impact of several hundred pounds of hot metal streaking fifty yards through the air and slamming against *Constitution*'s hull was . . . nothing. The eighteen-pound balls bounced off the dense southern oak and plunged harmlessly into the ocean.

"Huzzah!" a sailor shouted. "Her hull is made of iron, boys! She's untouched!"

"*Reload!*" demanded 4th Lt. Henry Ballard, the battery's commander, in a fit of anger at the outburst.

Cheered on despite the reprimand, gun crews delivered another volley into the British ship's starboard side. But in the time it took them to fire off one broadside, *Guerrière*'s gun crews responded with two, most of them now aimed at *Constitution*'s rigging. From above on the weather deck they heard a scream of agony and, seconds later, the dull thud of a body hitting the deck.

For a quarter hour the two ships sailed abreast, slugging it out broadside to broadside. From above came the cries of officers exhorting sailors and Marines to stand to amid a barrage of flying wooden splinters, ricocheting pellets of grapeshot and rifle fire, and steel fists of cannon balls smashing across a deck made slick by the blood of the dead and dying. But the gun crews paid scant attention to all that. It was do or die where they were. The fear of imminent death from a ball crashing through an open port drove them inexorably forward to the call to arms and a duty drilled into them from their first day at sea.

Amid the hue and cry of battle came an unholy *crack* from across the short expanse of sea. Jamie glanced out a port to confirm its source: *Guerrière*'s mizzenmast had gone by the boards. He could not see the broken mast, only its ragged stump, but he noted that the mizzen rigging remained attached to the ship and was hanging over her starboard quarter. Already British sailors were rushing to the raised quarterdeck, braving a hail of American rifle and swivel gun fire to attack the downed rigging with tomahawks and hatchets in a desperate effort to hack it free. In what seemed a suspended flicker of time, Jamie saw four British sailors fall, to be instantly replaced by four others.

Returning amidships, Jamie picked up the speaking trumpet and raised a hand to the seven-foot deckhead to balance himself. "Well done, boys!" he cried out. "We've made a brig of her! Now let's make her a sloop!"

As men cheered, *Constitution* pulled ahead of the wing-clipped *Guerrière*, slowed by the debris hanging off her stern that was acting as a sea anchor. Jamie sensed what was coming even before Henry Bancroft's head again appeared at the open hatchway. "The captain's compliments, Mr. Cutler," the perspiring midshipman shouted down, "and we shall rake the enemy from the bow!"

The worst punishment a ship-of-war could endure was a rake from the stern. A ship might turn certain defeat into victory if her captain managed to turn his ship around and train her guns on the stern of his adversary to deliver a crash of multiple round shot through stern windows and down the full length of two decks, pulverizing everything in their path. The second-worst punishment was a rake from the bow.

"*Starboard guns!*" Jamie cried. "*Prepare to fire in sequence!*"

His order echoed down the line to battery commanders and from them to individual gun captains.

Guerrière's captain also sensed what was coming. He fought to mirror *Constitution's* maneuver by turning his ship to starboard and keeping the two ships broadside to broadside, but the drag of her mizzen rigging prevented her helm from answering. For a reason Jamie could not fathom, *Constitution*, too, was having trouble making the turn.

Suddenly, *Guerrière* slewed toward *Constitution* in a last-ditch stab to get under her stern and be the one doing the raking. As she did so, her bowsprit became entangled in *Constitution's* larboard mizzen rigging, locking the two frigates in a macabre counterclockwise dance orchestrated by a combination of fresh breeze and frothing sea. Guns on the upper decks of both ships kept firing, but now *Constitution* held the upper hand. Her hull remained impervious to the onslaught of *Guerrière's* shot, even at point-blank range, as her more powerful guns staved in enemy planking and blasted top-hamper into matchwood. At *Guerrière's* bow, two gun ports were gored by twenty-four-pound shot, leaving two ugly gaping holes and guns upended and rendered useless.

A barrage of small arms fire from high up in *Constitution's* rigging and from behind netting on her weather deck kept would-be enemy boarders at bay, forcing them to crouch low behind whatever cover they could find amid the blood and mayhem on *Guerrière's* deck.

In the continuous roil of wind and sea, *Guerrière* managed to pull away from *Constitution's* grasp. But the incessant pounding of *Constitution's* massive ordnance was taking a toll; the British ship's very fabric was coming undone. A second deafening *crack* signaled *Guerrière's* mainmast toppling over, taking with it most of what remained of the ship's rigging. Seconds later, a third *crack* resounded as her foremast fell forward into the sea.

"*Cease fire!*" Isaac Hull shouted from above. Seconds later the great guns fell silent.

Guerrière lay dead in the water, bobbing up and down, the three stumps of her downed masts silhouetted in the soft light and calming winds of late afternoon. For several minutes an eerie quiet reigned on the Atlantic as officers and crews of both ships took stock of the devastation they had wrought in less than an hour's time. Then, slowly, *Constitution* sagged off the wind and sailed off to take station a hundred yards away.

In the continuing silence, Jamie Cutler walked up the hatchway steps to the weather deck. A quick survey of the deck and rigging revealed torn canvas and sprung rigging, and the bodies of two sailors and three Marines lying face-up against the larboard bulwark. Two of them Jamie instantly recognized. One was William Bush, lieutenant of Marines, an officer of strong character and fierce loyalties. But it was at the sight of the second body that he paused to make the sign of the cross at his forehead and torso. It was that of Seaman David Ayres.

Jamie walked slowly toward the helm amid the bang of hammers and rasp of sails as the ship's carpenter and sailmaker and their mates set to work fashioning what repairs and jury-rig they could in the fading light of day. At the mizzen Jamie nodded to his captain and touched his hat.

"Casualties on the gun deck, Lieutenant?" Hull inquired. The tone of his voice matched the look in his eyes: somber, distant, sorrowful.

"No, sir," Jamie replied forthrightly. "No casualties and no damage to speak of."

"That, at least, is a comfort," Hull replied in the same tone. "By the grace of God our butcher's bill is modest. Fewer than ten men, I believe. However, I regret to inform you that Mr. Morris has suffered a wound to his abdomen. He is below in the care of Dr. Carleton."

"I am indeed sorry to hear that, Captain," Jamie said, "but we can take heart that Dr. Carleton is one of the best surgeons in the Navy."

"He won't be up and about any time soon, from what I am told, but Dr. Carleton believes he will recover." Hull sighed. "I shall sorely miss his wise counsel in the meantime." Then, with a slight smile he added, "But despite such bad tidings, I now find myself in a most fortunate position in that Mr. Morris's current incapacity makes you my acting first." He clapped Jamie on the shoulder. "And in that role I should like you to take the cutter over to *Guerrière* to see what assistance we might offer her captain. More to the point, we need to confirm that he has indeed struck his colors. I assume he has, but we can't act on that assumption. Sergeant Brady and six of his Marines will accompany you, as will my coxswain."

"Aye, aye, sir." Jamie said.

As Coxswain Edward Henderson directed the cutter and its six oarsmen toward *Guerrière*, Lt. Jamie Cutler, seated in the stern sheets in front of the American ensign and a white flag, surveyed the damage *Constitution* had inflicted on the enemy frigate. Precious little of what he saw would bring either joy or pride to any Lord of the Admiralty. She appeared to be nothing more than a floating hulk, a navigational hazard. As they neared, Jamie heard the familiar mournful crank of pumps waging war against seawater gathering in the bilges. Seeing no damage at or below her waterline, he speculated that the pumps actually might be winning the battle to keep the frigate afloat.

With the coxswain's command of "Toss oars!" the cutter glided forward under its own momentum until it bumped gently against what had been *Guerrière*'s larboard fore-chains. There, two of the Marines, under the watchful eyes of the others, secured her in tight next to the nine steps cut into the hull. As the senior officer on board, Jamie was first to grab hold of the twin hand ropes leading up to the weather deck. After stepping through the entry port, he turned to salute the quarterdeck and saw an officer approaching him wearing the full regalia of a Royal Navy post captain. The expression on the man's face reflected the state of his uniform: Both looked as grim and forlorn as the wreckage strewn about the deck. A splotch of dark blood soiled the exquisite fabric on the right arm of his gold-trimmed coat.

Jamie removed his hat and offered a slight bow. "Good evening, Captain," he said courteously. "I am James Cutler, acting first lieutenant of the United States ship *Constitution*, at your service."

"Good evening to you, Lieutenant," the officer said in turn, the inflections in his voice suggesting a family lineage rich in England's peerage. "I am Captain James Dacres of his Britannic Majesty's ship *Guerrière*. I apologize for not assembling a side party to pipe you aboard properly. As I am sure you can appreciate, preparing such a courtesy is rather beyond our competence at the moment."

As Sergeant Brady and his six blue-coated Marines stood stoically by with the butts of their sea-service rifles resting on the deck, Jamie tucked his hat under his left armpit and bowed again. "Yes, of course, Captain. Please do not be concerned. Captain Isaac Hull of *Constitution* sends his compliments and desires me to inquire if you have struck your colors."

"Does he indeed?" Dacres responded tartly. Although his tone remained somber, a faint smile floated across his face. "Well, let me see if I can shed light on the matter. My first lieutenant is dead, as is my sailing master and more than seventy of my crew at last count. Many others are wounded. Half my guns are out of action, and as you can plainly discern, I have no mast on which to display my colors. So yes, you may safely conclude that I have struck them."

Jamie maintained his deadpan expression. "Very well, Captain. Captain Hull also desires me to inquire if he may be of any assistance to you or your crew. I see that you are wounded. May my ship's surgeon attend to your needs? Dr. Carleton is an excellent physician."

"As is the physician aboard this ship. You have your own wounded to attend to, Lieutenant. Allow me to attend to mine. Night is soon upon us. Might I suggest that we reconvene in the morrow and assess our best course of action at that time?" Dacres swept the deck with his uninjured left arm. "Please assure your captain that I have no intention of making a dash for it during the night." His laugh held no humor.

"Yes, sir," Jamie said evenly. "We shall stand off and on throughout the night. At first light I shall return. If in the meantime you require assistance, you need only signal us with lanterns. We shall come right over."

"That is most noble of you, Lieutenant. Please thank your captain for me." Dacres made to withdraw his sword from its sheath buckled to a belt at his right hip. "And please accept my sword on his behalf."

"That will not be necessary, Captain." Jamie motioned to Brady to return the Marines to the cutter and then bowed to the British captain a final time. "I shall convey your gratitude to my captain, sir. I wish you well this evening, and I shall see you in the morning."

Toward noon the next morning, having deemed *Guerrière* beyond salvage, Isaac Hull ordered her remaining crew transferred to

Constitution and the British frigate set ablaze. As Captain Dacres watched at the American frigate's taffrail beside Captain Hull, the flames of the fires set at *Guerrière*'s bow and stern licked their way amidships and down to the orlop deck. When they broached her magazine, the ship exploded with such violence that her midsection lifted up out of the ocean in an inverted V before collapsing down onto the ocean and sinking rapidly. Within minutes, what the previous day had been the proud command of Captain James Richard Dacres, RN, was now open water.

"Mr. Cutler," Captain Hull said quietly into the ensuing silence. "I have invited Captain Dacres and his senior officers to dine with me in my cabin at two bells. My cabin should have been put back to rights by then. And if Providence continues to smile upon us, my steward will have drummed up something fit to serve distinguished company. You are most welcome to join us."

"Thank you, sir. I would be honored."

"Very well, Lieutenant. Now, if you please, shape a course for home. Our ship is in need of repairs, and the sooner we return to Boston, the sooner we may return to action. Plus, we have prisoners to deliver."

"A course for Boston, aye, Captain."

CHAPTER TWO

Boston, Massachusetts

September 1812

CITIZENS OF HULL ABROAD EARLY ON SUNDAY, AUGUST 30, WERE greeted by a remarkable and unexpected sight. It was not the blaze of the late summer sun languishing above Nantasket Road and casting its golden hues over the approaches to Boston Harbor. That phenomenon, however glorious, was typical of this time of year. Nor was it the façade of Boston Light, the seventy-five-foot-high conical lighthouse on Little Brewster Island. That impressive edifice had originally been constructed in 1718 before being demolished by British forces evacuating Boston in 1776 and then rebuilt seven years later. No, what demanded the attention of these citizens and set their hearts and minds awhirl was what they saw sailing between the Brewster Islands and Allerton Point at the northern tip of the Nantasket Peninsula. *Constitution* was returning home, and judging by the blue British ensign fluttering listlessly beneath the Stars and Stripes high on her ensign halyard, she was returning victorious. *Victorious, by God!*

In short order, those who had a horse handy were galloping down the seven-mile stretch of peninsula to spread the glad tidings to the neighboring villages of Duxbury, Scituate, Cohasset, Hingham, and Weymouth, and on to points northwest into the very heart of Boston. Church bells ringing in one steeple were echoed by bells in another steeple, and so on and so on, until within an impossibly short span of time the entire South Shore resounded with the joyous pealing—to an extent not heard in these parts since that unforgettable day fifteen years ago when the Cutler schooner *Falcon* returned to Boston from North Africa, carrying home a crew of American merchant sailors forced to languish for ten years in an Algerian prison. All of New England had rejoiced with the Cutler family that day, and with the families of other seamen whose kin had also been seized by Barbary pirates and ruthlessly punished for the sole crime of being American citizens.

Richard Cutler heard the bells of First Parish and Second Parish, the two churches closest to his home on South Street in Hingham, as he was sitting in his comfortable parlor reading the latest issue of the Boston newspaper *Columbian Centinel.* The big news of the day once again centered on the ongoing effects of the various embargos enacted by the Madison administration since President Jefferson imposed the original Embargo Act of 1807. Since that year, the article reported, British men-of-war had seized 389 American merchant ships with a cumulative value of ships and cargoes exceeding $30 million. At the same time, several thousand sailors—the vast majority of whom could offer proof of American citizenship—had been impressed from these vessels. Such proof notwithstanding, precious few of these sailors had been released.

Of course, now that war had been declared against Great Britain, such statistics served only to justify the declaration—if one believed that Britain alone was responsible for this deplorable state of affairs. Richard Cutler did not believe that, nor did the editorial page of the *Columbian Centinel* and most other publications in New England. Such voices of Federalism placed primary blame on the incompetence of a government that overvalued the rantings of War Hawks in Congress and other Americans either unaffected by or unmindful of the vital trade routes that tied the United States economically to Great Britain. Such exponents of war with the Mother Country seemed to care little for the financial welfare of their own country, and not a fig for the financial future of the Cutlers and other New England shipping families.

Richard folded the newspaper and placed it on a side table. The bells indicated that something was afoot, and it was obviously of great import. His first inclination was to walk to Caleb's house on Main Street. As the proprietor of Cutler & Sons, Richard's younger brother always seemed to have his finger on the pulse of current events, no matter how recent those events might be. But then he remembered that Caleb wasn't home. He and his wife, Joan, had sailed to Boston the previous day.

A knock on the front door brought him to his feet.

"I'll get it," a reedy voice declared from the kitchen.

"Don't trouble yourself, Edna," Richard called out to Edna Stowe, the woman who had unceremoniously served four generations of Cutlers with a hand that was at once both strict and solicitous. "I'm up."

"So am I." Edna's stooped form emerged from the kitchen, walking with slow, deliberate steps toward the front hallway. "Mr. Cutler!" she admonished as she passed by the parlor, "I may be getting on in years, but please God, I am still capable of answering the door!"

Richard smiled at a tone of voice he had heard ever more frequently since Edna turned fifty a quarter century earlier. His smile broadened when, a few moments later, he heard the door creak open and a close friend being welcomed inside. Agreen Crabtree had been Richard's shipmate since the earliest days of the first war with England. They had served together as midshipmen in *Ranger* under Captain John Paul Jones, and years later Agreen had served as Richard's executive officer in USS *Portsmouth*, an *Essex*-class frigate that had seen hot action in the war with Tripoli. During the intervening years they had shared duty on numerous naval and merchant vessels and had rubbed shoulders with many of the saints, scoundrels, and scofflaws of the modern age.

"Care for a cup of coffee, Mr. Crabtree?"

Agreen nodded. "I would, thank you, Edna. Lizzy filled me up this morning, but as usual, Zeke somehow managed t' drain it all out of me." His wife, Elizabeth, was Richard's cousin, and their precocious fourteen-year-old son kept both of them at their wits' end.

"You realize," Richard commented dryly, "that what you just said makes not the slightest lick of sense."

"Makes perfect sense t' me," Agreen replied. "So what else matters?"

"Point taken."

As Edna padded off to the kitchen, Agreen gave Richard a hard look. "Heard the news?"

"No. Just the bells. I'm hoping you'll tell me the news."

"*Constitution*'s back. And she's flyin' a British jack."

"Beneath our ensign?"

"You got it, matey."

"A victory, then."

"That's how I figure it."

Richard squeezed Agreen's shoulder. "You do have a knack for figuring things out, my friend. That's one of the many things I like about you." He shook his head as a surge of elation coursed through him. "No wonder everyone's all stirred up. This is the first good news since the war started."

He paused as Edna reappeared in the parlor bearing a tray with a small silver pot of coffee and two cups that she placed on an oval table in front of the sofa. "Thank you, Edna," Richard said absently, lost in thought. Then, to Agreen: "Help yourself, Agee, and have a seat." He sat silently until Agreen handed him a cup. When he spoke, it was to the floor and in a distracted tone. "That is welcome news. This afternoon I'll send a dispatch to the Yard," referring to the Charlestown Navy Yard, home port of USS *Constitution*. "I need to know Jamie's all right. The timing of all this is fortuitous. Jamie should be up for shore leave next week, when Will is due home."

"So I've heard you say," Agreen laughed, "how many times now? Ten? Twelve? Fifteen? But seriously, I can only imagine how anxious Jamie is t' see you, and vice versa. It's been quite a spell."

Glancing up, Richard broke into a grin. "Perhaps. But my perspective is a bit different from yours. *I* can only imagine how anxious he is to see Mindy."

Agreen grinned in turn. "Well, he's a Cutler, isn't he? And Cutler men adore their women, right?"

Richard's smile faded and the light left his eyes. "Right," he said sotto voce.

In the ensuing silence, the two lifelong friends and shipmates sipped their coffee and listened to the ongoing chime of church bells in the distance.

Lt. James Cutler, along with every officer in *Constitution*, was granted extended shore leave shortly after she was warped in against a quay at the Charlestown Navy Yard and her crew was paid off and formally discharged. In her duel with *Guerrière* the frigate had suffered considerable damage to her top-hamper, and it would be weeks if not months before she could again put to sea. At a hastily called conference with his senior officers in the captain's day cabin, Isaac Hull related some startling and unexpected news. "I have just returned from a meeting with Mr. Heath," he informed them, referring to the Yard's commandant. "Effective immediately, I am relieved of command of this vessel."

After several moments of stunned silence, Acting 2nd Lt. John Cushing Alden asked, "To which ship are you being reassigned, sir?"

"That I don't know," Hull replied blithely. "There are several possibilities. But I am anxious to get back into action, so I am pleased with the decision. I will be receiving my orders directly from the Navy Department—as I suspect each of you will also within a month or two. Be assured that I have given each of you a strong commendation, both in my log and in my report to Mr. Hamilton," referring to Paul Hamilton, secretary of the Navy in Washington.

After additional moments of silence, Jamie asked, "Who is to command *Constitution*, sir?"

"Captain Lawrence let it be known that he wanted the job. Nonetheless, I believe the honor is to fall to Captain Bainbridge."

"I see." The captain's answer startled Jamie. Although known to be battle seasoned and highly intelligent, William Bainbridge had suffered several well-publicized setbacks in his naval career, the most distressing being the loss of the 1,240-ton, 36-gun frigate USS *Philadelphia* to Barbary pirates during the Barbary War. He was subsequently cleared of any wrongdoing or dereliction of duty because the ship had struck an uncharted reef off Tripoli Harbor and he had tried valiantly to defend and refloat her. Nonetheless, it was for him and for the U.S. Navy a day that would forever live in infamy.

"Further questions or comments?" Hull asked. When none were forthcoming, he said, to conclude the meeting, "Gentlemen, it has been an honor serving with you. I thank you for your loyal service, and I wish each of you Godspeed wherever this conflict may take you. May our tacks cross often in the years ahead." With that, *Constitution*'s lieutenants were dismissed from the captain's cabin and, the following morning, from the ship.

The day was warm, pleasantly so for the first week of September, evoking for Jamie fond memories of summers past spent sailing on Hingham Bay with his father and brother, and later, with his fiancée. As Jamie approached the stockade-style fence that set off the Navy Yard from the bustle of Charlestown, he answered the salute of a sailor on guard duty and then turned to gaze again upon the majestic ship that had defined his life since the day in '03 when he had first stepped aboard her as a midshipman. At the time she had seemed more like a derelict abandoned along the banks of the Charles River than the pride of New England. Several years earlier, at the conclusion of the naval war against France in the Caribbean, all naval vessels had fallen victim to a wave of demilitarization fostered by a government that believed it could not afford the luxury of a standing navy. Nor did it believe it had the need of one.

"Eliot Street, Cambridge, at the intersection of Bennett," he said to the driver of a coach-and-two for hire outside the fence. He opened the carriage door, tossed in his seabag, and climbed inside the dingy interior. At two thumps of his hand against the roof the carriage lurched forward, following a route that took it along a road leading to Charlestown Neck. After passing Breed's Hill and then Bunker Hill on the right, and Mill Pond on the left, it took a sharp left and followed another road past Cobble Hill before merging with the main road leading to the ivied brick enclaves of Harvard College.

In his rigorous training as a naval officer—and before that, under the tutelage of his father and other sea captains—James Cutler had learned to hold his emotions in check whatever the challenges and exigencies of a given set of circumstances, and never to reveal to friend or foe what was on his mind or in his heart. But as the coach veered onto the road once known as the King's Highway and now known as Brattle Street, all that training went out the windows. Gone, too, were thoughts of those killed or seriously wounded in the engagement with *Guerrière* and the devastation this had inflicted upon his family. Certainly all that and more would be covered in detail at a family gathering at the Endicott residence two days hence. But those concerns were for tomorrow. Today, only one thing mattered: He was close and getting closer. She knew he was coming. Yesterday he had sent word to her by post rider. Married less than three years ago in Hingham, they had been granted precious little time together before he had reported for duty in *Constitution*. Now, with God's blessing, he had a month with her, maybe more, before he received new orders. He leaned forward on the padded plank that served as a seat, willing that simple motion to spur the carriage to a healthier pace.

"We've arrived, Lieutenant," the coachman called down a few minutes later. "Eliot and Bennett, as requested."

A quick glance out the window forward confirmed that they had indeed arrived. The attractive three-story row house set among other freestanding homes of similar brick-and-wood construction had been the focus of his memory for so long. To Jamie, what differentiated this house from its neighbors was, of course, the soul of one who lived here. More precisely, the souls of three who lived here: one a husband blessed by divine Providence and the others two lifelong friends who had been inseparable since their earliest days as classmates at Derby Academy in Hingham.

Jamie had hardly stepped out of the carriage and flipped a gold quarter-eagle up to the driver when the door to the row house flew open and Diana Cutler Sprague came running out.

"*Jamie!*" she cried, throwing her arms around his neck. "At last! You have come home at last!"

As the coach-and-two rumbled off, Jamie gripped his sister's waist and lifted her off the ground, causing her to shriek with delight. As he set her down and gazed into her hazel eyes, he was once again, as always, captivated to look at the mirror image of their mother: the delicate facial features; the tall, svelte body; the curly chestnut hair tumbling down to her shoulders; the expressive features that spoke volumes before a single word was uttered.

"You look wonderful, Diana," he said from his heart.

"And you, Jamie!" she said from hers. "Are you as well as you look?"

"I daresay. Is Peter home?"

"Not until later. But he told me to let him know the moment you arrive. And I must go to the market right away to buy a roast for supper."

"So soon?"

"Yes, so soon." She glanced askance at the house and leaned in, whispering confidentially, "It's all a big plot, of course—a grand scheme. Please don't let on you know."

"I won't," Jamie promised. "But knowing her, she's up to her neck in whatever scheme you two have hatched."

"Perhaps," Diana laughed. "Well, I'm off. Back in four hours. That would be three-thirty," she emphasized. "Make the most of that time." She kissed her brother on the cheek, pressed two fingers on the spot of the kiss, and threw him another smile before walking off to where her husband practiced law with two other graduates of Harvard.

Jamie gathered up his seabag and walked up the short pathway to the front door left ajar by his sister. When he pushed it fully open, he saw her standing in the hallway a few feet away. She was wearing a simple but elegant crimson dress that emphasized a beauty that matched Diana's own, except that this woman was taller, almost his own height, and the silken curls that cascaded down over her shoulders were lighter, almost blonde. Without a word she stepped up to him and gently wrapped her arms around his neck as his arms came around her waist. For long moments they held each other, the only sound the rhythmic ticking of the Gütlin clock sitting on a mantle in the parlor. When at length Jamie tried to loosen his hold, she tightened hers, loath to let him go.

"Mindy?" he whispered in her ear.

"Mmm."

"Diana has given us four hours. I think we could make better use of them if we're not standing in the hallway."

When he felt the pressure ease around his neck, he took one step back and looked at her carefully. Although she was smiling at him, her eyes glistened with unshed tears, a sight that inflamed his heart. The heat spread through his body. "By God, Mindy, I have missed you so very much," he breathed. "I am utterly obsessed with you still. Utterly obsessed."

"And I with you, my love," she sighed. "And now you are here, with me, safe." She ran a hand down the right arm of his woolen blue undress coat, from the gilded epaulet on the shoulder to the cuff. When she reached his hand, she took it in hers and squeezed it. "And you know the effect a sea officer's uniform always has on me."

"I do. What's more, I am counting on it happening again, right here, right now. It seems an endless eternity since I last made love to you."

She lifted his hand and pressed it to her lips. When she spoke, her voice was thick with desire too long suppressed. "Then I suggest we dally no longer. I need every minute of those four hours. And a great many more after that."

Jamie showed a leg, placed his right hand over his heart, and bowed low in courtly French fashion. "I am your obedient servant, my lady."

———

Only a few years earlier the Endicott residence on Belknap Street had been a showpiece and the center of Beacon Hill society. Although it retained its imposing redbrick Georgian façade, its interior no longer reflected the opulence of the days when Jack Endicott held sway as the chief executive of C&E Enterprises. That global shipping operation had conveyed the treasures of the Dutch East Indies and the Qing dynasty in China to eager and well-heeled customers of many nations, and the ample profits into his own coffers. Many of the elegant European furnishings had been sold off now, replaced with simpler, less expensive American-made items. Since Endicott's disappearance at sea four years earlier on a voyage to southern Africa, his wife—a former French marquise and once the toast of *la crème de la crème* of Parisian aristocracy—had turned melancholy, as much from the loss of her former lifestyle as the loss of her husband. Starting with the first trade embargo in '07, the once mighty C&E Enterprises had suffered one business reversal after another. Fed up with what he viewed as suicidal government policies, Jack Endicott set out to sell C&E Enterprises to the company's competent administrator in Batavia and invest his share of the proceeds in New England's nascent textile industry. Endicott was on a voyage to

Cape Town to close the deal when disaster apparently struck *Falcon*, the swiftest vessel in the Cutler merchant fleet.

With Jack Endicott and *Falcon*'s crew declared dead *in absentia* by the courts, there seemed no way out of the financial quagmire. Had not Caleb Cutler stepped in to resume negotiations and close the deal, and had not the proceeds of the sale recently become available to her, Anne-Marie Endicott would likely have dismissed her two remaining servants and sold her Boston home. As it was, the financial windfall allowed her to continue to enjoy the trappings of wealth and privilege, albeit on a much reduced scale. The same set of circumstances held true, of course, for the Cutler family. As holders of 50 percent of C&E's equity, the family had received half of the transaction's net proceeds. But instead of dividing that amount equally among family members, as had been the custom in earlier years, the Cutlers were using the funds as working capital to help their company weather the storms of war.

When there was a rap on the front door, Anne-Marie called out, "Can you answer it, Will?" She had heard him coming down the grand stairway and preferred not to disarrange her carefully arrayed ensemble.

"I'm on my way, Mrs. Endicott," came the reply. "Adele will be down soon."

As the echo of Will's footsteps reached the long marble hallway, Anne-Marie turned back to the guest sitting across from her in the parlor. "It's so nice having so many family members in my home again," she remarked. "It's been too long. I must confess, however, that I wish your son would stop calling me 'Mrs. Endicott.' I appreciate that 'Mama' may be a bit off-putting, but surely there is a compromise? He is as dear to me as my own son would be, did I have one."

"I'll work with you on that," Richard Cutler said, his gaze lingering on hers a bit longer than he had allowed in earlier years. "Might something like 'Mother E' be appropriate? I have the same issue with Mindy and Adele. They insist on calling me 'Captain.'"

"I see," Anne-Marie said mock seriously. "Well, I agree that we shall have to work on this matter together if we expect to change things. Are you up to the task?"

Richard gave her a warm smile. "I am. With you."

Anne-Marie returned the smile as her blue eyes locked on his, the unspoken yet indelible message embedded in them the same as it had been for years. When Richard was a young midshipman serving in Paris as aide-de-camp to Captain Jones during the war with England, Anne-Marie Helvétian had introduced him to the glorious rites of manhood. Twelve years later, on the eve of the French Revolution, Richard had saved her life and the lives of her two young daughters. In Paris to confer with his former naval commander, he had secreted Anne-Marie, her daughters Adele and Frances, and a loyal family servant in the Cutler schooner *Falcon* just as the enemies of aristocracy were preparing to make an example of her—the same brutal example they had made of her first husband, the last royal governor of the Bastille. By then, Richard was blissfully married with three children of his own. On the subsequent voyage to America the two had established an affectionate but platonic friendship. Despite Anne-Marie's winsome ways and lingering affection for him, he had so far resisted her hints that they might rekindle dormant embers.

From the foyer came the cheerful sounds of Will greeting his brother and Mindy, and then his sister and Peter. When a few moments later the five of them walked into the parlor, Richard stood up, strode over to Jamie, and embraced him with the same intensity with which he had embraced Will the day before.

After the full array of emotions and greetings had made the rounds, the parlor was enhanced by the entry of Adele Endicott Cutler, at thirty a woman whose physical features reflected those of her lovely mother just as Diana Cutler Sprague's reflected those of her own beautiful mother. "Welcome home, Jamie! How wonderful to see you both," she said, embracing Jamie and Mindy in turn.

"It's good to be home, Adele," he replied, casting a knowing glance at Mindy. And it's good to see you and your mother. Frances is well, I trust?"

"She is, and she will be pleased to know that you asked after her. Unfortunately she is unable to be with us this evening. The baby still requires a great deal of her attention."

"Of course."

Richard Cutler caught the inflection of relief in his son's voice and understood its source. He had felt the same stab of relief earlier in the evening when Anne-Marie had informed him that her younger daughter would be absent this evening. For many years Frances Endicott had laid siege to the impenetrable fortress of Jamie Cutler's heart. After valiant efforts to scale the parapets, she had bitterly withdrawn from the campaign. Since then her attitude toward him had remained icy and aloof, despite her very advantageous marriage to Robert Pepperell, scion of a prominent Boston family, and the birth of their son.

"Shall we?" Anne-Marie said as the tides of excited chatter began to recede. "Supper is ready. I suggest we continue our conversations in the dining room."

The adjacent dining area was the one room on the first floor that retained its original splendor. A long, rectangular dark mahogany table set upon a plush Turkish carpet of intricate design dominated the space. Two richly appointed silver candelabra provided the chamber with additional light and a sense of conviviality. Eight elaborately carved armchairs surrounded the table, one at each end and three to a side. Oil paintings of seascapes and French country scenes adorned the walls. In the far corner, near the marble hearth and twin oriel windows, a grand Chippendale china cabinet displayed dishes and Wedgewood and Limoges tea sets.

"Richard, if you would sit at the head," Anne-Marie said, indicating the chair opposite her at the other end of the table. "Jamie, you are on his left and Adele is on his right. Will, here on my left, please, and Peter on my right. Mindy and Diana . . . well, you two figure it out. You both graduated from Derby, after all."

Diana and Mindy exchanged amused glances. Best friends since childhood, each knew without words that the other was amused by Anne-Marie's patrician airs.

Gentle laughter was followed by the muffled sound of chairs being pulled out and family members settling comfortably into them—except for one man, who remained standing as a servant filled each glass with a ten-year-old Bordeaux. When the room had gone quiet and all eyes were fixed upon him, he reached down and gripped the stem of his glass. "To family," he said, raising the glass and pausing to allow his gaze to linger on each person sitting at the table, as if to stress to that person that his remarks were meant for him or her alone. "To *my* family. No father has a greater source of pride."

"Hear, hear!" they all shouted before imbibing the rich liquid.

"*And*," Richard continued, his gaze now focused straight down the twelve-foot length of the mahogany table, "a toast to our host this evening. We owe her much gratitude—especially the Cutler men. Rarely in the course of human history has an assembly of such exquisite feminine beauty graced a room."

"Hear, hear!" the young men cried out, repeatedly slapping the palms of their hands on the table to express their approval. Down the table, Anne-Marie returned Richard's smile and raised her glass to him.

As two servants began setting out platters of salmon, roasted beef, and roasted potatoes and greens, and an assortment of cheeses, breads, and nuts made the rounds, the conversation shifted to a more serious topic.

"Will," Jamie said, looking across the table at his brother while cutting into a slice of beef, "how long is your leave?"

"Through October," Will replied.

"Where then? Back to New York?"

"Yes. But I am hoping we can share some time together in the meantime. On Thursday, Adele and I are sailing for Hingham. Will you and Mindy join us?"

"Count us in," Mindy put in. "We can have another family gathering there, perhaps with Aunt Ann and Aunt Lavinia," referring to Richard's two sisters, "and certainly Uncle Caleb. Besides, Hingham is where Jamie needs to go to await his orders. And it's where I need to go to stop being a parasite to Peter and Diana. I fear I am overstaying my welcome."

"Nonsense," Peter and Diana said together.

"Excellent," Will said.

Of the two brothers, Will Cutler had inherited the blond hair, blue eyes, square jaw, and finely chiseled Anglo-Saxon features of his father. Even in the plain brown civilian trousers and white shirt and waistcoat he was wearing this evening he looked every thread and sinew the military officer—a strong man on whom those under his command and those who commanded him could trust and rely. In contrast, Jamie and Diana had inherited the gentler and more intellectual personality of their mother, along with her slender build, fresh coloring, and eye-catching beauty.

"Then it's settled," Richard said. "You are all most welcome in Hingham. There's plenty of room in my house and in Caleb's. Not to mention your own home, Will. And it will mean so much to Agreen and Lizzy to have you all nearby. Not to mention what it will mean to me."

"Where is your next post?" Peter asked Will several moments later. "After New York?"

"Presque Isle Bay."

"Where is that?"

"In northwestern Pennsylvania. Near a village called Erie. My orders are to report there by the middle of May. Captain Perry is supervising the building of warships, and I am to report when the vessels are near completion."

"Why there?"

"Erie has a natural harbor that is easily defended. And there is plenty of oak and pine in the surrounding forests for shipbuilding. The British are constructing their own flotilla across the lake in Canada, at a town called Kingston. It's a race of sorts, and the stakes are high. But until these vessels are ready, any military action will be limited and restricted to land."

"What are the stakes you mentioned?" Mindy asked.

When he noticed Will contemplating a platter of salmon held before him by a servant, Richard answered in his stead.

"The stakes, Mindy," he said, "are control of the lakes. Will is right. They couldn't be higher. Who controls the Great Lakes controls the lines of supply. The *lifelines* of supply. Whoever controls them will win this war. We cannot defeat the British without attacking them in Canada, and they cannot defeat us without attacking us from Canada. Either way, an army advancing into enemy territory must have secure supply lines. Taking nothing away from your victory over *Guerrière*, Jamie, it accomplished little beyond giving our nation hope and something to cheer about. The Royal Navy still has more than five hundred warships to our thirty. This war may be catastrophic for America and for our family, but now that we are in it, we must, must win it.

"Sooner or later the Royal Navy will extend its blockade to New England, and when it does, commerce in and out of Boston will cease just as it has in Baltimore. It will no longer be just our country's warships bottled up in port. It will be our family's merchant ships as well. We'd be forced to release all our sailors to serve in privateers because we'd have no work for them. And God help the United States if Napoleon is defeated before the end of this war. We would then have to face the British Empire alone. So it's essential that we succeed in Canada, and as quickly as possible.

"Mark my words: This war will not be won or lost in the Atlantic. Britain has indisputable control of the seas. Our warships and privateers, effective as they are, cannot stop the Royal Navy. No, the war will be won or lost on Lake Erie and Lake Ontario. You will be in the thick of it, Will, which is why I am grateful that you are serving under Captain Perry. His father was a brilliant naval officer, and from everything I hear, his son is cut from the same cloth. He is one of our best naval officers. As for our generals, that is another story. And a much sadder one." He looked at his son. "Do I state your sentiments accurately?"

"You do," Will replied. "And I agree with your assessment of our generals. The debacle at Fort Detroit should convince anyone of that. Do you know what happened there, Jamie?"

Jamie nodded. "We had hardly docked at the Navy Yard when Captain Hull received word. He was devastated."

Four days before Capt. Isaac Hull's defeat of *Guerrière*, his uncle, Brig. Gen. William Hull, governor of the Michigan Territory and commander of three Ohio and Michigan militia units earmarked to lead one prong of a proposed three-pronged invasion of Upper Canada, had surrendered the fort and town of Detroit without a fight. After his command had been repulsed and forced back over the Canadian border, Hull had been duped into thinking that the force opposing him at his headquarters in Detroit was vastly superior to his own. Hard-pressed to avoid the senseless slaughter of innocent men, women, and children seeking refuge in the fort—a threat articulated by British major general Isaac

33

Brock when he informed Hull that an Indian massacre was inevitable unless Hull surrendered the fort to the British—Hull had ordered the Stars and Stripes lowered and a white flag run up in its place. As it turned out, Brock and his Indian ally, Tecumseh, commanded but a handful of British regulars, Canadian militia, and Shawnee warriors. As a result of the surrender, the citizenry of Upper Canada—many of whom were descendants of Tories in the previous war but were by now beginning to harbor pro-America sentiments—stiffened their allegiance to the Crown. Meanwhile, other Indian tribes in the Northwest, loath to be pushed further off their lands by the Americans, deemed the time right to cast their lot with the British.

"Does what happened in Detroit make you want to enter the fray, Captain?" Adele asked. "You certainly have not lost your grip on military strategy."

Richard gazed affectionately at his daughter-in-law. Her question was not out of character or place, despite the fact that most young women of genteel breeding would not have broached the subject on such an occasion. Adele possessed a candor that he greatly admired.

"No, Adele," he said. "Although I will admit, Hamilton and Secretary of War Eustis are trying to convince me otherwise. Not to mention former shipmates. But no, I believe the future and the fighting are best left to younger and better men than I."

"I know of no finer officer than you," Anne-Marie remarked from her end of the table. "And I certainly have never known a finer man."

"Thank you, my dear," Richard said as all eyes swung back to him. "But my decision stands. I love the Navy and I love my country. But these days, whatever skills I possess must be devoted to Cutler & Sons. Caleb needs all the help he can get to see us through these difficult times."

An interlude of silence ensued, as if to acknowledge the full weight of that statement. When at length Diana stole a glance at her husband, he gave her a brief nod in reply.

"Father," she said, in an oddly casual tone, "you should know that there are at least three people present tonight who are delighted to learn that you are staying put and not going back into the Navy. I am one, and Peter is another."

Her father gave her a quizzical look. "Who is the third, pray?"

Again Diana exchanged a glance with her husband before returning her gaze to her father. "Well," she replied in that same even tone of voice, "as the saying goes, baby makes three."

Stunned silence reigned until Will asked, "Who's the lucky sire?" at which point pandemonium broke out. Amid the excited banter and embraces and handshakes, Richard Cutler found it hard to make his own congratulations heard. It was not until later, with the meal concluded and his family preparing to depart, that he managed to steal a moment alone with his daughter.

"Bless you for your surprise tonight, Poppet," he said, his voice laced with emotion. "Your mother would be so happy, so proud."

Diana brought her right arm tight around her father's neck. She kissed him on the cheek and then brought her lips to his ear. "She knows, Father," she whispered reverently. "She knows."

CHAPTER THREE

Lynnhaven Bay, Virginia

April 1813

LT. SETH CUTLER SAT QUIETLY IN THE AFT DAY CABIN OF HMS *Marl-borough*, his eyes taking in the splendor of a space that to his mind captured what the headmaster's office at Eton or Harrow must look like. He had not attended either school, of course. He had sailed to England from Barbados but three times in his life, twice as a young boy in the company of his father, Robin Cutler. So while in matters of seamanship and courage he considered himself the equal of the other officers around him, who had been born into some of England's finest families, he did not consider himself their social equal. He was, as the saying went, a colonial who had arrived on the quarterdeck through the hawsehole, not the wardroom. The fact that he had scored high marks on his lieutenant's exam and that he commanded the esteem of the captain and crew of HMS *Seahorse* did not and never could counteract that deficiency.

While those seated around him at the table chatted amicably, Seth's gaze wandered from the array of leather-bound books crammed into specially designed shelves secured to the bulkhead to the intricate side table hosting fine wines and spirits, to the decorative black-and-white diamond flooring that tied all that together into a snug space. For a fleeting moment he dared to wonder if his naval career would ever take him to such daunting heights. In the next instant, however, he dismissed the notion as pure poppycock.

The door leading from the admiral's private quarters creaked open, cutting short the muted conversations as with a sword. Everyone stood as Rear Adm. Sir George Cockburn strode into the open space. He cut an imposing figure: tall and sinewy, dressed simply but elegantly in black cotton trousers and a uniform coat to match save for the gold rings at the cuffs and two rows of nine gold buttons down the front. Not yet forty-one years of age, Cockburn had already achieved a reputation known to every officer in that room, and indeed to every officer in the Royal Navy. In 1797, at the Battle of Cape St. Vincent, he had served with distinction with Adm. John Jervis and Capt. Horatio Nelson in thrashing a considerably larger Spanish fleet, thus handing Napoleon and his ally a devastating defeat. A decade later he had commanded naval operations when British forces wrested the West Indian island of Martinique from the French. In recognition of these and other significant contributions to the glory of the Crown, he was awarded a baronetcy and inducted into the Most Honorable Order of the Bath.

Cockburn walked to the head of the rectangular table and set down upon it a roll of paper. "Good evening, gentlemen."

"Good evening, sir," the assembly responded.

"Please be seated."

As the officers complied, Cockburn remained standing. "Gentlemen, I believe you know why you were summoned here this evening," he drawled in patrician tones. "We have an important mission to undertake, one that will send a message to Washington that 'little Jemmy' and his cronies will not soon forget."

The use of the derogatory nickname for President Madison, a reference to his diminutive size, inspired a round of polite tittering among the twelve lieutenants and five senior midshipmen.

"But before we discuss the specifics of our expedition, I shall apprise you of the *real* reason our squadron is gathered here in Lynnhaven Bay and what we may expect to accomplish as a result. What I am about to tell you was told to me yesterday by Admiral Warren," referring to Cockburn's immediate superior, Adm. Sir John Barlace Warren, commander of the North American Station, "who received his instructions from My Lords of the Admiralty. Yesterday noon, over dinner here in my stateroom, I informed each of your captains. They in turn have chosen you to carry out the mission. Whilst the expedition is not major in scope, it has major implications for this war. It is, in fact, the first action in a strategy that, God willing, will *win* this war."

Cockburn paused to allow the officers to digest his words, then continued, "We need not dwell on our current situation. The facts are quite clear and known to you all. At home we are engaged in a mighty struggle with France for control of the Continent. So the bulk of our military forces are committed there. That is especially true of our land forces, creating an unfortunate state of affairs that leaves us precious few regulars in Canada. We have the local militia, of course, but those chaps are hardly worthy of serious consideration—as is true, of course, of our so-called allies among the Natives. Let us just say that they too fall somewhat short of British army standards."

Another round of polite titters.

"So what does all this mean?" Cockburn asked rhetorically. "Allow me to tell you, gentlemen. What it means is that king and country are depending on the Royal Navy—on us—to achieve victory in America. Since we now have nearly every American warship bottled up in port and the Americans still refuse to concede, there is but one action we can undertake to bring the United States to its knees. That action, gentlemen, is to blockade the entire American seacoast, a process that is already well under way. At the moment we have forty-three vessels on station from New Orleans to St. Marys in Georgia to Sandy Hook and Montauk Point in New York. The Admiralty has promised us additional vessels within a matter of weeks. In the interval we must use what we have to our maximum advantage.

"Understand, gentlemen: The United States has never been and is not now a naval power. The defeat of *Guerrière* matters naught. She was a worn-out ship in dire need of repairs, and the Jonathans got lucky. What *does* matter is that the United States Navy, such as it is, poses no threat to us. As I have indicated, its ships are mostly out of action, and that includes *Constellation*. Make no mistake, she and her sister frigates are fine vessels. But at the moment the Americans have her rammed so far up a Virginia river that she is no longer able to distinguish her head from her arse!"

Cockburn raised a hand to stem another, heartier round of titters. "Mind you, the war is not yet won. Whilst the United States is not a naval power, it is most definitely a maritime power. The Johnnies possess hundreds of merchant vessels, many of which are being converted into privateers. These privateers are now our primary targets. Many of them are fine and fast vessels—the Baltimore clipper is one, the Bermuda sloop another—and we are hard put to chase them down. But chase them down we shall! As long as these vessels sail the seas, our supply lines from England are in jeopardy."

Again Cockburn paused. When he continued, it was in a softer tone of voice. "And how do we stop them? The answer is no mystery. We stop them, first, by expanding our convoy system; no British merchantman sails today from Europe or the Indies without Royal Navy protection. And we stop them by striking at the heart of their operations, here in the Chesapeake. Thus the basis for our cutting-out expedition tomorrow night, which I shall discuss in detail after each of you has had an opportunity to study this map." He held up the roll of paper and handed it to the first lieutenant of his flagship, seated on his immediate right. "Mr. Polkinghorne, if you would start passing it around."

"You will note," Cockburn explained as the map made the rounds, "that the map shows the location of each Royal Navy vessel stationed off the American coast. In addition, you will note that the map partitions the United States into three sections.

"Gentlemen, here's the nub of it." Cockburn held out his arms expansively. "The Royal Navy shall employ a different strategy for each section. In the South our strategy is to prevent a single merchant ship from either leaving or entering a port. We shall thus cut off their ability to deliver and receive seaborne commerce of any kind. As you can appreciate, that is just the ticket for destroying their economy.

"Now then, as to what the map calls the mid-states, our strategy is twofold. We first do what we are doing in the South: We blockade the approaches to the Chesapeake from Cape Henry to Cape Charles and allow not a vessel in or out. And second, we institute a series of quick raids ashore directed at specific targets and designed to create havoc and panic amongst the citizenry. Our objective here is not to cause harm to civilians; rather, it is to demoralize them and give them cause to turn against their government."

Around the table, officers exchanged quick glances before returning their attention to Cockburn.

"And now, gentlemen, we come to the third section on the map." For the first time that evening a trace of a smile bracketed his lips. "As is my wont, I have saved the best for last—the plum duff after a feast of good English beef, as it were. Gentlemen, I give you New England, where our strategy will continue to be . . . naught."

"Naught, sir?" a midshipman's voice piped up at last.

"That is correct, Mr. Dunn," Cockburn replied. "Naught. Whilst there is opposition to this war in every state of the Union, that opposition is most vociferous in the four New England states. As you are aware, we have been allowing New England merchantmen to slip through our patrols and trade openly with Spain. My lord the Duke of Wellington requires grain to feed his army on the Peninsula, and New England farmers and merchants are only too happy to oblige him. Which raises an interesting point. As you are no doubt aware, many of our vessels on blockade duty are being supplied not from our bases in Bermuda and Jamaica but by American vessels trading illegally with us. We are, of course, all too happy to oblige *them*."

That remark inspired open laughter.

"But there is more involved in all of this than a few American vessels treating with their enemy," Cockburn went on. "Much more. You may be interested to learn about an enterprising chap named John Henry. Mr. Henry is a double agent who has delivered papers to President Madison in which he details covert conversations he has had with Sir John Craig, our governor-general in Canada. These papers—which, I might add, Mr. Henry sold to the United States government for the admirable sum of twenty thousand pounds sterling—list the names and dispositions of prominent Federalists in the northern states who advocate a separate peace with Great Britain. What's more, these Federalists and their cohorts in local governments are urging New England to secede from the

United States, form a new and separate country, and return to the fold of the British Empire."

Into the profound silence that greeted that remark, Cockburn said, "So now you understand why it is in our best interests to maintain a *laissez-faire* policy toward New England, at least for the moment, in all matters related to commerce. Such benevolence, however, does *not* apply to ships of the American navy. Aside from *Constellation* here in Portsmouth, we have *United States*, *Macedonia*, and *Hornet* licking their wounds in the Thames in New London. And *Shannon* has *Chesapeake*, *President*, and *Constitution* bottled up in Boston Harbor. Woe to any captain who attempts to escape.

"And now, gentlemen, the reason you in particular are seated here today—your mission. Each of you will captain a small boat . . ."

⌁

Seth Cutler had been here before. Back in '07 he had served as midshipman in HMS *Leopard*, Captain Salisbury Pryce-Humphreys commanding, in a confrontation with a U.S. Navy frigate that the American press dubbed "the *Chesapeake* debacle." Before the actual event, he and three shipmates had sailed in one of *Leopard*'s small boats from Lynnhaven Bay twenty miles to the mouth of the Potomac and beyond to Baltimore. There, in a local tavern frequented by sailors of many nations, they had happened upon four well-oiled jack tars from *Chesapeake* whose sailor's garb might have come from an American vessel's slop chest but whose slurred speech was decidedly British. A few days later, after *Leopard* had fired three unanswered broadsides into *Chesapeake* off the Virginia Capes, Seth joined a detachment of Royal Marines and boarded the American frigate to retrieve these four sailors, plus two others accused of desertion, to face certain death by hanging.

Now, on a moonless night with a wisp of a breeze that carried the refreshing scents of early spring, Seth gazed out upon unruffled Lynnhaven Bay at the outline of seventeen ship's boats conveying a strike force of six hundred sailors and Marines northward around the contours of the small bay. Each man was wearing everyday dark garb distributed from a slop chest, and each sported a strip of white cloth wrapped around his upper left arm. At anchor out in the larger bay, the squadron of two ships of the line, four frigates, two brigs, and a schooner trained their collective firepower on the three-mile-wide mouth of the Rappahannock. Had the enemy somehow caught wind of their intent and were lying in wait for them, those naval guns would quickly send them packing.

Seth's eyes lingered for a moment on the faint deck lights on the frigate *Seahorse*, his ship, before shifting them ahead to the sailors and Marines facing aft as they sat on thwarts with stony expressions. A few Marines held muskets vertically in front of them; the rest were armed with steel. Beyond them and to his left, the dim outline of the low-lying shore was drawing ever closer with each pull of the oars.

No one spoke, by order of the boats' commanders. Even the oar handles were shrouded in cloth to prevent telltale squeaks from escaping the thole pins and alerting a passerby ashore. Close by on Seth's right, the launch of the commander of the expedition, Lt. James Polkinghorne, kept pace in the lead. When their eyes met, Seth touched his forehead in silent salute and Polkinghorne replied in kind.

As the boats rounded the corner at the northwestern tip of Lynn-haven Bay and approached their initial landmark, Seth strained to see through the darkness. What gave him comfort was not what he saw; rather, it was the two words being relayed in whispers down the thirty-foot length of the launch to his post in the stern sheets, "Nothing unusual."

Seth nudged the coxswain and pointed slightly to larboard at the southern reaches of Northern Neck between Stingray Point and Wind-mill Point. The coxswain jogged the tiller to starboard, and the launch swung into the massive mouth of a river that wound its way nearly two hundred miles from its source near the Blue Ridge Mountains before emptying its vast outflow into Chesapeake Bay. The chart of the river that the boat commanders had reviewed the previous evening in Cock-burn's cabin confirmed a minimum three fathoms of water extending well inland past an especially wide and deep expanse of water located three miles upriver around a sharp bend. That lake-like expanse, an hour's row on a night like this, was their ultimate destination.

As the pinnaces, barges, longboats, and launches knifed through the slow-moving brackish tidal estuary, lookouts in the bows kept as sharp an eye out as possible in the feeble glow of starlight for hidden shoals and other navigational hazards, and for any tipoff of human activity ashore. It was unlikely that enemy military personnel would be out and about in such wilderness on such a night. But all it would take to abort the mission was for one idler out gathering crabs or oysters to spot them and fire off a gun in warning.

But they saw no one, and no one spotted them. The silence remained piercing. When word was passed aft to Seth Cutler that, according to the chart and the slight narrowing of the river, they were approaching the bend, Seth pointed ahead and to the right. The coxswain nodded and jogged the tiller to larboard, in keeping with Lieutenant Polkinghorne's launch and a pinnace commanded by Lt. Samuel Harding off HMS *Acosta*. A quick glance behind revealed one other boat, a barge with a 12-pounder gun mounted on blocks in the bow, holding its own in mid-river. The remaining thirteen boats were nowhere to be seen.

When the bows of the three boats hissed onto the sandy bank, the three British officers stepped out into the shallow water and splashed ashore. Without a word to each other they started walking up the river-bank. When, after a few minutes, they sensed as much as saw the bend in the river ahead, they turned inland across a blunt-tipped peninsula jutting out into the Rappahannock. Moving stealthily among clusters of ferns and tall, scraggly pines, they crossed to the river on the other side of the peninsula. As one, they crouched low as Seth Cutler drew out his waistcoat watch.

"The time?" whispered Polkinghorne.

"One bell in the morning watch," Seth whispered back.

"So far, so good," Lieutenant Harding remarked softly. He pointed across the river. "Have a look."

Seth and Polkinghorne required no prompting. They had spotted their quarry—the dark profiles of four vessels at anchor—an instant before dropping to a knee. All four vessels were schooner-rigged—three of them with three masts and the smallest one with two—and all four, they knew, had been built in Baltimore. Two of the schooners carried six guns. *Dolphin*, the largest and most seasoned of the lot, carried twelve 6-pounders, and the small two-master carried no guns. This much the officers knew from intelligence gathered by British spies during the previous fortnight. What the spies could not tell them was the size of each schooner's complement of privateers. Admiral Cockburn had assumed that by now their crews would be small because the vessels had been holed up here for more than two weeks.

"We haven't much time," Seth cautioned. "It's coming on dawn."

"Right," Polkinghorne agreed. He had withdrawn a small night glass from a coat pocket and was peering through it. Although the images in the glass appeared upside down to him, he had no trouble interpreting what he saw. "I can see the lights of lanterns clear enough. But I see no movement on the decks. Have they not posted sentries?"

"Likely not," Seth whispered. "They think they're safe up here and don't see the need. Besides, were they to post sentries, they would have posted them where our boats are pulled up."

"Quite. Well, it seems our good admiral was right. Gentlemen, let us be on our way. Pray that our luck holds."

Beneath the first feeble fingers of light on the eastern sky they returned to the boats. During the time they were gone, one additional boat had joined the small flotilla to make a total of five boats. Twelve boats remained unaccounted for somewhere in the awakening darkness astern.

"We can't wait for them," Polkinghorne said. "We'll just have to make do. At least we have the 12-pounder. Seth, you and I will take *Dolphin*. Sam, you take the schooner next to her. That leaves the other two for Robert and William," referring to the lieutenants commanding the two boats at mid-river. "I'll confer with them on the way out. Good luck, gentlemen. Heed the signal."

A few minutes later the five boats were gliding in short spurts toward the sterns of the four American privateers. Seth sat stock still in the stern sheets of his launch, his senses alert for the sudden jar of a ship's bell or a shrill cry. But . . . no. No sound intruded into the uneasy silence. As his boat approached *Dolphin*'s starboard side, the morning had grown sufficiently bright to make out details on her stern and the displacement of her gaff rigging, including the topsail yard high on her foremast. When the coxswain raised his right arm, the oarsmen lifted their oars out of the water, tossed them to the vertical, and then boated them quietly against the thwarts. For the third time that hour Seth lifted the frizzen on the pair of pistols he was carrying at his belt to verify priming powder in the flash pan.

With a gentle bump fended off by sailors in the launch, they were lying alongside the American schooner. Seth instinctively brought a finger to his lips, commanding silence from a crew already holding its collective breath. And so they waited. One minute. Two. Three. A Marine corporal seated on the sternmost thwart was giving Seth a questioning look when there came the crushing report of a 12-pounder round ball being fired point-blank into cedar planking, which buckled with an almighty *crack*!

"*Reload!*" he heard the voice of Lt. William Sweeney in command.

"Let's go, boys!" Seth shouted even as he leapt up, grabbed the schooner's railing, and hauled himself aboard. A horde of sailors and Marines, cheering madly with the release of pent-up emotions, followed close at his heels. In the launch a handful of Marines stood with their rifles held at the ready to take out any Johnny who appeared on deck.

Seth Cutler met John Polkinghorne amidships. "You take the bow, Seth. I have the stern. Don't let the bastards scuttle her!"

"*Seahorses, to me!*" Seth shouted and started running between the six guns mounted on either side of the weather deck toward the fore companionway just as a man's naked torso materialized there, pistol in hand. He fired, and a Marine private running beside Seth whirled around, clutching his forearm. "*Bloody 'ell!*" he cursed as Seth brought up his pistol, took aim, and sent a bullet straight into the man's forehead. As the privateer slumped down out of sight, Seth discarded the pistol, unclipped his other one, and unsheathed his sword. He stopped just short of the hatchway and trained the ends of his weapons on the open space.

"Surrender!" he shouted down. "Surrender or die! We have you outmanned and outgunned!"

"Come down and get us, limey!" growled a raspy voice from the depths.

There was no further response. Seth imagined the crew preparing to sink their own ship to keep her from the British. But to go down that ladder meant certain death.

He spun around. "Corporal!"

"Sah!" A Marine stepped forward.

"A grenade, if you please!"

"Sah!"

The Marine corporal reached into a thick leather bag he was carrying and handed over a thin metal canister crammed with black powder with a six-inch fuse leading out of the cap. That fuse consisted of two inches of fast match blended into a four-inch coil of slow match behind it. Seth took the grenade, sliced off the length of slow match with a pocketknife, and then fired his pistol with the frizzen placed next to the short coil of fast match. Two seconds after the fuse sizzled to life from the spark of the frizzen, he dropped the grenade down the hatch.

The blast shook the deck beneath his feet and sent a shudder down the eighty-foot length of the schooner. Below, men screamed in agony, their skin and organs pierced by hot metal shards and seared by exploding powder.

"Want more of that?" Seth shouted down into the smoke and stench.

"Quarter!" someone cried, wheezing and coughing. "For the love of God, quarter!"

"Right, then. Those of you who can walk, come up on deck. Slowly. Your wounded may remain below. We will tend to them."

The fight had lasted a matter of minutes. A glance to larboard confirmed that two other schooners had been captured; the fourth, the smallest and of least value to the British, was listing badly and would soon find her grave on the riverbed. Behind, in the river, the twelve missing boats of the flotilla were drawing near. To landward, Seth saw a band of men swimming frantically for shore.

"Let's clap on sail and get out of here," Polkinghorne said to Seth Cutler. "We'll secure the prisoners and tow the boats." Extending his right arm to Seth, he added, "Well done, Lieutenant. Admiral Cockburn shall hear of this."

Seth felt the strong grip of his superior's hand. "Thank you, sir."

Within the half hour, three schooners were sailing down the Rappahannock into the spreading warmth of day, the British jacks high up in their mizzen halyards stirring to life in the morning breeze. Within the week, Seth knew, these highly coveted vessels would be added to the squadron of Rear Adm. Sir George Cockburn and put to work chasing down American privateers in the shallow bays, inlets, and estuaries of Chesapeake Bay that no longer served as safe havens for any American vessel.

Chapter Four

Lake Ontario

May 1813

MANY AMERICANS VIEWED ANNEXATION OF CANADA AS A NATURAL goal of their nation's manifest destiny. In December 1775, at the dawn of the war against England, Gen. Richard Montgomery and Col. Benedict Arnold led Patriot forces to the very gates of British-occupied Québec. The invasion ended in failure, however, and with defeat went all hope of gaining Canadians' support for America's cause.

Nearly forty years later, with the first inklings of war drums on the American frontier and on warships in the Atlantic, Congress and the War Department again cast covetous eyes on the ripe plum to the north. With the bulk of British land forces hunkered down on European battlefields fighting Napoleon, few leaders in Washington expected the conquest of Canada to be anything more than a cursory exercise. Even former president Thomas Jefferson predicted that conquest was simply a matter of marching north. After all, who would stop the invading American army? Many of the 500,000 Canadian citizens in 1812 were of American or French descent. Would they not welcome liberation from tyrannical British rule just as Americans had thirty-five years earlier?

American military strategy, such as it was, was centered on a three-pronged invasion of Upper Canada, a vast area differentiated from the primarily French-speaking territory of Lower Canada. In the first prong, two thousand militiamen assaulted Fort Malden, a British fortress located across the Detroit River from the American fortress of Detroit.

Not only did the assault fail, but the British returned the favor, crossed the river, and took Detroit. The blame for that humiliating disaster fell squarely on the epaulets of Gen. William Hull. To the east, Gen. Stephen van Rensselaer led a force across the Niagara River to attack the British position at Queenston Heights. Although the Americans briefly held the high ground, they were subsequently driven back across the river with the loss of 330 lives. A third prong of five thousand troops under the command of Gen. Henry Dearborn marched to Lake Champlain with orders to advance on Montreal. As it turned out, however, Dearborn's army never took one step into Canada, and the dead and wounded it recorded were of its own making when American troops accidentally opened fire on each other.

Just a month earlier, an American force commanded by Brig. Gen. Zebulon Pike and supported by a naval flotilla had attacked York, a city of major political but minor military significance. The heavily outnumbered British regulars soon abandoned the town, blowing up the fort's magazine and leaving behind civilians, units of Canadian militia, and their Ojibway Indian allies. American soldiers lost no time in torching and looting the city before withdrawing across Lake Ontario. York was an American victory of sorts, but the only thing gained was the antipathy of Canadians and British outraged over the mindless and needless sacking of their provincial capital.

Three reasons were offered for these military debacles. The first was inept leadership. As summed up in a January 1813 editorial in the Vermont *Green Mountain Farmer*, the Canadian campaign had to date resulted in nothing but "disaster, defeat, disgrace, and ruin and death." The second reason offered was that in each campaign a sizable portion of the state militias had refused to leave American soil. But it was the third reason—the inability to establish and maintain lines of supply and communication—that a small cadre of qualified military strategists deemed to be the most germane and critical. Men such as Army officers Winfield Scott and William Henry Harrison, and Navy officers such as Oliver Hazard Perry and Stephen Decatur understood that victory on this northern border depended on wresting control of Lake Ontario and

Lake Erie from the British. Only then could these vital lines of supply and communication be secured.

—~—

The journey to the Great Lakes had been more challenging than Will Cutler had anticipated. He was already a week behind schedule, and if he could not quickly secure transportation from Oswego on the southern shore of Lake Ontario to Presque Isle Bay on the southern shore of Lake Erie, he could be in Dutch with his commanding officer.

He had left New York City nearly three weeks earlier, sailing up the Hudson River as far as Albany and then canoeing upstream along the Mohawk River to the small settlement of Rome, an ancient Iroquois portage site. From there he and his small entourage had trekked overland to the Wood Creek–Oneida Lake waterway system and finally to the Oswego River flowing into Lake Ontario. Strong headwinds on the Hudson coupled with powerful river currents caused by heavy winter snowmelt had slowed their progress to a crawl, making for a tedious journey made even more miserable by the incessant swarms of mosquitoes and blackflies. As bad as it was for Will, he, at least, was traveling light. He could not imagine the challenge of lugging the thirty-seven cannon that were currently somewhere en route to Presque Isle Bay from a foundry in Frenchtown, Maryland, to be added to the twenty-eight cannon already there. Now he understood why Pittsburgh was becoming such an important hub of manufacturing and supply to U.S. forces on the lakes and along the Appalachian frontier. Pittsburgh was not only located much closer to these arenas of war, it was blessed with a host of natural resources and navigable rivers.

As it turned out, Will needn't have worried. When he finally reached Oswego in the early morning of Tuesday, May 15, and sought a boat to continue his journey, he discovered, much to his relief and surprise, that his commanding officer was just a few miles to the east at Sackets Harbor. That very afternoon he secured passage on a small mail packet and joined Perry's forces.

Sackets Harbor might once have been a picturesque lakeside village—its Main Street was wide and lined on both sides with cozy-looking log homes and shops—but today it was a military compound of considerable proportions. Here, there, and everywhere, Army tents had sprouted amid homes, and personnel mingled with the town's citizens. As his little packet sailed into the wide, semicircular harbor populated by merchant and naval brigs, schooners, and sloops, Will was impressed by the massive earthworks, shore batteries, barracks, and ramparts the U.S. Army had erected to defend and maintain this most vital U.S. Navy shipyard that served as military headquarters for the Great Lakes.

Once ashore and walking into the semi-chaos that seemed to define the town, Will singled out a young man walking purposefully and wearing the loose-fitting garb of a sailor. "Excuse me, please," he said to get the sailor's attention. When the sailor turned to face him, Will said, "Where might I find Captain Perry?"

The look the sailor gave him bordered on contempt, and Will understood why. At that moment there wasn't much about him to impress anyone. He was dressed in simple frontier deerskin and balancing a soiled duffel on his shoulder. His thick blond hair was a dirty, matted mess, and his cheeks and square jaw were in serious need of both a shave and salve for insect bites.

"Who?"

"Captain Oliver Hazard Perry."

"Sorry. Never heard of him."

"Well, then, can you tell me where I might find Commodore Isaac Chauncey?"

The sailor narrowed his eyes. "Who the hell are you, if ye don't mind me asking?"

"I don't mind," Will replied pleasantly. "My name is William Cutler. I hold the rank of first lieutenant in the United States Navy. I am here on the orders of Mr. Armstrong, Mr. Jones, Commodore Chauncey, and Captain Perry." He was uncertain whether the sailor would know that John Armstrong was the newly appointed secretary of war and that William Jones had a few months earlier replaced Paul Hamilton as secretary of the Navy, but Chauncey and Perry should be familiar names.

The sailor's jaw dropped slightly. Then his body went taut as he snapped a crisp salute. "Sorry, sir," he said, his gaze ahead as rigid as his body. "I didn't know."

Will returned the salute. "How could you? Be at your ease." When the sailor noticeably relaxed, Will added, "Can you now direct me to the commodore's headquarters?"

"Aye, sir." The sailor pointed down Main Street. "Do ye see that long, single-story building there at the end? That's the Old Meetinghouse. It's used for church meetings on Sundays and by the commodore on other days."

One God to another, thought Will. "Thank you, sailor. Your assistance is noted and appreciated."

"Sir!" the sailor fairly shouted.

At the door to the meetinghouse Will presented his papers to two soldiers on guard duty and was admitted to the home office of the commander-in-chief of U.S. naval forces on the Great Lakes. As he stepped inside the spacious but sparsely appointed chamber, Will's first impression was that the man's headquarters was far more modest than his titles.

"Welcome to Sackets Harbor, Mr. Cutler," Commodore Chauncey said graciously after an orderly had formally introduced him. The two men shook hands. "This is indeed an unexpected pleasure."

"For me as well, sir. I arrived in Oswego just this morning after a rather difficult passage from New York. When I was told that Captain Perry was in Sackets Harbor, I decided to come here before going on to Lake Erie."

"A fortuitous decision, Lieutenant. You will understand why later today. And be assured that *every* journey here from New York is a difficult one. The St. Lawrence offers a better alternative, certainly, but sailing blithely through the heart of enemy territory would hardly be in an American's best interests, now, would it?" Chauncey chuckled at his own wit.

"No, sir, it would not," Will replied. Despite his expectations, he took to this rotund, prematurely balding, and decidedly unmilitary-looking man, who must have been in his mid-thirties. While Chauncey's service in the Caribbean and Mediterranean had been noteworthy, to Will's mind a number of other naval officers were far more deserving of this exalted post. For one thing, Capt. Edward Preble had never counted Isaac Chauncey as one of his "boys."

"Well," Chauncey said after each man had taken the measure of the other, "you will want to get settled. An orderly will show you to your quarters. As a senior naval officer you will be assigned to a room in a private residence. I doubt, however, that you will find your accommodations luxurious. Luxury is a forgotten commodity here on the lakes. Sacrifice and self-denial are the rule for us all, I fear."

"Yes, sir," Will said. Silently he wondered what comforts the commodore had been denying himself since his own arrival here. Clearly, eating well was not one of them. "Whatever is available will suit just fine, thank you."

"Very well, Lieutenant. I will expect to see you back here at the start of the first dogwatch. And Lieutenant," he added with a hint of a smile, "may I suggest that you . . . um . . . tidy up a bit before then? We don't stand on ceremony here. No need for that in a place like this. But a good wash-off might do you wonders."

"Yes, sir. I do apologize for my appearance."

"Tut tut, my good man. You've just come through a vast wilderness alive. Not everyone is so fortunate."

At three-thirty, just as Will had finished shaving and dressing, there came a soft rap on his door. "Just a moment," he called out, thinking it was the mistress of the home to which he had been assigned. He was grateful that she seemed a gentle and kind woman who welcomed his presence. Hardly had he settled in when she brought a bowl of fish stew and a plate of freshly baked bread into his modest but comfortable room. "Have at it," she encouraged, and she took great delight in watching him wolf down the food.

But when he opened the door he found not Mrs. Carson but a man of similar height, build, and age to his own. He was wearing, as Will was, close-fitting buff trousers and a reasonably clean white linen shirt. His hair was thick and dark, and his finely chiseled facial features bespoke a highbrow descent from one of America's first families. The direct hazel eyes that bore into Will's blue eyes were those of one who valued the bond between men of high calling and high station, and who suffered gladly neither fools nor sycophants. As well, they were the eyes of a man of destiny who understood where Providence had placed him, and why.

"Captain Perry," Will gulped, fashioning a quick salute.

Perry offered his hand, and Will took it in his own. "Good to see you again, Lieutenant. Based on how well you look, you must have had a relaxing journey."

Will grinned. "Looks can be deceiving, sir."

Perry grinned in turn. "Yes, quite. I must say that I was most delighted to learn of your arrival. You see, I came to Sackets Harbor several weeks ago to requisition additional sailors and supplies from the commodore. My written requests had gone unanswered. Dobbins"—referring to Daniel Dobbins, the naval shipwright charged with the construction of naval vessels at Presque Isle Bay—"is doing a commendable job, as you will soon discover for yourself. But even the finest ships are not much use without a proper crew and armament."

"Have your requests now been met?"

"Yes, and no." Perry left that detail dangling. "As you have been invited to attend this afternoon's briefing, we had best be on our way. It would not do to keep the commodore waiting."

"No, sir. I imagine it would not."

Perry ushered Will outside and motioned down the street. Their destination lay a quarter mile away, but the press of soldiers, sailors, military wagons, and farmers' carts clogging the narrow dirt byway made for slow going.

"And now, in truth, you had a decent trip?" Perry inquired.

Will laughed wryly. "Frankly, no. I was bitten raw and so scratched by branches that I look as though I've been subjected to a shipboard lashing. The netting I was provided for protection against the insects did little good, and when our food supply ran out, the land offered little. I experienced heaven on Earth when I arrived here and washed off in the lake.

The water was almost ice, but I have never felt anything so refreshing, nor have I ever tasted water so pure and delicious."

Perry chuckled. "Spoken like a true sailor. But if Sackets Harbor is your idea of heaven on Earth, then by God you *did* have a difficult journey. In truth, however, it was the same for me. This land is lovely to look down upon from the vantage point of a mountaintop. But try battling your way through it! It would seem, Lieutenant, that you and I have come a long way from the beaches of Newport and Hingham."

"That we have, sir."

"Everything is well in New York?"

"It is. Your gunboats are all fitted out and ready for service. And I have seen to the final disposition of *Revenge*. That went according to plan."

Perry's last command, the sloop-of-war *Revenge*, had sunk in a storm soon after running aground in Narragansett Bay in Rhode Island. After hearing testimony from all concerned, the mandatory court-martial had placed blame for the incident on the sloop's pilot. Further, the court had commended Master Commandant Perry for repeatedly risking his life to save the lives of his crew.

"Good man. I knew I could depend on you." As they approached the Old Meetinghouse they came across several grandly attired Army officers heading in that direction. Perry recognized one of them and touched his hat. "Good afternoon, Colonel."

"Captain," the man replied tersely before hurrying on.

"Who was that?" Will asked.

"Colonel Winfield Scott," Perry replied. Lowering his voice, he added, "He's Dearborn's adjunct general and one of the few Army officers I have come to respect. Listen carefully to what he says this afternoon. The commodore *did* explain the purpose of the meeting, did he not?"

"He did not. He simply stated that my arrival here was most fortuitous. Can you explain what he meant by that?"

"Certainly. We are going to attack Fort George."

"Fort George? Forgive me, but where is Fort George?"

"Westward across the lake, at the Niagara River."

"Who is the 'we' you are referring to? Who will attack it?"

"You and me and damn near everyone else you see around here. We're planning an amphibious assault. I'm to command the brig *Oneida*, and you, Lieutenant, will join me. *That* is why your arrival is so fortuitous."

"When will this assault take place?" Will asked in bewilderment.

To Will's astonishment he answered, "On Thursday, the day after tomorrow." Perry faced Will and swept his left arm toward the front door of the meetinghouse. "Shall we go inside and review the details?"

Will listened intently as Commodore Chauncey conducted the briefing. The British had three forts of consequence on Lake Ontario, he learned. The fort at York was located on its northwestern shore and had been neutralized when the Americans captured the fort and sacked the town. A second fort to the east at Kingston, located near where the waters of Lake Ontario flow into the St. Lawrence River, was of far greater military significance because the Royal Navy and the Provincial Marine, a military transport service, harbored many of their ships there. American intelligence believed that the fort was defended by eight thousand British regulars, a situation comparable to the American position at Sackets Harbor. Any assault on Kingston, Maj. Gen. Henry Dearborn declared, was simply too risky at this stage. That would have to wait for reinforcements and for a shift in the winds of war.

That left Fort George, which defended the westernmost approaches to Lake Erie just as Fort Kingston defended the easternmost approaches to the St. Lawrence. Built as a counterbalance to Fort Niagara, which the British were forced to cede to the Americans in 1796 as a result of Jay's Treaty, it was commanded by Brig. Gen. John Vincent. According to American spies, the garrison included elements of the 8th King's Regiment, the 49th Regiment of Foot, a troop of Royal Newfoundlanders, and Glengarry Light Infantry—in total about a thousand British army regulars. The garrison also included several hundred Canadian militiamen and a handful of Indian allies. American observers had counted only five fieldpieces of modest caliber. All of that intelligence had inspired Chauncey to conclude that an American force of four thousand Army regulars conveyed across the lake by a schooner, a brig-of-war, and a dozen gunboats could carry the day. The Royal Navy had no vessels of consequence in the area, and Fort Niagara was expected to throw its weight of cannon into the fray.

—◦—

The rising sun on Thursday, May 27, gradually dispersed the grayish-white fog that had stubbornly clung to the surface waters surrounding Fort George to the north, east, and south. Standing on the foredeck of the brig-of war *Oneida*, Oliver Hazard Perry peered southwestward through a spyglass and saw Fort George in the distance silhouetted against the feeble rays of sunlight forcing their way through the thinning mist. Across the river, on the American side, he could just now make out the separation of land that defined the mouth of the Niagara River, and beyond that, to the east, the dark nub of Fort Niagara.

"Lieutenant," he said, as he continued peering through his glass, "there is a question I have been meaning to ask you."

Will lowered his own glass. "Sir?"

"Your father has an enviable reputation in our Navy."

"Yes, sir?"

"I mean no disrespect to him or to you. But can you please tell me why he has repeatedly refused Secretary Jones's call to return to duty? Secretary Hamilton made the same request of him. So did Secretary Smith. I grant you, your father has every right—and no doubt every reason—to decline. He served our country with distinction in three wars. But I daresay our military could use a man of his talents and instincts and caliber."

Will took a moment, then: "I believe the answer to your question lies in a promise my father once made."

Perry's gaze shifted slightly to starboard where USS *Madison*, the three-masted schooner leading the U.S. force into battle, was shortening sail. "A promise? To whom, pray?"

"To Admiral Nelson."

Perry lowered his glass and gave Will a quizzical look. "Your father *knew* Lord Nelson?"

"He did. He first met him in Barbados in '74, just before the war with England. Nelson was a midshipman at the time. Years later, my father met him in Antigua and then once again in the Mediterranean when we were at war with Tripoli. By then Nelson had attained the rank of vice admiral and was serving as commander-in-chief of British forces in the Mediterranean. Father has told me the story many times."

Perry lifted his eyebrows. "How very interesting. What sort of promise did your father make to him?"

"As I understand it, sir, he promised never again to take up arms against England or against men such as Nelson."

"My word. Your father must have known Nelson quite well to have made a pledge like that."

"He did. You see, my mother was once engaged to marry Lord Nelson."

Perry's jaw went slack. "*Engaged?* Your mother was *engaged* to *marry* Admiral Horatio Lord Nelson?"

"Yes, sir. My mother was born in England. Her family lived in Fareham, a town where my father's uncle also lived. My father was staying with his uncle in '74 when he first met my mother. That was the same voyage on which he later met Nelson in the Indies. In any event, my father and mother fell in love with each other, as much as two young people can. He met her again several years later after he was paroled from Old Mill Prison into the custody of his uncle in Fareham. At that time, as it turned out, my mother was engaged to Lord Nelson."

"But not for long, I take it?"

"No, sir. Not for long."

Perry shook his head. "Well, I'll be damned to hell and back. That's one of the most remarkable stories I have ever heard. I hadn't realized I was keeping company with such a luminary."

"Indeed you are not, sir. I have nothing to do with any of this."

"Oh, I'd say you have quite a bit to do with it, Lieutenant. If your mother hadn't thrown over the greatest naval hero in history to marry your father, you, sir, would not be standing with me on this deck at the moment."

Will cracked a smile. "Point taken, sir."

"I should very much like to hear more about this fascinating love triangle, but at the moment we have work to do." Perry brought his glass back up to his eye and studied Fort George and the river flowing south-to-north to the east of it. "Unless I am mistaken," he said, "they are indeed expecting us to attack from the river. Do you see that battery they've erected before the fort? It was not there a week ago."

Will trained his glass on the western riverbank. The freshening northwesterly breeze had pushed *Oneida* along sufficiently for him to clearly profile the shore battery Perry meant. It was strategically placed behind a natural outgrowth of rock ledge fortified by man-made earthworks and positioned halfway between the river in front of it and the gates of Fort George behind it. The battery faced Fort Niagara on the eastern side of the river, but the cannon in that fort were mounted too high to pose much of a threat to a position placed so low to the ground. At the same time, the battery was well positioned to make short work of an enemy assaulting Fort George from the riverbank. Its sole vulnerability appeared to be on its northern end, which did not seem to be heavily fortified. Will suspected the reason was because that northern opening provided the only means to redeploy the fieldpieces positioned inside the battery.

"I daresay your theory is correct, sir," Will commented. "Otherwise, why would the British have erected that battery?"

"Quite," Perry said, his tone sharp and crisp. It had been his recommendation to attack the fort not from the riverbank but from the southwestern tip of Lake Ontario. His reasoning was based more on common sense than on a reconnoitering of the area he had performed on his way from Erie to Sackets Harbor. Quite simply, the riverbank offered the most direct approach to Fort George and therefore would be where the British would expect an assault to commence. Not every senior American officer had agreed with him. They had argued that the shallow waters of the lake would force the Americans to wade ashore, making them extremely vulnerable until they managed to reach land. In addition, these officers argued that an American assault from the riverbank could be covered by cannon fire from Fort Niagara. The lakeshore, however, lay open and exposed. If the British caught wind of their plan, it could mean a massacre.

Upon due reflection Commodore Chauncey had decided to reject that argument and accept Perry's recommendation. So had Winfield Scott.

To starboard, USS *Madison* had come into the wind and was lying to, her sails set to counteract one another and render her motionless. On her deck, the imposing figure of Col. Winfield Scott in his grand fore-and-aft bicorn hat was discernible to the naked eye. He was about to step down into one of the scows towed behind *Madison* and each of the twelve gunboats—miniature two-masted schooners, each mounting a sizable gun on the foredeck—that had been sailing in her wake. Each scow was earmarked to convey forty to fifty soldiers ashore. Scott was to lead the first of four waves, each wave comprising one thousand soldiers. Commodore Chauncey had announced at the briefing that he would remain aboard *Madison* and direct operations from there.

"Lieutenant," Perry said, turning aft, "it's time. We wouldn't want our friends in that battery to think we've forgotten about them."

Minutes later, the assault began. The twelve gunboats began firing twenty-four-pound shot at Fort George's north-facing wall, which was built of long, round wooden stakes bundled close together and driven deep into the porous soil. Beneath the screeching projectiles, Colonel Scott, his sword raised high, was ordering his men out of the scows and into the waist-deep water. The scows, having unloaded their men, returned immediately to *Madison* and the gunboats, where the second wave, to be led by Brig. Gen. John Parker Boyd, was making ready.

At first there was no response from the fort. Colonel Scott had reached dry land and was urging his men to follow him ashore when rifle fire from inside the fort began peppering the water around the Americans and a force of British soldiers came charging outside with fixed bayonets, firing upon Americans on the beach and in the water. One American fell in the hail of bullets. Two fell. Three. Four. Five. At Scott's command, the Americans ashore knelt and returned disciplined fire as the shallow-draft and highly maneuverable gunboats closed in to rain death and destruction on the fort and on the enemy soldiers deployed outside its walls.

Watching from *Oneida*'s foredeck, Perry noticed a fieldpiece being slowly wheeled out of the fort's northern end onto open ground.

From the midsection of the battery a cannon roared, and a plume of white water rose high into the air dead ahead of *Oneida*. A second cannon roared; its shot plunged into the lake, closer.

Perry looked hard at Will. "We're about as close in as we're going to get. Have at it, Lieutenant."

"Aye, aye, sir."

As the brig sailed on a broad reach, her bowsprit aimed southward at the mouth of the river, Will stepped to the first of four long nines mounted on her starboard side. Often employed as bow chasers on larger warships, a long nine was the weapon of choice for accuracy. Its extra-long brass barrel was loaded with a cylindrical flannel bag firmly packed with four pounds of black powder and a nine-pound ball rammed down the bore of the breech. A rammer, sponger, loader, and wormer were stationed at each gun. Will served as gun captain for all.

He knelt low beside the forwardmost gun and peered over the top of the barrel. Using a series of hand signals relayed to the helmsman, he waited until the brig came slightly off the wind, an evolution that brought the gun to bear on the shore battery, which by now was a mere hundred yards away. When he had its northern end wavering in his sights, he stood up and stepped aside.

"Firing!" he shouted. With a yank on the firing mechanism he struck hammer on flint. Sparks sizzled down a quill to the main powder charge in the breech, hurtling the 9-pound ball forward in an outrage of orange flame and white sparks as the 2,800-pound gun carriage careened backward until checked by its breeching ropes. Seconds later, the northern end of the battery exploded in a torrent of wooden shards. A distinct *clang* sounded when the fieldpiece was struck and overturned. As *Oneida*'s crew cheered in exultation, men ashore screamed in agony, some of them struck by the ball, others harpooned by thin pieces of jagged wood ripping into vital organs.

"Reload!" Will shouted. Quickly he strode to the next gun and unleashed another version of hell into the British battery. By the time he reached the third long nine, British soldiers were streaming out of the battery, some running to the fort while others followed their officer charging the Americans now gathering in force on the shores of Lake Ontario.

"Firing!" Will cried out again, and the third long nine erupted, followed in short order by the fourth. Ashore, green sod thrown high into the air mingled with a red spray of blood and body parts.

"Stations to wear ship!" Perry shouted. Sailors responded by turning *Oneida* around on a reciprocal course to avoid the shallowing water ahead and to bring her larboard guns to bear on the shore.

At that same moment the guns of Fort Niagara roared. Will glanced up to see glowing balls of iron shot careening over the wooden walls of Fort George before exploding in a burst of sparks. "Hot shot!" he breathed. It was the first time he had witnessed the tactic in which metal balls were heated in a furnace, quickly loaded in a cannon, and launched against an inflammable target—in this case the wooden structures inside the fort. Smoke and flames wafted up from the confines of the fort as the Americans stormed the edifice, sending British soldiers fleeing outward toward the perceived safety of the dense forest.

Perry joined Will. "Cease fire, Lieutenant. The battle is over. Winder is evacuating the fort—I'd wager to get the hell out before he's surrounded. If I know Colonel Scott, he'll pursue him to the gates of hell if necessary." He clasped Will's shoulder. "That was mighty fine work you did just now, Will," he said confidentially. "Who taught you to shoot like that?"

"My father's executive officer in *Portsmouth*, sir. A man named Agreen Crabtree."

"Yes, I've heard of Crabtree. He's a legend of sorts, and his is a hard name to forget. I am most grateful for his tutelage." Perry jabbed a finger at Fort George, where gray smoke was turning a sickening black. "I suggest we go ashore and help douse those fires. The poor bastards Winder so ungallantly left to their fate have serious need of our assistance."

Chapter Five

Boston, Massachusetts

June 1, 1813

McMurray's Tavern had long been one of Richard Cutler's favorite haunts in Boston, just as in earlier days it had been for his father. Located in Faneuil Hall, a short walk from the offices of Cutler & Sons on Long Wharf, it was widely touted for its hearty fare and fine beverages served on heavy oaken tables surrounded by matching Windsor chairs. This noon, after a monthly meeting with his brother Caleb and George Hunt, the elderly but still highly capable administrator of the company's Boston office, Richard and Caleb were enjoying a rare meal together, watching with anticipation as an aproned waiter placed before each of them a tankard of frothy ale and a heavy pewter plate heaped with a generous serving of shepherd's pie. Richard gripped the tankard's handle and downed a healthy swig before slowly placing the tankard back on the table.

"I wish George had joined us," he said with a sigh. "He's always good company, and he so enjoys his food."

"Not as much these days," Caleb said after taking a sip from his own tankard. "He no longer has much appetite for food. The consequence of old age, I suppose."

Richard Cutler nodded, his expression somber.

"Today's circumstances are enough to age any man," Caleb snorted. "Three years ago we were shipping our own rum, sugar, and molasses to ports near and far. With C&E we added the luxuries of the China trade.

We made good money. Damn good money—for our family and for the families of those who sailed with us. Today we're reduced to shipping other people's goods and American grain to Spain, and for what purpose? To supply Wellington in his fight against Napoleon. And who is Napoleon? To cite your old friend Dr. Franklin, he is the enemy of our enemy and therefore our friend. But Napoleon is no more a friend of ours than is King George!

"Where's the sense in any of this?" he sputtered. "Where's the *profit*? You saw the books this morning. There *are* no profits. We barely make enough these days to pay our crews a reduced wage. Hell, we barely earn enough from everything we do to pay for this meal!"

Richard gazed down at his plate, said nothing.

"What else *can* we do?" Caleb asked the world at large. "We have closed our Baltimore office and consolidated everything here. And we have lost half our sailors to privateers. I hate to see that, but at least I can understand it. Starvation is too high a price to pay for loyalty. Even so, most of those men did not want to leave our employ."

Richard nodded but continued to sit in silence. He ate slowly, as if deep in thought. Then: "I ran into Phoebe yesterday morning in Hingham."

Phoebe Hardcastle was the widow of Hugh Hardcastle, Richard's brother-in-law and a Royal Navy post captain attached to the Windward Squadron in Barbados before leaving the service and immigrating to America with his bride. Hugh had been in command of *Falcon* on her fateful last voyage to Cape Town.

"How is she?"

"About the same," Richard replied. "She still believes that Hugh will return to her someday."

"Good God. It's been five years."

Richard shrugged. "Were it fifty years it wouldn't matter to her. She is convinced he is alive somewhere in Africa and trying to find his way home. Her family in England wants her to return to them, but she won't go. Hingham is where the memories are, and Hingham is where she is convinced Hugh will return to look for her. She still keeps in her Bible the letter Hugh wrote her from Santa Cruz on the voyage to Africa."

Caleb sighed. "Poor dear. She is a lovely lady and doesn't deserve any of this. Joan and I will look in on her next week when we're back in Hingham. She may have family in England, but she also has family here. I need to remind her that we will never abandon her. We will always be there for her."

"Thank you, Caleb. I've told her that many times, but I know she'll appreciate hearing it from you and Joan as well."

The two brothers ate in silence until Caleb said, with a glint of mischief in his eye, "Speaking of lovely women, Richard, how are you and Anne-Marie getting on?"

Richard cast a wary eye at him. "I'm not sure what you mean by 'getting on.'"

"Of course you know what I mean. Anne-Marie's feelings for you are legendary, and Lord knows she's a beautiful woman. Since you two have been seeing a lot of each other in recent months, I naturally assumed—"

"Stow it, Caleb," Richard interrupted, his voice stiff. "You don't give up, do you? You keep hammering away on a bent nail. If I have told you once I have told you a hundred times: Yes, I care deeply for Anne-Marie. I always have and I always will. That is no secret to anyone. We have shared a lot over many years, not to mention the marriage between her daughter and my son. But for all that, my feelings have not changed. Nor will they. I have truly loved only one woman in my life, and that is the way it shall forever be, however much you and others scheme to have it otherwise."

"I am not scheming, Richard," Caleb said evenly. "I am only interested in your happiness."

"So am I. Which is why I would appreciate changing the subject."

A little later, as noontime patrons of McMurray's began filing out, Caleb leaned across the table and gave his brother a meaningful look. "All joking aside, Richard, now that dinner is over I do have something to discuss with you. Something important that has come to light. It has nothing to do with Anne-Marie or any other woman."

Richard returned the look. "Well, what is it?"

"Not here. It's too public. Let's return to Long Wharf, shall we?"

In years gone by, Long Wharf had been the commercial hub of Boston and of the entire East Coast of the United States. Along its half-mile stretch of wood and stone, sailors, clerks, ship owners, and ship's masters strolled or toiled amid the clutter of merchant vessels of various sizes and rigs moored hard against its south side or nested against each other, their yards set acockbill to avoid entanglement in the rigging of a neighboring vessel. Lining the wharf's north side was a community of buildings, constructed one against another, devoted to the business of maritime trade: warehouses, countinghouses, shipping offices, sail lofts, coopers stations, and other suppliers and providers of a merchant fleet that served the globe.

On this Tuesday, June 1, 1813, the buildings remained, but the wharf was largely deserted. The handful of merchantmen tied up at its bollards appeared as lonely and forlorn as the city that looked down upon them. Even the weather seemed out of sorts. Although the sun was finally managing to peek through a persistent cloud cover and the wind remained light from the southwest, grayish-white clouds continued to dominate the heavens, and the chill off the Atlantic made the day reminiscent of one in late October.

Halfway down the massive structure were the offices of Cutler & Sons, coupled with the now-vacant offices of C&E Enterprises. As soon as Caleb and Richard entered through the front door, George Hunt was there to greet them and take their coats. Within the brick-lined walls a handful of clerks scratched away on sheets of lined paper, a shadow of the fifty-odd who had once witnessed the comings and goings of these two once-powerful commercial juggernauts.

"May I offer you a cup of tea or coffee on this chilly afternoon?" George Hunt inquired pleasantly.

"Thank you, no, George," Richard said with affection. "Caleb and I just had dinner. All we require is a room with privacy. We missed you at McMurray's."

"I missed you as well, Mr. Cutler. It was my loss. Please, if you need privacy, take my office."

"Thank you, George. We will do that. We shouldn't be too long." The two brothers quickly settled into Hunt's comfortable office, which offered a panoramic view across the quay through a large mullioned window. There, secured by a bow line, a stern line, and a spring line running diagonally forward from the stern to the dock, bobbed the single-masted company packet boat earmarked to convey Richard Cutler home to Hingham later that afternoon.

"Well, let's have it," Richard said. "What's on your mind?"

From his perch on George Hunt's chair, Caleb folded his hands on the desk and eyed his brother. "I have been approached," he said.

Richard waved that away. "You've been approached all your life, Caleb. I've told you before: Keep away from loose women. They have only one thing on their mind. You're a married man now. Joan will have none of it, nor will I."

Caleb's expression remained deadpan. "I was not approached by a woman, Richard. I was approached by Caleb Strong."

"The governor?"

"The same."

"What did he want?"

"He wanted to know if I would consider running for the state legislature. He predicts the Federalists will win next year, here in Massachusetts and in the other three New England states. If that prediction holds, we may finally be in a position to redress injustices."

Richard digested that. "By 'redress,'" he said carefully, "I assume you mean take steps in defiance of the federal government."

Caleb leaned forward. "Think on it, Richard," he said earnestly. "Think on what I said at McMurray's only an hour ago. Our family has been nigh ruined by Madison and his Republicans. Were it not for the proceeds from the sale of C&E, we would be on the brink of bankruptcy. Christ, our government should be filing for bankruptcy. It has no source of money beyond what it takes in from customs duties, which are pretty damn paltry these days with no ships sailing. It's surviving on public credit, and how long can that continue? The availability of borrowed funds is limited. They will soon dry up. When that happens, who will then have the wealth—not to mention the will—to keep the government running?

"Now Madison has pushed us into a war we cannot win. Why should we support it? What do we gain by supporting it? *Nothing*, that's what. We have nothing to gain and everything to lose—what we have not lost already, that is. Good God, man, even Samuel Dexter, the Republican candidate for governor, is sympathetic to our plight." Caleb became increasingly agitated as he went on.

"Our New England brethren certainly agree with me. Massachusetts is finally taking a stand. It is refusing to subject our militia to the whims of the War Department. Connecticut, Rhode Island, and New Hampshire are expected to follow suit. Think on it, Richard. *Think* on it. Did we not receive a letter from Robin telling us that Seth is now attached to a Royal Navy frigate in the Chesapeake? Seth is our nephew! Our *nephew*, Richard! Our own flesh and blood is fighting against us! This war is *insane!*"

Richard took a few moments to reply, giving Caleb time to collect himself and Richard time to collect his own thoughts. "Your tone suggests that I disagree with you," he said at last. "But I don't. You know precisely where I stand on these issues. I agree. This war *is* insane."

Caleb leaned back in his chair just as Richard leaned forward in his. "What is this *really* about, Caleb? What do you want from me?"

"What I want, Richard," Caleb said quietly, "is for you to join us. Will you do that? Will you put aside your notions of duty and honor and love of country and consider, just for a moment, where your country truly abides? Will you join those of us whose loyalty to New England is unquestioned and who, like me, are now prepared to do whatever is necessary to save ourselves and our families?"

Richard's blue eyes bored into his brother's. "No."

"No? No? *Why*, in heaven's name?"

Before Richard could answer, his attention was drawn to the window and the surprising sight of a throng of men running at full tilt toward the outer end of the wharf. "What is going on?" he wondered aloud.

He received his answer when they heard a shrill cry of what sounded like a newsboy standing outside the front door of Cutler & Sons. His high-pitched voice easily pierced the thick oaken walls of George Hunt's office.

"It's *Chesapeake!*" he cried. "Captain Lawrence is taking her out at last!"

In an instant Richard and Caleb were up and out the door onto Long Wharf. A quick glance seaward confirmed that USS *Chesapeake* was sailing eastward out of Boston Harbor. Under a panoply of fighting sail— topsails, spanker, and jibs—she was approaching the channel between Deer Island and the northern tip of Long Island. From the tip of each of her three masts an American ensign flew above flags and banners of various sizes, colors, and descriptions clapped on to her standing rigging. Farther out to sea, beyond The Graves, they could make out the tiny white triangle of another ship that had been standing off and on the harbor for two months, serving as a constant thorn in Boston's side. Often sailing in consort with one or two smaller warships, today HMS *Shannon* stood alone.

"Son of a *bitch!*" Richard Cutler breathed. "What is Jim *doing?* Has he lost his *mind?*" He touched Caleb's arm and pointed to the packet boat. "Get your coat. We're going out there."

Billy McDermott, the packet's helmsman, had emerged from the small cabin at the sound of the hubbub and was standing on the bow, a hand on the forestay, staring ahead out to sea. Near him, on the wharf and all along the adjacent shoreline, citizens of Boston were running about and chattering excitedly, each vying for a favorable vantage point from which to watch the drama unfold.

"Where's Alan?" Richard demanded of McDermott when he and Caleb had crossed the wharf, referring to Alan Beech, the packet's mate.

"Gone into town," was the reply. "I'd warrant with all this excitement he's hurrying back."

"Leave him. We can sail her. Prepare to cast off, Caleb."

Within minutes the thirty-foot craft was sailing wing-and-wing in pursuit of *Chesapeake*, the steady offshore breeze filling her canvas and pushing her along at a fair clip past Calf Island and then Green Island on the starboard side of the channel. Before they reached The Graves at the outer perimeter of the harbor, Richard went below to retrieve a long glass.

There was nothing to do but wait and let the minutes and the hour slip by in observation and speculation. Without question, the fierce storm that had been brewing for ten days—since the day James Lawrence had assumed command of the American frigate—was about to unleash its wrath. Several days earlier, Philip Bowes Vere Broke, *Shannon*'s captain, had sent a message to Lawrence. It was delivered by a sailor aboard an American merchantman that had been captured off Outer Brewster Island and battered to a floating hulk before she was released to all but drift into Boston harbor on the incoming tide. As reported in local newspapers, the message was a challenge to Lawrence to come out and fight.

"You took the bait, Jim, damn you," Richard muttered bitterly as the packet veered to starboard in *Chesapeake*'s wake. "You couldn't lay off, could you? You had to call his bluff."

It was not that Richard held James Lawrence in disdain. Quite the contrary. As naval officers the two had fought together in the Mediterranean. And last February off the coast of Guyana in South America, Master Commandant Lawrence had led his brig-rigged sloop-of-war *Hornet* to victory over the more formidable HMS *Peacock*. As a result, Lawrence was promoted to captain and given command of *Chesapeake*, one of a small treasure of heavy frigates flying the American flag.

To Richard's mind, Lawrence had all the makings of an effective naval commander. What he lacked in this instance was sufficient time to train a green crew that had replaced the ship's original crew following a dispute over prize money.

As the packet boat continued to follow *Chesapeake*—which in turn was following *Shannon* farther out to sea—Richard reviewed what he knew about the relative strengths of these two frigates—which was considerable given his knowledge of Royal Navy pedigrees and the length of time *Shannon* had remained on station off Boston. Both ships were 150 feet long, and both carried thirty-eight long guns in addition to an array of carronades on the weather deck. It followed, then, that the two ships' complements of sailors and Marines would be about equal. So it would be a fair fight, Richard concluded, were it not for British superiority in gunnery inspired by a British captain renowned for drilling his men hard and for introducing innovations in gun sightings and accurate shooting.

When they reached the open ocean roughly midway between Cape Ann and Cape Cod, the southwesterly breeze stiffened. On the western horizon the skyline of Boston and the harbor islands was reduced to a low, dark mass stretched out under the gold of a late afternoon sun. Peering ahead through the spyglass, Richard noted *Shannon's* sudden turn to the southeast, shifting the wind from her stern to her beam. From this perspective, perhaps two miles distant, the closest Richard had ever been to *Shannon*, she looked the worse for wear. Her sails were no longer pure white, and the paint on her hull was chipped and cracked—the natural consequence of serving so many continuous months at sea.

Chesapeake quickly mirrored *Shannon's* turn, retaining the weather gauge by keeping the British ship to windward. High on her foremast a large white banner was unfurled, emblazoned with the words *Free Trade and Sailors' Rights*. Richard noted the time: 5:30 p.m.

Chesapeake was pulling even with *Shannon*, a hundred feet off to larboard. Both ships had opened their ports and run out their guns. Time crept by as the American frigate slowly pulled even with the British frigate. Richard and Caleb said not a word to each other, nor did Caleb accept the glass when Richard offered it to him. They remained spellbound by this spectacle of war and the armada of other small boats rushing out from Boston and South Shore harbors to witness the action and stake their claim to history. Even at this distance Richard could see with his naked eye what appeared to be so many spiders on both ships clawing along a web of rigging to take position with rifles and swivel guns.

Another check of his pocket watch: 5:59.

Just then, *Shannon's* starboard side erupted in an explosion of cannon fire. Through the spyglass Richard saw *Chesapeake* shudder with the impact of hundreds of pounds of hot metal slamming against her hull. One of her forward gun ports exploded just as *Chesapeake* returned fire with a broadside of her own. But because she was heeling slightly to larboard in the stiffening breeze, her shot hit either the water or the copper on *Shannon's* bottom, causing little damage to the British ship's hull or top-hamper.

Chesapeake edged closer to *Shannon* even as the British vessel's carronades were ripping into her rigging and onto her deck. Royal Marines kept American personnel pinned down with constant fire from the three fighting tops and from behind bedroll-packed netting on the quarterdeck railing. Still *Chesapeake* edged closer. Below on the gun deck and above in the rigging, American sailors and Marines returned fire. But their best efforts were falling short.

What happened next, as Richard saw it, happened quickly. As *Chesapeake* pulled ahead of *Shannon*, she made a slight veer into the wind, apparently to slow her and keep the two ships abreast. That turn to windward and the resulting luff in her sails further exposed her quarterdeck to the efficiency and ferocity of British gunnery. In a matter of seconds her binnacle was blown away, followed in sickening sequence by a direct hit to her foretopsail yard. Richard watched in despair as the shattered yard plunged downward to slam against the weather deck railing and slide into the Atlantic. The impact sounded like a pistol shot.

Richard dropped the spyglass. "Damn," he said quietly. "Damn."

"What's happened, Richard?" Caleb asked.

"*Chesapeake* is dead in the water. Lawrence should not have brought her in so close."

Reluctantly he brought the glass back up to his eye. What he saw now was what he had expected to see. With her wheel and critical topsail rendered impotent, *Chesapeake* had lost her ability to maneuver. In the swirl of breeze and ocean turbulence at close quarters, *Chesapeake's* larboard quarter yawed against *Shannon's* starboard midsection just as her mizzen boom swung across *Shannon's* deck. A swarm of British tars seized hold of the boom and lashed it to their ship just as Captain Broke, his sword raised high, polished steel blade glistening in the setting sun, led a boarding party onto *Chesapeake*, meeting no meaningful resistance that Richard could see. The battle was over. A third glance at his watch revealed the time to be 6:10.

He collapsed the glass. "Take her in," he barked disgustedly to McDermott at the helm. "We've seen enough.

CHAPTER SIX

Lake Erie

September 1813

THE FIGHT CONTINUED AFTER THE BATTLE FOR FORT GEORGE WAS over. Col. Winfield Scott remained hot on the British general's heels, harrying Winder's rearguard while American gunboats and the cannon of Fort Niagara pounded the enemy's main body until the men disappeared into the thick forest. To the northeast, two companies of American light dragoons had landed to cut off Winder's retreat. That contingent had encountered unexpected British resistance on the shores of Lake Ontario, allowing Winder and the bulk of his infantry and his Indian allies to outrun their pursuers. Still, the British had suffered significant casualties and the Americans had captured not one but two forts.

When word of the fall of Fort George reached the small British garrison in Fort Erie at the source of the Niagara River, the British, sensing the futility of their position, abandoned the fort. Of greater significance for Captain Perry, the capture of Fort Erie meant that three armed American schooners that the fort's cannon had kept pinned down at Black Rock could now be added to Perry's squadron on Lake Erie. Of still greater significance to 1st Lt. William Cutler, he was given command of the little squadron, with orders to take it with all due haste to Presque Isle Bay. Perry, meanwhile, sailed back to Sackets Harbor to requisition additional personnel and ordnance from Commodore Chauncey.

❧

Presque Isle's strategic importance was made abundantly clear to Will Cutler long before his schooner *Somers* entered the bay. Even without its massive batteries and redoubts, the position appeared impregnable. A substantial peninsula jutted out into the lake; at its tip was a curl of land that reminded Will of the tip of Cape Cod at Provincetown in that it formed a bay within the larger bay. Within that smaller bay several vessels bobbed at anchor, one of them a sloop-of-war carrying six carronades, three to a side. The other was a sleek schooner named *Tigress*. The name immediately caught Will's attention. At Fort Erie, Perry had informed him that this newly built fifty-foot vessel was to be his new command. Added to her armament of six carronades, three to a side, would be *Oneida*'s four long nines that Perry would soon be bringing with him from Sackets Harbor.

Closer to shore, beyond the sandbar that ran across the mouth of the bay, two other naval vessels rode at anchor. USS *Caledonia* was a captured British brig of 180 tons that was now under the command of Lt. Daniel Turner. Counting the three schooners of Will's squadron, the U.S. Navy now had seven vessels in the waters of Presque Isle Bay.

Ashore, not far up from a sandy beach, two other vessels—from what Perry had told him, Will thought they were the brigs *Lawrence* and *Niagara*—lay on stocks, braced up by a series of stout beams that looked like giant oars protruding out from their starboard and larboard sides. Much work had been done on these two brigs in recent weeks, judging from what Perry had described as their status when he had left Presque Isle for Sackets Harbor in late April.

On his way into the larger bay, Will kept a weather eye on the sandbar as it approached and then slowly passed beneath *Somers*'s keel. Because there were no ebbs and flows of tides to consider, there was no need to throw out a lead line. The water's depth at the bar measured a consistent five feet even after days of heavy downpour, and the draft of the schooner was less than four feet. Still, Will breathed a silent sigh of relief when *Somers* passed over the bar. It would not do to have any misadventure out here under the hard scrutiny of those in the shipyard and earthworks watching every move of this newcomer naval officer.

"Stations to drop anchor!" he barked out from the helm. "Trim the sheets there! Stand by to douse the jib!" Will coaxed the helm to larboard, bringing the schooner to starboard and into the northwesterly breeze, allowing the single jib and the trapezoidal foresail to flutter and shiver. "Away anchor!" he commanded. In short order the schooner's jib and foresail were doused and furled and the flukes of her wrought-iron anchor were buried in the bay's sandy bottom, holding her firm and steady.

Behind him, the acting captains of the schooners *Trippe* and *Ohio* mirrored his evolutions.

"Handsomely done!" Will called out to his crew.

"Mr. Walsh," he said to the man standing next to him. Although rated a sailing master, Walsh had acted as Will's executive officer during the eighty-mile voyage from Black Rock, New York. Of the nineteen men in the schooner, he was one of the few with sailing credentials. The remainder were mostly Army soldiers who would have contributed little to the voyage beyond commenting on the passing scenery had not Walsh pressed them into service. "I am going ashore. Once *Somers* is properly secured, you and the men may follow me. See what you can do about securing accommodations for us." He offered his hand and lowered his voice. "Thank you for your help on this cruise, Tom. I would have been in rough water without you. I swear, you can turn a deuce of a lubber into a credible sailor in just one watch." Both men chuckled before Will said in a more serious tone, "I intend to submit a formal request that you be promoted to the rank of lieutenant and assigned to *Tigress*. I am confident that Captain Perry and Commodore Chauncey will approve my request."

"Thank you, sir," Walsh said earnestly. "I would be proud to sail into battle with you."

The western sky was a glorious twilight of red, blue, and yellow hues when Will stepped ashore from a ship's boat and walked up from the beach. What he saw was pleasing to the eye—a landscape of sand dunes, marshes, ponds, and dense forests thick with ferns tucked around a community of boat sheds, joiner's and blacksmith shops, and lofts housing sailmakers, sawyers, coopers, ropemakers, and glaziers. But what most assailed Will's senses was not what he saw but what he smelled and heard: the heady scent of freshly hewn wood and the exhortations of men hard at work on the two brigs despite the late hour.

As Will approached the blocks, he spied a man with a high forehead and bushy black hair who seemed to be in charge despite wearing trousers and shirt covered in grime and wood shavings. When Will approached him, he turned from two men he was conferring with.

"May I help you?" he asked politely. His smile was genuine, though he was clearly showing the strains of stress and accountability.

"Are you Mr. Dobbins?" Will asked, seeking the man charged with oversight for ship construction at Presque Isle Bay.

"No, I'm not," the man replied, "although many mistake me for him. We look somewhat alike." Despite the cool air, he wiped his brow with a stained kerchief drawn from a side pocket. "My name is Noah Brown."

Will knew of Brown, as did most other American seamen. A ship-wright from New York, he had constructed numerous vessels for the U.S. Navy as well as other vessels that were either built as or converted into privateers. Perhaps his greatest fame was earned in the construction of USS *Demologos*, the Navy's first steam-powered warship. Designed by Robert Fulton, its purpose was to defend New York Harbor from the British. Noah and his brother Adam were widely recognized as among the elite in ship construction, and the fact that both brothers were here in Presque Isle Bay—along with Dobbins, three hundred axmen and shipwrights, and two thousand Pennsylvania militia and a contingent of Army regulars—spoke volumes about American resolve to wrest control of Lake Erie from the British.

"Your reputation precedes you, Mr. Brown," Will said, offering his hand. "I am Lt. William Cutler."

"Yes, Mr. Cutler. Captain Perry spoke of you on several occasions, and with great respect, if I may say so. Welcome to Presque Isle Bay. We are pleased to have you here with us."

"And I am pleased to be here," Will rejoined before motioning toward the two brigs. "How goes the battle?"

Brown followed Will's gaze. "Well, we're on schedule. Perhaps a tad ahead. But you're right, Lieutenant, it *is* a battle. A battle against circum-stances and against time."

Will had a general idea what Noah Brown meant. Captain Perry had told him certain details of the situation back in Sackets Harbor. Having to construct six warships in five months—two of them of substantial tonnage—was challenge enough for shipwrights. But they had to do it with a lack of proper supplies and fittings. A scarcity of nails forced them to use old-fashioned wooden pegs in the ships' planking. And a dearth of oakum and pitch with which to caulk the vessels necessitated the substitution of thin strips of lead. But most frustrating to skilled shipwrights such as the Brown brothers was the lack of time to properly season the planks and spars, either by immersing them in a pond or exposing them over time to rain or snow. Without such seasoning the wood of the planks and spars remained green and brittle. Nevertheless, as Brown pointed out to Will, at least the wood they had was black oak, second only to southern live-oak as the preferred material with which to build a warship. And there was plenty of it in these forests of Erie, Pennsylvania.

"I understand your predicament," Will sympathized. "Given all that, when do you expect to have the brigs ready?"

"Well, now, that's a good question," Brown replied. "We should have them in the water by mid- to late July, assuming this weather holds and the British leave us be. They've increased their patrols on these waters, but thus far have only fired a few shots at us, which we've answered threefold. They don't dare get too close to our batteries, and they can't get into the bay any better than we can get out of it. So we're safe from an attack from the lake. From the land? Now that's a different matter. Still, those damn Indian friends of theirs won't surprise us, as crafty as they are. We have our own Indian friends keeping an eye on them. And they're damn fierce fighters."

Will was listening to Brown with only half his attention. His eyes were riveted on the two brigs. Each vessel was about 110 feet in length and would soon carry eighteen 32-pounder carronades. In addition, *Lawrence* would mount two long 12-pounder guns, one on each side. "So what you're telling me is that we'll have them in and fitted out by the middle of August."

"Likely," Brown replied. He gave Will a sardonic look. "Ye itchin' for a fight, Lieutenant?"

"I am, Mr. Brown. More to the point, so is Captain Perry."

—— ⁓ ——

Perry arrived two weeks later in a flotilla of small craft laden with extra hands to help crew his squadron. The flotilla had hugged the shoreline of New York and Pennsylvania, ready at a moment's notice to duck into any backwater that might serve as a refuge from a prowling Royal Navy vessel. None was sighted, and under cover of a providential mist that stayed with them throughout the voyage, Perry made it to Presque Isle Bay without incident. As soon as he stepped ashore he was all business.

"Assemble the officers, Lieutenant," he said to Jesse Elliott, his second-in-command, there to greet him. "Two bells in the second dogwatch."

Elliott was a man of some thirty years with a wide, round head and deep-set, piercing eyes. Born to a prominent Maryland family, he had earned distinction earlier in the war by capturing the brigs HMS *Caledonia* and HMS *Detroit* from the British. Although *Detroit* had been swept down the Niagara River and pummeled to matchwood by the cannon of Fort George, *Caledonia* managed to make it safely to Presque Isle Bay. Because of that action Elliott believed that the honor of commanding the Lake Erie squadron should rightly fall to him, and not to a man who had received the appointment simply because he had asked for it and because his family had better connections in Washington.

Without a word, Elliott offered Perry a cursory salute and turned on his heels to carry out the order. Only then did Perry allow his gaze to settle on the fine sheer of the hulls of the two brigs on stocks. The oarlike supporting beams had been removed, and tubs of grease had been placed near the cradle. When the time came—and that time had to be soon, else the tubs wouldn't be there—the tallow would grease the skids to ease the brigs off the cradle and into the deepest arm of the bay. Too, he noticed with satisfaction the lettering that had been applied to the stern of one of them. To Perry, *Lawrence* was more than the name of a new vessel. It was the name of a dear friend—James Lawrence, captain of the ill-fated

Chesapeake. Never had there been a question for whom Perry would name his flagship.

In a rectangular log cabin that served as command center for the shipyard, the other squadron commanders were gathering. Although the summer solstice had long since passed, the evening air had a bite to it. A fire crackled agreeably in the substantial stone hearth as the officers chatted quietly. When Perry entered the room, conversation abruptly ceased. Those who were seated stood.

Perry looked up and down the table before speaking. "Good evening, gentlemen. I have returned with as many men as I could requisition from Commodore Chauncey. We should now have enough to man our ships. That is the good news. The bad news is that you will find many of them sorely lacking in seafaring skills. For the most part, they are soldiers, not sailors. Nevertheless, they are what we have, and you as commanders will have to make do with them. As will I. I shall leave it to Lieutenant Elliott to assign them to your vessels.

"Rest assured, the British at Fort Malden"—referring to the fortification near the town of Amherstburg in Upper Canada that served as naval headquarters for the British squadron on Lake Erie—"are in worse straits than we are. Our spies and reconnaissance agents confirm that their vessels are largely manned either by sailors of the Provincial Marine or by Royal Army regulars drawn from the ranks of Major General Proctor, the fort's commander. My counterpart, Commander Richard Heriot Barclay, has requested additional supplies and men from Commodore Yeo in Kingston—just as I have from Commodore Chauncey in Sackets Harbor—but apparently Yeo has even less to offer than Chauncey does. Since we now control Lake Ontario, what supplies Yeo can spare must come overland four hundred miles from Kingston to reach the British. And *that*, gentlemen, is no easy matter. From everything we hear, Barclay's position is rapidly becoming untenable, and we shall be pleased to make it more untenable by preventing any supply ship from bringing relief to the British garrison. Are there questions?"

There were none. What Perry had stated thus far was either already known or the subject of serious speculation.

"Very well." Perry paused to look at each officer in turn. Suddenly he pounded his fist on the table. "Gentlemen, this is it. *This* is the time to strike. We have our enemy right where we want him, and we must not hesitate. The moment *Lawrence* and *Niagara* are launched and fitted out, we shall set sail for Sandusky to pick up additional manpower from Major General Harrison. From there we sail to Put-in-Bay, and we shall remain there until the British come out and fight. And come out and fight they will. Barclay has only one other option. He either fights us for control of the lake or he remains where he is and withers. As you are well aware, Barclay is Royal Navy to his core. So we already know which option he'll choose. Mark well: Whoever wins this battle wins Lake Erie. And dare I say it? Whoever wins Lake Erie wins this war."

Put-in-Bay was a horseshoe-shaped refuge on the northern coast of South Bass Island. Located three miles north of the southern shore of Lake Erie and thirty miles south of the Canadian mainland at the mouth of the Detroit River, it had long served as a safe harbor for lake craft "putting in" during inclement weather. If winds were howling from the north, as they frequently did during the gales of November, Gibraltar Island in the heart of the bay provided additional shelter for vessels anchored in its lee. The bay and the terrain of the two landmasses connected by an isthmus reminded Will Cutler of Nantucket Harbor.

In the early afternoon of September 9, *Tigress* was standing off and on the confines of Fort Malden under foresail, mainsail, fore staysail, and outer jib. Under close study were the six warships under the command of Capt. Robert Barclay. Not once since Perry had initiated these patrols had a British vessel sailed out to challenge the American ships blockading their ports. Probably, Will thought, because the British knew that giving chase to a fleet American schooner was an exercise in futility.

By now Will was not the only American officer questioning the British resolve to fight. True, the enemy had been waiting for Barclay's flagship, the ship-rigged *Detroit*, to come off her cradle and be armed with cannon stripped from the parapets of Fort Malden. But she had been at her mooring for two weeks now, the cannon had been transferred to her weather deck, and nothing untoward seemed to be happening anywhere on land or lake. Until yesterday, when Will had spotted Royal Navy officers dressed in blue coats and buff trousers congregating ashore while lighters and other small craft were being rowed about the squadron with barrels of what clearly were extra supplies and ordnance.

"Shall we pick up Wheeler?" Tom Walsh asked Will. The *Tigress* sailor, who had a prominent West Country accent, had gone ashore in the dead of night clad in the slop chest garments common to both navies. "Whatever information he's going to get, he should already have. And the hour of pickup is nigh."

"My thought exactly, Lieutenant," Will said. "See to it."

Tigress came off the westerly breeze and followed the northern contours of Lake Erie until she reached the drop-off point, a secluded cove indenting the rocky, forested coastline five miles east of Fort Malden. There she hove to and waited. And waited. Four bells sounded, followed a half hour later by five bells—the designated hour of pickup—followed by six bells in another half hour. At Will's command, everyone's gaze was directed either on shore or to westward, their senses alert for any sign that they had sailed into a trap.

"We may lose the wind if we wait much longer," Walsh cautioned. His glass, too, was trained on the cove. Alongside *Tigress*, an oarsman stood by in the ship's cutter.

"We'll give him to seven bells. It's the most we can allow."

Will bit his lower lip and uttered a silent prayer. To his mind, Sam Wheeler was a skilled and loyal American. To the British, he was a traitor and would be treated accordingly if his ruse should be detected. Will had feared for his safety and was loath to send him on this reconnaissance mission. But that mission was vital, and the tawny-haired young sailor born in the English county of Lancashire was the obvious choice to carry it out. Will could not deny Wheeler when the lad had stepped up to volunteer.

As the minutes ticked by, the strain of being hove to so close to enemy territory, and so helpless, was taking its toll. Suddenly, Walsh pointed ashore. "There, sir. It's Wheeler."

Will swept his glass to the left and brought the figure in the lens into sharp focus. "So it is. Send over the cutter, pick him up, and get us out of here."

⬩⬩⬩

At dawn the next morning, September 10, after reviewing the battle plan a final time, Oliver Hazard Perry issued a general order to the eight captains of his squadron:

Commanding officers are particularly enjoined to pay attention to preserving their stations in the line and in all cases to keep as near the Lawrence as possible. Engage your designated enemy in close action at half cable's length.

He looked up. "Questions?"

There were none. What Perry had just read might have been lifted from a page in Admiral Lord Nelson's diary, and every officer worth his salt was familiar with those fighting instructions. It was textbook Royal Navy. Nonetheless, Seaman Wheeler's reconnaissance at Fort Malden the previous day had added crucial details. From what information he was able to gather, and from what the Admiralty's *Fighting Instructions* mandated, the British would place their larger vessels—*Detroit*, the brig *General Hunter*, and the ship-rigged schooner *Queen Charlotte*—in the center of their line. Perry, therefore, would place his larger vessels at the front of his line, to more quickly engage the enemy in close ship-to-ship action. *Tigress* would sail in the vanguard, followed by *Lawrence*, *Caledonia*, and *Niagara*, with the remaining schooners and a sloop-of-war bringing up the rear guard.

Everyone in the room understood the fundamentals of battle. The Americans had nine vessels, the British, six. Whereas the British possessed more guns overall, the Americans carried guns of larger caliber and thus a greater weight of broadside. What did surprise many of the officers—most of all Lieutenant Elliott—was Perry's decision to place *Caledonia* between *Lawrence* and *Niagara*. *Caledonia* was British-built and beamy, and slower than either of the two other brigs. Plus, as Perry's second-in-command, Elliott's rightful place in line was directly behind the acting commodore.

At midmorning the British squadron appeared on the northern horizon, bearing due south. Perry immediately ordered anchors and sails raised and guns loaded and run out. The breeze was light from the southeast at about five knots. Sailing northward on a broad reach, the American squadron slowly approached the British warships, their weather leeches held taut by bowlines as they sailed on the wind, one behind the other, on a larboard tack.

"They hold the weather gauge," Tom Walsh commented to Will Cutler, stating the painfully obvious. They stood together at *Tigress's* bow absorbing the terrifying beauty of white canvas drawing near in line of battle.

"So I see," Will said, struggling to keep his voice calm while a witch's brew of fear, awe, and dread was coursing wildly through his veins. "That will make it hard for us to close on them in this wind." He paused to again peer through his spyglass to starboard, focusing on the ship-rigged vessel at the center of the formation. "And it appears that Captain Perry was right. Signal the flagship: 'Line of battle confirmed.'"

"Aye, aye, sir."

As the British line neared, details of the vessels and the men in them took form, first through the glass and then with the naked eye. At the vanguard of the British squadron sailed the schooner *Lady Provost*, her sail plan a spitting image of that of *Tigress*. High above her stern on the ensign halyard the Union flag was stirring to life in a gathering breeze that had suddenly shifted ninety degrees to the southwest, thus transferring the weather gauge to the American squadron.

"Look behind you, sir."

Will turned to see a sight that was at once both inspiring and confounding. High on *Lawrence's* foremast an enormous blue flag had been unfurled. On it were emblazoned the words *Don't Give Up the Ship*—the dying words of Capt. James Lawrence as he was carried below during *Chesapeake's* engagement with HMS *Shannon*. Fashioned by the women of Erie, the banner had been presented to Perry yesterday; it served today as Perry's battle flag, and would ever after as an inspiration to history.

But Will's eyes were not on that flag. He was staring at the extra press of sails being clapped on to *Lawrence*. She was surging ahead to starboard, directly at the British flagship *Detroit* with the wind at her back. It was as though, having suddenly been blessed with the weather gauge, she was determined to "go right at them"—as Nelson always exhorted his officers to do—and engage *Detroit* in close quarters.

Behind him, *Caledonia* struggled to keep up but could not. Incredibly, to Will, *Niagara* remained on station on a northerly course, as though Elliott was oblivious to the peril of *Lawrence* going alone into the lion's den.

"Aim for that schooner," Will said to Walsh, pointing at *Lady Provost*. Just then *Detroit*'s larboard battery erupted in orange flame and white sparks. Will watched plumes of water shoot up on each side of *Lawrence*, followed instantaneously by four direct hits, one at her bow, one on her foremast, and two others bowling over anyone on deck standing in the path of a streaking round shot. When the smoke cleared, *Lawrence* lay stricken with a broken jib boom and a mast with a giant chunk of green wood blown out of it.

"Bring her up!" Will cried. "Firing!" he shouted a moment later, yanking the lanyard of a starboard long nine and sending a ball streaking toward *Detroit*. He cursed aloud when the ball missed its mark and plunged into the lake. "Reload!" he cried just before firing the other long nine. That, too, missed its mark. Like Captain Perry, Will was still too far away to bring his heavy carronades to bear.

The shot from *Tigress*'s long nines had failed to draw fire away from *Lawrence*. *Detroit* continued to pound her with long guns and with swivel gun and musket fire. Despite five, ten, fifteen minutes of unmerciful pounding, *Lawrence* sailed on, unable to answer the incessant shelling because she lacked bow chasers.

"Firing!" Will cried again. A more careful aim scored a hit on *Detroit*'s railing, sending up shards of wood and evoking faint cries from her crew. The cheers on *Tigress* stopped short when *Queen Charlotte* swerved into the wind to present her starboard broadside.

Despite this new threat, Will kept a sharp eye on *Lawrence*. She had finally swung up to unleash a round at *Detroit*. One round. One gun. It must be all Perry had left, Will reasoned. He turned back to the long nines and fired into the British schooner. "Come up!" he yelled at Walsh. As *Tigress* veered into the wind, her two starboard carronades roared, unleashing a lethal barrage of grapeshot across the enemy schooner's deck and into her top-hamper, springing rigging free and ripping into canvas. *Queen Charlotte* suddenly lost headway.

Astern, to starboard, Will saw Perry's battle flag being hauled down. A ship's boat had been drawn up on *Lawrence*'s windward side, and Perry was stepping down into it. In a paralyzing state of stupefaction, Will watched as Perry settled into the stern sheets and was rowed away from the crippled *Lawrence*, battle flag in hand, toward *Niagara*. Plumes of water shot up in all directions as all six British vessels opened fire on Perry's little boat. Small arms fire peppered the lake, making it look as though a downpour was consuming the boat in a pounding deluge. Will saw an oarsman slump over and fall off his thwart. Perry ducked over to the vacant slot, filled it, and rowed with all his might until the boat bumped against the hull of *Niagara*. In a flash he was on her deck, miraculously unharmed, and his blue standard was raised high over her stern. With the transfer of that standard, *Niagara* became Perry's new flagship.

What happened next was forever seared into Will's memory. As Elliott was sent off in the ship's boat toward the rest of the American line, presumably to urge them onward into battle, Perry again steered his flagship toward the center of the British line, still determined to break it. This time, *Caledonia* was close enough to fall in behind the flagship. *Tigress* fell in behind *Caledonia*, and *Somers* behind her. Together the four men-of-war, with their cohorts quickly forming ranks behind them, closed on the British line, taking the punishment that comes from attacking head-on to deliver the ultimate punishment of a rake to the bow on one side and a rake to the stern on the other, with the enemy unable to answer either onslaught. When *Tigress* passed through the British line with her starboard and larboard batteries firing simultaneously, there wasn't much left for her to fire at. The 32-pounder carronades in *Niagara* and *Caledonia* had done their job.

That evening, ashore in Put-in-Bay, Perry and his squadron commanders shared a bottle of prime Madeira, a gift to Perry from his wife, Elizabeth, as Perry was preparing to depart Rhode Island for Lake Erie. For a reason Will did not know—and for the moment did not care to know—Lt. James Elliott was not in attendance. The others toasted the victory as they savored the spirits. For the first time in Great Britain's history, an entire Royal Navy squadron had surrendered to an enemy. As a result Perry was free to ferry Maj. Gen. William Henry Harrison's Army of the Northwest to Detroit to take on Major General Proctor and his Indian ally, Tecumseh.

In the warm glow of the evening's conclusion, Perry read from a communication he planned to send the next day to Harrison:

Dear General: We have met the enemy and they are ours: two ships, two brigs, one schooner and one sloop. Yours with great respect and esteem, O. H. Perry

CHAPTER SEVEN

Thames River, Upper Canada

October 5, 1813

AFTER THE BATTLE OF LAKE ERIE, MAJOR GENERAL HARRISON AND Captain Perry truly did have their enemies where they wanted them. Maj. Gen. Henry Proctor had run out of choices. The land adjacent to the Detroit River could barely sustain enough cattle and crops to feed the local populace, let alone the garrison at Fort Malden. Far worse, the fort had but several light cannon, the heavier guns having been transferred to *Detroit*, and now Barclay's flagship and the squadron she led lay either in American hands or at the bottom of Lake Erie. Unable to be resupplied or reinforced by British positions to the east, Proctor abandoned the city of Detroit and the fort at Amherstburg and fled with his nine-hundred-man Right Division of the Army of Upper Canada northeastward along the Thames River. His destination: Burlington Heights, a British army post located 175 miles away across the rolling hills, fields, and forests of Upper Canada.

Tecumseh, the Shawnee leader who had allied his tribe with the British long before the war broke out, was furious over Proctor's decision to retreat. Nonetheless, he had no choice but to follow him. His scouts had spotted a thousand mounted troops heading northward along the western shore of Lake Erie, and he suffered no doubts that a larger force would soon be conveyed across the lake. He and his brother, the Prophet, had confronted Major General Harrison before, at Tippecanoe, and the memory of that humiliating defeat continued to weigh heavily upon him.

He wanted to stay and fight. To abandon his Indian confederates in the Michigan Territory to the whims of the despised Americans was anathema to him. Plus, he had a score to settle. But the five hundred Shawnees under his command were no match for what was coming against him. He could not take on the Americans alone. So he, too, fled.

"Over here, sir."

Will Cutler nudged his horse to the right and followed Oliver Hazard Perry off the road leading from Detroit to Burlington Heights. Behind him, ten mounted Kentucky volunteers reined in, holding their long-barreled rifles at the ready.

"What is it, Corporal?" Perry asked just as his eyes answered his own question. Before them, drawn up on the riverbank, were four scowlike barges laden with what the corporal confirmed were barrels of food and other supplies devoted to sustaining an army in the field.

Will studied the river. It had narrowed during the last several miles to a width that a horse with a running start could easily leap across. Ahead, in the middle of the river, he noted water swirling around forest debris entangled in shallows and snagged on low-hanging branches. "It seems the boats could go no further," he remarked. "That must be why they left them here."

Perry followed Will's gaze. "But why leave the food?"

Will pondered that. "I can think of two reasons. Either the British want to travel light, or they are preparing to make a stand somewhere close to where we are now."

"Agreed. So which is it?"

"The latter."

Perry nodded. "I knew there was a reason I invited you along on this little excursion. By the bye, Lieutenant, who taught you to ride so well?"

"My mother, sir. She was a superb equestrian."

"Do tell! Well, there's something we have in common. My mother was as well." He wielded his steed around. "I suggest we return posthaste and make our report to Colonel Johnson."

⌐ ⌐

Oliver Hazard Perry, Will Cutler, and other officers in General Harrison's command gazed eastward at the battlefield laid out before them like a giant sideways V. The American flanks—the sides of the V—were anchored on the right by the river and on the left by a great soggy swamp thick with beech, red maple, oak, and black ash trees displaying the full splendor of a Canadian autumn. Between the flanks—in the middle of the V—was a smaller swamp bounded on each side by solid ground with scattered trees, fallen timber, ferns, and tall shrubs. On this ground, two hundred yards distant on both sides of the swamp, the British lines were drawn up in open order. It was this British deployment in open formation rather than the traditional close formation that prompted Harrison to order a cavalry charge at full tilt against the two forward enemy lines.

Two smaller lines stood in back of that first line. Tecumseh and his force of three hundred Shawnee, Ottawa, Delaware, Chippewa, and other warriors of his Indian confederacy were concentrated near the large swamp on the American left flank. That flank was defended by the Second Division of Kentucky Militia commanded by Maj. Gen. Joseph Desha, a soldier with a long and successful career of fighting Indians under Gen. "Mad Anthony" Wayne.

Two miles farther east, behind the British formation, lay the village of Moraviantown, a community of Delaware Indians converted to Christianity by Moravian missionaries. Indian scouts loyal to the United States had discovered that the British women and children who had fled Fort Malden were being housed here to await the outcome of battle.

"I figure we outnumber them three to one," Will remarked.

"I don't doubt it." Perry, too, was pointing ahead at a figure riding along the British front line. That figure was clearly an Indian. "Have a close gander yonder, Lieutenant. If I'm not mistaken, that fellow a-horse is none other than the great Tecumseh."

Will squinted through a glass. Yes, there could be no mistaking the tall, broad-shouldered Indian dressed in deerskin with colorful feathers in his hair. "Well, I'm a son-of-a-bitch," he muttered. He watched, fascinated, as Tecumseh rode slowly down the line, shaking hands with each British officer in turn before joining his Indian cohorts at the edge of the black ash swamp.

"I don't doubt it," Perry deadpanned. He turned in the saddle to once again survey the force arrayed behind him. Col. Richard Johnson, sitting astride a white pony, and his brother, Lt. Col. James Johnson, would lead the charge with their regiments of mounted Kentucky riflemen. Behind the cavalry stood five brigades of buckskin-clad Kentucky militia commanded by Maj. Gen. Isaac Shelby, the sixty-three-year-old governor of Ohio. General Harrison had asked Shelby, a hero at King's Mountain during the first war with England, to assemble an army of 2,500 volunteers with which to invade Upper Canada. Shelby had without question turned to the Kentucky militia and its regiment of cavalry commanded by Colonel Johnson, a popular Kentucky lawyer, politician, and War Hawk in Congress. The Kentucky militiamen were widely admired as fierce fighters who also had a score to settle. The previous January, during the Battle of the River Raisin in the Michigan Territory, five hundred of their fellow Kentuckians had been taken prisoner by Proctor and Tecumseh and then summarily massacred despite Proctor's promise of British protection from the Indians and Tecumseh's efforts to quell the bloodlust. That reckless and senseless slaughter had earned Tecumseh the antipathy of Kentucky and Proctor the epithet "Butcher."

For a span of time difficult to determine, men on both sides waited in tense silence. The Americans and British faced each other from across an open countryside, their battle flags and standards fluttering listlessly in the gentle westerly breeze. Overheard, a bright sun in a nearly cloudless sky cast a golden glow upon the unusually warm October afternoon.

A rider approached Col. Richard Johnson from the direction of General Harrison's field headquarters near the river and handed him a message. Johnson read it and handed it back to the dispatch rider. In the next instant he unsheathed his sword, held it high for several moments, and then sliced it downward.

"*Remember the River Raisin!*" he shouted, spurring his horse forward. A bugle sounded. Behind him, those in his command and in the command of his brother took up the cry. Across the open terrain of Upper Canada thundered a horde of one thousand Kentucky volunteers.

A volley of British musketry cracked to life from one end of the front lines to the other. Two Americans fell. The distance closed to a hundred yards, seventy yards, fifty yards. Another line of musketry flashed sparks and smoke. Two more Americans fell. But the charge never faltered. Irreversible momentum and a fierce force of will propelled them forward. Before the British front line could reload a second time, the Kentuckians burst through it and were hurtling like demented demons toward the second line of Redcoats. On the right, that line wavered and then buckled as the Kentucky cavalry punched through it and took position behind it. Outnumbered, outgunned, and outmaneuvered, the British laid down their arms and surrendered en masse just as Oliver Hazard Perry and Will Cutler neutralized a fieldpiece before it could fire a shot. Less than ten minutes had elapsed since the bugle's call to arms. Col. Richard Johnson, meanwhile, led a small force through the small swamp to join his brother fighting on its other side.

"Sergeant Choate!" Perry called out to a man he recognized.

"Sir!" the sergeant replied, trotting up on his horse.

"Secure the prisoners and send them down to General Harrison. Then follow me and Lieutenant Cutler into the swamp with as many men as you can muster."

Choate saluted. "Yes, sir!"

On the other side of the smaller swamp, between it and the larger swamp, the fighting was intense and bloody, inspired by the resolve of Tecumseh's Indians to stand firm and British soldiers' resolve not to be outdone by their Indian allies. Charging forward from the American lines were soldiers of the Kentucky militia, many of them riding two to a horse to reach the fighting more quickly. At their lead rode Colonel Johnson. The colonel commanded his troops to dismount and fight hand-to-hand, knife-to-knife while he remained a-horse.

"The colonel's a sitting duck on that pony," Perry said to Will as the two men took stock at the northern edge of the small swamp. "Who the hell does he think he is? Admiral Nelson on his quarterdeck?"

Just as he said that, Johnson jerked backward in his saddle, recovered, and then slumped forward as another bullet found its mark. Slowly he began to slide off his saddle onto the ground.

Will dug his heels into his horse's flanks and took off at a full gallop. Covering the short distance in a matter of seconds, he reined in and jumped off his horse. Before he could turn to the wounded colonel, two Indians came at him. In a single fluid motion he drew a pistol from his waist belt, cocked it, and squeezed the trigger. One Indian dropped just as the other raised his tomahawk. He was set to hurl it at Will when a bullet tore into his forehead, sending him lurching backward, dead.

"A hand here!" Will cried to the mounted rifleman who had fired the shot. "The colonel's been hit."

The Kentuckian dismounted, and together he and Will lifted the wounded officer and placed him face down across the neck of Will's horse. Will swung himself back on board just as another bullet ripped into the colonel's thigh, causing him to grunt and his body to shudder. Crouching low over Johnson's body, Will drove his horse against the tide of charging Americans as bullets whined and pinged through the air. Gathering speed on open ground, he raced to the hospital wagon at the rear of the American lines.

Orderlies and soldiers materialized on both sides of him. In the distance Will spotted General Harrison and his entourage hurrying toward the wagon. Will slid from his saddle and with the aid of the others gently coaxed Johnson onto the ground and over onto his back. Behind them, two men came running with a canvas stretcher.

Will knelt down beside Johnson. "Can you hear me, Colonel?" he said slowly and clearly. He counted five bullet holes in Johnson's arms, wrist, leg, and shoulder. His uniform was everywhere splotched with blood. "Hang on, sir. Help is on the way."

Johnson's eyes fluttered open. "I can hear you," he wheezed. Then, to Will's astonishment, the colonel's mouth creased into a ghost of a smile. "You owe me one, Lieutenant. That last bullet was meant for you."

Will smiled. "Yes, sir. Thank you, sir."

Will slung himself back onto his horse and wheeled around. He saluted Harrison as the general came striding up and then flicked the reins, urging his horse onward. As he broke into a gallop back toward the swamp, he could feel Harrison's eyes on him.

In the time it took Will to convey Colonel Johnson to the field hospital, Major General Desha had moved his division into the western reaches of the large swamp and was pushing hard to eastward, forcing the

Indians into an ever smaller defensive position. By now, the bulk of Colonel Johnson's cavalry had emerged from the smaller swamp and taken up the fight. The few British soldiers remaining in the fray, seeing the hopelessness of their situation, began to surrender. Tecumseh's Indians fought on savagely until a great war whoop sounded, not from the Indians but from a contingent of Kentucky militia. Will was there to see a tall Indian sink to his knees and then fall over onto his back in the underbrush. The large peace medallion hanging around his neck, engraved with the head of the British sovereign and the words *Georgius III, Dei Gratia*, made his identity unmistakable. Tecumseh, the legendary leader of a vast Indian confederacy stretching from the Fox and Sauk tribes of the Michigan Territory to the Seminoles of Florida, was dead.

With the death of their leader, Indian resistance faltered. Warriors melted into the swamp and forests, hotly pursued by the Americans.

"Do we have Proctor?" Will asked Perry when Perry joined him.

"No. From what we can gather, he and fifty of his party hightailed it for Moraviantown before the battle started. He left his second-in-command in charge, that dejected-looking colonel you see sitting over there against a tree. I imagine Proctor is well on his way to Burlington Heights by now."

"Shall we pursue him?"

"Why bother? We'll leave it to a British court-martial to pass judgment on him. I doubt it will be a pretty affair, wouldn't you agree, Lieutenant?"

"I do agree," Will said. He paused, then: "What now, sir?"

"*Now*," Perry said, "we await further orders. One thing is damned certain: Wherever Fate may take us, our job here is over. Tecumseh is dead, the lakes are ours, and the British army is either under guard or underground. This part of Upper Canada is secure."

CHAPTER EIGHT

Alexandria, Virginia

February 1814

HE AWOKE IN THE STILL LIGHT OF EARLY MORN, HIS SEA SENSES ALERT even though he'd been land-bound since *Constitution* put into Boston for repairs more than a year ago. Again this morning there was nothing for his senses to take in beyond her soft, rhythmic breathing as she slept naked beside him, his left arm wrapped around her and cupping her breast.

When he gently lifted his arm away, she stirred in the depths of spent passion and sighed contentedly. For several moments his eyes lingered on her tousled hair and rosy cheeks, still brightened by the rouge she had meticulously applied the previous evening to accentuate her God-given beauty and feminine charms. The mere sight of her naked flesh inspired the familiar stirrings in his loins. He laid a hand on her shoulder, thinking to coax her out of sleep and into the fierce hunger that had yet to slake. But she needed sleep. As did he. In recent days sleep had eluded him, and not just because of the fire raging in his heart and loins.

Slipping out of bed, careful not to disturb her, he kissed her forehead and drew the blanket up over her shoulders. Pulling on a simple woolen nightshirt that covered him from his neck to his knees, he walked into the parlor of their row house and rebuilt the fire of the previous evening. When delicious warmth had permeated the cozy, well-appointed space, he crossed the room to stand before the large mullioned window, shading his eyes against the glare of the rising sun. There, across the Potomac

River from their home at the base of Queen Street in Alexandria, a newly constructed three-masted sloop-of-war lay moored against a quay at the Washington Navy Yard. He noted with keen satisfaction that all three of her masts had been stepped and her jib boom adjoined to the bowsprit, a long, thin, graceful arm jutting out from the ship's stem and pointing heavenward at a forty-five-degree angle.

Within the hour, Jamie knew, shipwrights would be back at work on her standing rigging, preparing for a shakedown cruise scheduled for later in the week. After the cruise, with final adjustments made to her rigging and framework, her eighteen guns would be hoisted aboard and mounted. Only then would her full complement of crew be formally mustered and USS *Truxtun* formally commissioned into the U.S. Navy.

Jamie slowly exhaled in satisfaction, his eyes fixed on his first command. *His first command.* The very thought sent a stab of pride surging through him, quickly tempered by the full weight of what the word *command* meant.

He felt Mindy behind him moments before she wrapped her arms around his waist. She, too, was clad in a simple slip-on woolen nightshirt. "Tell me, good sir," she cooed into his ear, "who is the fairest of them all? Me, your former lady friends, or that ship yonder?"

"That is not an easy question," he replied demurely, continuing to stare out across the Potomac. "The answer to such a question requires a good amount of prayerful consideration at a time when I am not quite so flubbery."

She took a step back. "Flubbery? What does that word mean?"

"Whatever I want it to mean. I just made it up. But I'm sure you can grasp its general meaning in the current context."

She stepped forward and again wrapped her arms around him. "Well then," she purred as her right hand dipped lower to where his strength was gathering, "tell me this. What does that ship yonder have that I do not?"

Jamie looked down at where her hand was stroking him. "A sense of decorum and a rounder bottom."

She laughed. "All right, my love. You win. I will cease and desist if that is what you wish."

He turned around. "I shall never wish for that, sweet Mindy," he said, his voice thickening.

She gave his midsection an appreciative glance. "So I see. Now *that* is something I can grasp!" She pressed her loins hard against his strength and looked deep into his hazel eyes. "Shall we?"

"We shall. But be forewarned. I must report to Commodore Tingey in two hours."

She took his hand and led him back to their bedroom. "Then we shall come straight to the point. And after you report to me, you may report to the commandant. You mustn't keep him waiting." Her brown eyes danced. "But neither shall you be early!"

———

The options for a shakedown cruise in Chesapeake Bay were limited and dangerous. Royal Navy ships based in Lynnhaven Bay had blockaded the southern approaches to the bay and could sail when and where they wished within the bay. Seemingly at will, British naval commanders landed Royal Marines ashore to harry local militias and destroy enemy foundries, arsenals, and batteries. As Admiral Cockburn had escalated his tactics of devastation and destruction in the Chesapeake, more and more towns had gone up in flames and been reduced to skeletal clusters of smoking timbers. Local citizens could do little beyond taking sniper shots at the invaders, a tactic that infuriated the British and sparked brutal reprisals.

For an American naval or merchant vessel to slip through this web of Royal Navy cruisers required the cover of darkness or fog—preferably both—coupled with a healthy dose of derring-do and a healthier dose of luck.

———

Once free of the Potomac and in the bay proper, Jamie Cutler gently coaxed *Truxtun* onto a beam reach heading for the Maryland Eastern Shore. A stiff westerly breeze set the leeches of her sails thrumming and sent moans of warning through the standing rigging. Hard on a larboard tack, she heeled to starboard. Seawater creamed off her stem, and white-crested waves broke against her bow, sending showers of spray into the air and across her deck. Despite the strain on the rigging, Jamie ordered additional sail clapped on, including her full complement of jibs and foresails—crucial sets of canvas on any vessel. Only the foremast topsail commanded greater influence in the proper maneuvering of a ship under sail at sea.

"You have the helm!" he shouted to Robert Manning, the lanky Norwegian-born lieutenant who was acting as first officer on this cruise. "Tack her back and forth as far north as the Tad Avon. We'll plan to wear ship there for the return voyage. That includes her stays'ls and stuns'ls," referring to two sets of sail normally deployed only in light winds.

"They'll likely tear in this wind, sir," Manning cautioned. Long strands of blond hair freed from their queue brushed back and forth across the weathered skin of his forehead.

"I am aware of that, Mr. Manning. Thank you. If and when they do, we'll better understand what strain they can take. That is why we are out here, is it not? My father once told me that if a vessel has a flaw, a storm at sea will find it. And he was right." He surrendered the helm. "I'm going up and then below. Send word if you have need of me."

Manning gripped the wheel. "Very good, sir."

Jamie strode to the foremast larboard chain-wale, a structure protruding horizontally from the ship's side to widen the base for the shrouds. Using the ship's heel to aid his climb, he clambered up the ratlines to the fighting top, and from there to the horizontal stubs of the crosstrees. In the far distance ahead he could just make out what he knew to be the brick façade of the Methodist church on the shore of St. Michaels. About him, both out in the bay and closer to shore, he noted that a number of brightly colored buoys had been recently set. He had seen these sorts of buoys before. They were there to mark a channel or a sandbar, and they had been put there not by the Americans but by the British. That troubled him. Why was the Royal Navy going to such lengths to take soundings of the Chesapeake and to mark deep water from Lynnhaven Bay to the northern reaches of the bay? There was only one logical explanation.

Today he was not on lookout duty up there, as he would have been as a midshipman or lieutenant. He was captain of this ship, and he was searching not for another vessel at sea but for any manifestation of weakness or opportunity for improvement in the masts and rigging. When he was fully satisfied that the shipwrights at the Washington Navy Yard had done their job with the foremast, he repeated the process in the mainmast and again in the mizzen. In time, with the full agenda of observations complete, he slid hand under hand down a backstay onto the afterdeck.

From there he went below two decks to the hold and the bilge, where he searched for excessive seepage between the difficult-to-caulk garboard strakes. Finding nothing that normal swelling of the wood would not rectify over time, he climbed to the main deck, which in a few months would accommodate the entire ship's crew—sailors in the bow and officers in the stern, separated by the ship's contingent of Marines berthed in the middle. He paused in his cabin to allow his eyes to contemplate for several delicious moments the modest yet meaningful space that defined the ultimate privilege of high rank in the U.S. Navy. He was studying a chart he had laid out on a table when he heard the cry from above.

"Sail ho! Ship fine on our larboard quarter!"

"Can you make her out, Vaughn?" Jamie heard Manning call up to the lookout. Jamie tensed, waiting for the reply.

"She's British, sir. A brig. She's coming at us, chock on!"

"Very well. I'll inform the captain."

Jamie was nearly all the way up the aft companionway when he met the young midshipman Manning had sent below. The midshipman handed Jamie his long glass once Jamie had pulled himself up onto the weather deck. A quick scan to northward revealed tips of sail on the horizon.

"Wear ship *now!*" Jamie ordered Manning at the helm. "Shape a course to the Potomac. If we clap on all sail, we'll outrun her, God willing."

In a race between a sloop-of-war and a brig, the sloop normally held sway because it was a slightly smaller vessel—essentially a smaller-scale frigate—and carried a larger set of sails. Sloops were built for speed—ideal for chasing down swift pirates or other miscreants ducking into an estuary or inlet—and carried a similar number of guns, albeit of smaller caliber. This noon, as *Truxtun* knifed through the slight chop toward the Western Shore, Jamie was not particularly worried. That his vessel carried no guns at all made her lighter and faster than would otherwise be the case, and that gave her a critical advantage over her adversary. He watched with satisfaction as the tops of the brig's masts dipped lower on the horizon. It was then that he heard the second cry from high in the crosstrees.

"Deck there! Sails on the horizon!"

"Where away?" Jamie called up through cupped hands.

"To larboard, sir," Seaman Vaughn shouted down. "Ten to twelve miles distant, I reckon. A squadron. Six ships, by my count. One looks to be a seventy-four. They're following a course north by northeast."

A seventy-four, Jamie knew only too well, was a third-rate ship of the line. One of them, HMS *Marlborough*, was Admiral Cockburn's flagship. Jamie was well versed about that ship. His cousin Seth Cutler served as a lieutenant in her. It was possible, although not likely, that Cockburn might bring his ship this far north into the bay. It would be a dangerous move. Well-concealed shore batteries could play havoc with so fat a target sailing in such confined waters. Another seventy-four, HMS *Victorious*, was rumored to be sailing toward the Chesapeake. Could this be her?

"Hold your course, Mr. Manning," Jamie said. He removed a long glass from its becket by the binnacle, slung the lanyard across his shoulder, and scrambled up the ratlines of the mainmast to the crosstrees. After securing himself, he trained the glass southward. Yes, there was the squadron, all six vessels accounted for. And Vaughn was right. The lead ship was indeed a seventy-four, although he did not recognize her. Or did he?

Jamie held the glass as steady as he was able and focused the lens directly on the third-rate. He let the glass fall, sifted through his thoughts for several moments, and then brought it back up to his right eye. Again he peered through it, squinting, his vision and memory taking in a *Culloden*-class ship of the line. From what his father had told him, only a handful of these capital ships were ever constructed, and only one of them sailed in American waters: HMS *Ramillies*, commanded by Capt.

Sir Thomas Hardy, Admiral Nelson's flag captain at the Battle of Trafalgar. But if that ship was *Ramillies*—and he could not be certain; he could only make out the unique cut of her sails, the sharp sheer of her bow, and the rake of her masts—what was Hardy doing in these waters? The last he had heard, Hardy was in Long Island Sound keeping Captain Decatur and USS *United States* bottled up in the Thames River at New London, Connecticut. If the Admiralty had dispatched Hardy and his seventy-four from New York to the Chesapeake, that could signal a fundamental shift in British war strategy.

Jamie slid down a backstay to the deck. "Change course to southwest by south," he told Manning.

"Sir?" Manning shouted over the wind.

"You heard me. Southwest by south."

"Sir," the lieutenant protested, "that's a course of interception with the British squadron."

Jamie stepped close to the helm. "Mr. Manning," he said sotto voce, "you are in the habit of informing me of facts of which I am already painfully aware. I would advise you to desist and put this vessel on the course I prescribed."

"Aye, sir," Manning said woodenly. "Southwest by south."

As *Truxtun* fell off the wind, Jamie said to a midshipman standing nearby, "I will have white flags flown from the truck of all three masts, Mr. Early. That will make them visible enough, I should think."

The midshipman snapped a salute. "Aye, aye, sir."

To Manning, Jamie explained, "Those flags will signal the squadron that we carry no guns. I am gambling on the fact that the squadron's commodore, whoever he is, is of England's peerage. As such, he may seize or sink as many unarmed merchantmen as he can, but he would consider it dishonorable—'bad form,' as he would put it—to attack an unarmed naval vessel that is not showing him her heels. I'm thinking they will let us go on our merry way."

"It may just work, sir," Manning conceded. His tone, however, suggested doubt.

"It damn well better work," Jamie rejoined. "Else for us, the war is over."

An hour later *Truxtun* veered upwind on a course to the Potomac and the safety of a series of batteries the British had not yet been able to overpower. By then, Jamie had the intelligence he had sought.

———

"What did Mr. Tingey have to say? Did he agree with you?" Mindy asked as she started serving out a supper of roasted beef, gingered carrots, and boiled onions and potatoes. Jamie had been recounting his day to her as she stirred, basted, and tasted the meat and vegetables. He had concluded his narrative with the sighting of the mysterious British squadron. The wrought-iron wood stove infused the small kitchen with welcome warmth, and the crackling logs added a note of cozy intimacy to the evening meal.

"I didn't offer an opinion," Jamie replied as she set a well-laden pewter dish before him.

"Why not?"

Jamie shrugged. "He didn't ask, for one, and it's not my place to offer an opinion to a superior officer unless it is requested."

Mindy served another plate for herself, then sat down and took a sip of the Bordeaux her husband had poured several minutes earlier. "Well that's a hell of a note. Welcome to the United States Navy, where junior officers are mute until ordered to speak. I should think Mr. Tingey would be more than a little interested in your theory that the presence of Captain Hardy in the Chesapeake means that the British are planning something big here."

"I daresay Mr. Tingey has drawn that same conclusion," Jamie said with a smile. He savored a morsel of beef and washed it down with a sip of wine. Then: "He wasn't appointed commandant of the Navy Yard because he is a good shipwright, you know. Besides, he has direct access to the president and his cabinet. And that includes Mr. Armstrong, Mr. Monroe, and Mr. Jones," referring respectively to Secretary of War John Armstrong, Secretary of State James Monroe, and Secretary of the Navy William Jones. "All those men are highly capable and intelligent, and all are far better versed in the affairs of this nation than I. Why would they require my opinion on something any fool could deduce?"

"Because they need it," Mindy stated firmly. "Because they may not be as capable and intelligent as you believe. Remember, these are the same 'brilliant' men who, along with President Madison—let's not forget him—got us into this dreadful war in the first place!" As if to emphasize her point, she seized her wine glass and downed a healthy swig. "They are a bunch of rascals and wastrels and scoundrels, the whole sorry lot of them!"

Jamie let the moment pass. He was accustomed to his wife's outspokenness. Like his sister, Diana—and like his sister-in-law, Adele Cutler, Will's wife—Mindy Cutler was a well-educated and resolute young woman who was not averse to speaking her mind, even when such behavior flew in the face of social conventions. Jamie knew that the subject of war—especially this war—was anathema to Mindy, despite her pride in his service to their country. Nevertheless, her outburst this evening was unexpected and set his sails aback.

He gave her a bemused smile. "What you just said could be construed as treason by some."

"Ha! Is it really treason?" she said hotly. Then, more calmly, "Or is it just plain common sense? Good God, Jamie. Look around you! Who is supporting this war? The New England states certainly are not. They are refusing to send their militias beyond their states' borders. Many soldiers are refusing to serve altogether. What's more, a number of their congressmen and business leaders are calling for a convention to discuss taking the four states out of the Union."

"That will never happen," Jamie said emphatically.

"You think not? Then I suggest you talk to your uncle Caleb. He's one of the leaders."

Jamie went silent. He knew Mindy was right. Caleb Cutler *was* part of a subversive movement aimed at divorcing New England from the federal government, and his involvement worried everyone in the family—especially Jamie's father, Caleb's brother Richard. And there was cause for concern. Several months earlier an American double agent and opportunist was widely rumored to have sold secret documents to

President Madison for the sum of $50,000. Those documents contained what the American press claimed was secret correspondence with Sir George Prévost, the governor-general of Canada. Among the letters was a list of prominent Federalists in New England who were advocating secession from the United States and a return to the British Empire and had approached Prévost regarding Britain's likeliness to support such a move. Jamie had no doubt that Caleb's name was on that list. Although the authenticity of these letters had been called into question, Madison and his cadre of supporters in the cabinet were taking them seriously. What might happen to Caleb and others of the Cutler family and their acquaintance for possibly being branded as traitors to the United States had yet to be determined. But Jamie was convinced that the consequences could be dire.

"I'm sorry, Jamie," Mindy said contritely into the ensuing silence. "I spoke rashly, and I am truly sorry. You have a great deal on your mind, and I don't mean to add to your burdens. But what you told me this evening has shaken me. You are my husband, and I love you above all else in this world. If anything should ever happen to you . . ."

"Nothing will happen to me," Jamie soothed. "I will not be blamed for Uncle Caleb's activities, and I believe Commodore Tingey does have matters in hand here." The words sounded lame to him even as he uttered them.

Mindy averted her eyes, looked down at her plate of mostly uneaten food. "Yes, of course. We must always believe that God is watching over us. You are too good a man, Jamie, to be taken down by such foolish government policy." She glanced up and shook her curls. "Now, I suggest we get on with our supper and talk no more about this. The night is young, and we have fires to put out, you and I."

Jamie grinned and lifted the bottle. "More wine, my dear?"

CHAPTER NINE

Hingham, Massachusetts

May 1814

THE MORNING WAS DELICIOUSLY COOL, MORE REMINISCENT OF A DAY IN mid-October than one in mid-May. Nevertheless, a warm yellow sun highlighted the splendor of a New England spring and warmed his skin, while a persistent breeze ruffled his still healthy shock of blondish hair as he made his way up South Street. Just an hour earlier, as he stood shaving before a mirror in his washroom, he had noted what seemed to be an increasing amount of white streaking the thick strands, and toeholds of white whiskers on his chin and jaw. But such signals of advancing age bothered him not at all. Not on this day. Not after reading the dispatch he had received late the previous afternoon. It had arrived, posthaste, at his home in Hingham direct on a coach-and-four from a naval vessel recently docked at Long Wharf.

At the intersection of South Street and Main Street, Richard Cutler turned right and headed past Old Ship Church toward the family seat. Although Caleb now occupied their parents' old home, Richard knew that his brother was away in Boston staying at the mansion of his wife, Joan, daughter of the lordly Cabot family of Louisburg Square.

Caleb. The very thought of him caused Richard to shake his head in worry and dismay. Caleb's ongoing resistance to the government in Washington was well documented in these parts, and Richard feared it was now simply a matter of how much longer the government would tolerate what it considered to be dangerously subversive behavior. After all, had not the president and Congress recently repealed the embargo and non-importation acts that had so angered New Englanders? And did that repeal not allow merchantmen to sail wherever they wanted to go and sell whatever they wished? Assuming, of course, that they could first cut through the British blockade that now extended from New Orleans to the Canadian border. But Yankee sea captains were widely admired for their ingenuity, and outrunning or outfoxing a Royal Navy blockade was second nature to them.

That anger against Washington was fading even further now that Britain had extended the blockade to include the entire New England coastline. Many formerly pro-British residents who believed that New England deserved a "favored nation" status with Great Britain, given its widespread anti-Washington sentiments, were furious. Their desire for a convention in Hartford to address their grievances against Washington and discuss possible secession was dwindling as more and more Yankee traders experienced a sudden influx of specie from the lifting of the embargo. But a few stalwart Yankees, including Caleb Cutler, remained both adamant and dangerously vocal. Richard was beginning to fear that after spending ten years rotting in a stinking Algerian prison as a young man, Caleb might end his days in a federal prison for the crime of treason.

A hundred paces beyond Caleb's house Richard turned left onto Pleasant Street—a street that to his mind had always seemed aptly named. A row of stately elms graced each side of the street, their branches intertwining high above the narrow thoroughfare to form a tunnel that came alive with green in the spring, provided cooling shade in the summer, and blazed with color in the fall. Halfway down the street stood a modest but lovely two-story wood-framed home that housed three people near and dear to him.

Richard walked up the home's flagstone pathway set between two attractively landscaped flower and vegetable gardens. At the front stoop he removed his tricorne hat, swept back his hair with his fingers, and lifted the brass knocker to rap twice. From within he could hear a faint echo reverberating down the hallway and a female voice calling out, "Would you see who that is, Zeke?"

"On my way, Mother," a young man's voice answered.

The front door opened to reveal a square-shouldered, square-jawed youth of sixteen years. His shoulder-length hair was equal to Richard's in length and was blondish-red, in keeping with one-half of his heritage. The bright blue eyes that held Richard's own bespoke the other half.

"Good morning, Zeke," Richard said affectionately. "You're looking fit. Are your parents at home?"

Zeke opened the door wider. "Good morning, Captain Cutler. My mother is home. Father went into town to fetch a few items. He should be back any moment. Please come in. May I fetch you some tea?"

"I'd prefer coffee, if you don't mind."

"A pleasure."

As Zeke Crabtree went off through the parlor into the kitchen, Richard glanced up at the curved stairway down which Elizabeth Cutler Crabtree was descending. "Hello, cousin," she greeted him happily. "How nice of you to drop by. We've missed seeing you these past several weeks."

"Sorry, Liz," he apologized. "I've been away."

"In Boston, perchance?" she inquired.

"Perchance." Lizzy's overly casual tone was not lost on Richard. "I had several meetings with Caleb and Mr. Hunt," he explained.

When Lizzy reached the bottom of the stairway she walked over to Richard and embraced him fondly. In the same all-too-casual tone she said, "Hmm, yes. Those meetings on Long Wharf do tend to become quite lengthy, don't they? By the bye, how is young Katherine? I assume you saw her? Perchance on more than one occasion?"

Richard smiled a bit sheepishly. "Do you know, Lizzy, you have barely changed since I first saw you in Fareham all those years ago? And I can still read you like a book." He shook her gently, then continued, "My sweet granddaughter looks more like her namesake every time I see her." Richard's face reflected his unending grief at the loss of his wife, the first Katherine Cutler, who had been Lizzy's lifelong friend and confidante. "Will and Adele are doing well too. And I also had occasion to visit with Diana and Peter in Cambridge. Young Thomas is walking like a jack tar and singing like one too. Hard to believe he's more than a year old already. I wager he'll soon be taking his rightful place on the quarterdeck of some frigate. Does a grandfather proud."

"He won't be on any quarterdeck if Diana has anything to say about it," Lizzy quipped.

"Which, of course, she does," Richard quipped in reply.

Lizzy took a step away from her cousin and placed a hand upon his shoulder. Gazing into his eyes, she said softly, "We both know what we are really talking about, don't we, Richard? Even if you choose not to admit it. All teasing aside, I am delighted that you and Anne-Marie are seeing more of each other. Many years ago—years after I had lost my beloved Jamie—after he died in your arms on *Serapis*—Katherine encouraged me to find a new love, despite—or because of—the terrible grief I could not seem to shake. Jamie was her own brother, and still she urged me to love again. I remember the day as though it were yesterday. I was here in Hingham visiting with Father, and Katherine and I were out riding on World's End on a lovely spring day. She told me that Jamie would be the first to want that for me. I didn't understand at the time. I resisted and resented the notion of another man in my life and in my bed. But I certainly understand it now after all these years with Agee and Zeke. And I am certain Katherine would want that for you, too. She would want you and Anne-Marie to be together. She told you that herself before she died, did she not?

Richard looked down at his feet. "Yes," he said so softly Lizzy could barely hear him. "Yes, she did."

"And you have feelings for Anne-Marie, don't you? I mean, *feelings* for her."

Richard nodded. He lifted his eyes to hers. "Yes, I do. It has all been perfectly innocent thus far. But yes, I do. And the fact that I do both excites and troubles me."

She brushed the back of her hand against his cheek. "That's understandable. You loved Katherine with your whole heart, just as she loved you. You two had a marriage for the ages. Everyone who knew you thought so. But she is gone now. She is now in heaven, blissfully happy knowing that you will someday join her there. Meanwhile, here on this earth, life continues. Life is for the living, Richard, and you, sir, are still very much alive—a vital and hearty man. Don't waste the years remaining to you!"

Richard blinked, then lifted her hand and pressed her fingers against his lips. "Thank you, dear Lizzy," he whispered. "You always have been my best and most loyal advocate. You have always watched out for me. Thank you and God bless you."

Just then the front door flew open and Agreen Crabtree strode in. He stopped short and narrowed his eyes at the tableau in front of him. "If you don't mind, Captain Cutler," he stated emphatically, "kindly take your filthy paws off my wife. I care not a fig that you two are cousins. Experience has taught me time and again that you are not to be trusted around beautiful women!"

Richard bowed gracefully. "My apologies, Lieutenant," he intoned. "And of course you are correct. In the future I shall endeavor to restrain my animal desires despite the stunning beauty and quality of the woman in question. When all is said and done, let it be recorded in the ship's log that no man's virtue was ever more sorely tested."

"What a pile of chicken shit. No, matey, such fancy talk will not serve here. Not in my house, and not with my wife."

"All right, you two," Lizzy interjected with a laugh, "that's quite enough. I'm off to request the butler of this grand establishment to convey a pot of coffee into the parlor."

Moments later, Zeke entered the room bearing a tray laden with a silver coffee pot, two porcelain cups, a small bowl of sugar, another of cream, and a round Wedgewood plate featuring an assortment of sweet cakes. He placed the tray on a table set between the two deep-backed upholstered chairs occupied by his father on one side and Richard on the other. Agreen took one of the cakes, popped it whole into his mouth, and washed it down with a sip of black coffee.

"Thank you, son," he said, wiping his mouth with his shirtsleeve. "Much obliged."

"You're welcome, Father," Zeke said, bowing low in his best imitation of a butler before departing upstairs.

Richard watched him go. "A fine young man you have there, Agee."

"That he is," Agreen replied. "But I'll be damned to hell if he doesn't aspire to become a teacher. A *teacher*, of all things!"

"What's wrong with that? It's an honorable and much-needed profession. Joseph is a teacher, and he loves his job. That's why he's so good at it."

Joseph, the son of Richard's cousin John Cutler and John's wife, Cynthia, had seemed a lost soul when Richard and Katherine first met him on the Cutler sugar plantation on Barbados. Katherine had recognized a rare gift in the withdrawn young man, and at her urging he sailed with Richard and Katherine from Bridgetown to Hingham to accept a position teaching mathematics at Derby Academy, the alma mater of Richard and Katherine's three children, and the oldest coeducational institution in the United States. Since those fateful days the young man had blossomed into adulthood and was now engaged to be married to the much-sought-after Abigail Whiton.

"Don't remind me," Agreen grumbled. "Joseph is Zeke's hero."

"Then you should be grateful to him."

Agreen's glare left Richard with no doubt as to where he stood on that issue. "Enough chit-chat," he said with a wave of his arm. "What say we get down to business? I know you better than any man alive, and this here is no social call. There's a reason you wanted t' see me, correct?"

"Correct."

"Well, what's on your mind?"

Richard topped off his mug of coffee and stirred in a teaspoon of sugar. "Does the name Lafitte mean anything to you? Jean Lafitte?"

"Lafitte? Sure. He's that pirate chap you and Katherine cuddled up to several years ago after he seized your vessel and held you prisoner in New Orleans."

"He's the one. You got the story all wrong, but what's new about that?"

"Like hell. In fact, as I recall, he took quite a fancy t' your wife. Lucky for you he didn't have you thrown t' the sharks and her sailin' off with him to the Spanish Main. Can't say I'd have blamed him. And it'd've been quite a big step up the romance ladder for poor Katherine. Why dredge up his name now?"

"Yesterday I received a dispatch from Secretary Armstrong. It was countersigned by Secretary Jones and sent with the knowledge and blessings of both President Madison and Secretary Monroe."

Agreen whistled. "You've got some right powerful blessings goin' on there. Makes a fellow sit back and wonder how you managed that. Promised t' mend their shirts for 'em, did ya?"

"Thanks for the compliment. But actually it involves a bit more than sewing circles."

"Oh? They want more, do they? Mend their trousers as well? Or maybe mend Lafitte's trousers?"

"A bit more than that, too. But you're getting warmer."

Agreen threw up his hands. "All right, matey," he sighed. "Enough of these silly games. Out with it. Tell this poor old ignorant sod the answer to your riddle."

"Right." Richard drained his mug and placed it gently on the tray. "As you know," he said, "we haven't seen much action in this war in recent months. We've scored several small victories at places like Sackets Harbor and Fort Erie, and Captain Porter's engagement off Valparaiso was brilliantly fought, despite the loss of *Essex*. The British have taken some land from us in eastern Maine, but nothing else of great import. It's as though they've been marking time until they defeated Napoleon and could send the bulk of their army here to America. Since this war began, the British have had to rely mostly on Canadian militia and their Indian allies. And, of course, the Colonial Marines."

Agreen nodded at the mention of the latter. The well-trained, hard-fighting former slaves who had flocked to the royal standard in search of freedom had struck fear into the hearts and minds of many Americans, especially those who owned slaves on southern plantations.

"During most of this time," Richard went on, "Cockburn has continued playing the devil in the Chesapeake. But thus far his raids have yielded precious little of lasting value to the British. The fact is, the number and intensity of his raids have been declining, although I believe that is for a reason."

"Oh? What reason?"

"I believe it's part of British strategy, and the lull in fighting is about to change. More to the point, so does Jamie. He is in the front lines in the Chesapeake, and he can see the change coming. In his estimation, the British are getting ready for an all-out push in the Chesapeake."

"Which explains Tilghman Island," Agreen remarked. That three-square-mile island in the Maryland side of the Chesapeake had recently been overrun by the British and now flew the Union Jack.

"You're right. Tilghman is an excellent case in point. I'll return to it in a moment." Richard crossed one leg over the other and leaned across the table. "As I said, everything is about to change. I believe that major new initiatives by the British are imminent. And those initiatives are aimed not just at the Chesapeake. In Canada, Governor-General Prévost has been named commander-in-chief of British land forces in North America. Intelligence reports I have read indicate that he is assembling an army to march south to attack us through New York and Vermont. In other words, down Lake Champlain. To have a chance for success, they need to control that lake."

"For supplies and lines of communication."

"Exactly. Just as on Lake Ontario and Lake Erie."

"Those lakes, God be praised, are now ours. Where does that leave Will?"

"Good news there. He has written to inform me that he will soon be transferred to Captain Macdonough's squadron on Lake Champlain."

"Then Will is in good hands, Richard. Macdonough is a fine man and an excellent naval officer. And a fearless one. His exploits at Tripoli are legendary. Few men could have done what he did. And far fewer would have dared to try."

"I agree. It's why both Commodore Preble and Captain Decatur think so highly of him. He truly is one of Preble's Boys—and one of the best of them at that."

A decade earlier, during the Barbary Wars, young Lt. Thomas Macdonough had volunteered to sail with Decatur into Tripoli Harbor, where they forced their way onto the captured American frigate *Philadelphia* and burned her where she lay at anchor to keep her thirty-eight guns out of enemy hands. Later, during an assault on Tripoli, Macdonough had again joined Decatur in chasing down the assassin of Decatur's brother, Lt. James Decatur, who had been shot in the head while accepting the surrender of an enemy gunboat. Although outnumbered five to one, they had chased down the fleeing assassin, engaged in fierce hand-to-hand fighting with him and a band of Arab soldiers, and won the day, delivering ultimate justice to the assassin and those of his command who refused to lay down their arms.

"What about Perry?" Agreen asked after a moment.

"Commodore Perry is apparently soon to depart Lake Erie for Washington. Perhaps he already has done so."

"Well that's that, then. Go on, Captain. You have my full attention. May I assume that all this has a suitable conclusion? One that reveals the great mystery of why you decided to grace my home today? Aside from flirting with my wife?"

"You may. Bear with me for just a moment longer. In the Atlantic, Warren has been replaced as commander-in-chief by Sir Alexander Cochrane. His second-in-command is, of course, Admiral Cockburn. Cochrane is one of Nelson's own and has earned many accolades in his engagements with the French. He is now leading a fleet of ships from Europe, presumably to the British naval base in Bermuda. From there they will likely sail to the base in Jamaica. Aboard those ships are four thousand veterans of Wellington's Peninsula campaign against Napoleon. They are the finest soldiers in Britain."

"Quite inconsiderate of that no-account Napoleon to lose and allow his sorry ass t' get shipped off to Elba, or so I hear?"

"So it is reported."

"Must be a nasty place."

"*Secluded* might be a better word. In any event, his abdication has allowed the British to turn their full attention to us. That brings us back to Tilghman Island. If what I hear and believe is correct, Cochrane chose Tilghman as a staging area for new initiatives in the Chesapeake. If that were not the case, why else would he defend the island so vigorously? We have tried to wrest the island back, but so far we have failed. And why would Admiral Hardy already be in the Chesapeake?"

"Let me guess. To launch new initiatives against us."

"Yes. That is what Jamie believes. And what Stephen Decatur and David Porter and Oliver Perry believe. And what I believe."

"And what I also now believe. You've convinced me. So we have a threat to our north and a threat to our midsection. May I assume we also have a threat to our south? And that's where you and Lafitte come in?"

Richard sketched a salute. "Very good! One thing I have always admired about you, Lieutenant, is your ability to cut through the crap and see things as they truly are. I knew there was a reason why I always insisted on you serving as my first officer. Yes, the British are also building up forces in Louisiana and sending spies and even a few soldiers to snoop around New Orleans, Mobile, and Pensacola. From the information we can gather, they are actively courting Lafitte to ensure he brings his impressive array of men and ships—not to mention his vast knowledge of the local landscape and culture—into the war on their side."

Agreen nodded. "Let me guess again. To ensure that Lafitte does the opposite and in fact comes in on *our* side, the powers that be in Washington want you t' use your good looks, your Boston charm, and Lafitte's blissful memory of the lovely Katherine t' close the deal."

"You got it."

"Damn, I *am* good. What are they offerin' you as payment for services rendered?"

"I am to be reinstated in the Navy with the rank of captain and given the additional title of presidential envoy. That is simply to give me credibility. Lafitte must be convinced that what I say to him carries weight in Washington. Otherwise, I am to act simply as a representative of my country. The powers that be, as you call them, believe that such a nonthreatening approach would be more acceptable to Lafitte, and for once I think they're right. He is a proud man who would not take kindly to threats."

For a moment, a light seemed to flicker in Agreen's eyes. "Sort of how you and Hugh Hardcastle negotiated with Toussaint L'Ouverture in Saint Domingue back in '98. In Haiti, I should say, as it's now called that."

"Something like that, yes."

"So, will you do it?"

"I will, under one condition."

"What is that, pray?"

"That you accompany me."

Agreen started. "What? Didn't see that comin'."

"You heard me. You accompany me. Oh, I forgot to mention that should you decide to accept, you too would be reinstated into the Navy with the rank and pay of captain—that would be a promotion, you lump—and you too would be given the grand title of presidential envoy. We would work as equals. After we're done, you can return to retirement with a nice little increase in retirement pay."

"They've *agreed* to these terms?"

"Not yet," Richard grinned. "But they will."

"How can you be so cock-sure?"

"Because the powers that be think as highly of you as I do. Besides, agreeing to these terms is the only way they're going to get me."

"Aha," Agreen chortled. "The truth comes out. So let me get this straight. What you're suggestin' I do is forsake my life of leisure, say goodbye t' my gorgeous wife and dutiful son, and go with you into some godforsaken, snake-infested swamp from which I may never return. And you are asking me t' do this t' help you negotiate a deal with a pirate who's as likely as not t' have me skinned alive and fed to the 'gators before they feast on your sorry carcass. Does that about sum it up?"

"It does. Except you omitted a few small parts."

"Oh? What parts?"

"The part about how much I enjoy your company; *and* the part about how I dearly need your wise counsel; *and* the part about how we have waged many a campaign together over the years; *and* the part about how we have saved each other's life more than once; *and* the part about how we have never let each other down; *and* the part about how your career in the Navy and at Cutler & Sons was helped along by me; *and* especially the part about how if it weren't for Katherine and me, you would not likely be married to that gorgeous woman waiting impatiently for you upstairs. Now *that* about sums it up."

Agreen stared slack-jawed at Richard, who sat there grinning at him. Slowly he shook his head. "You beat all, you know that? In no time flat you can make a man feel lower than a duck's ass in mating season."

"Yes, I know. It's another one of my unique skills." Richard stood up. "Think about it, Agee. Please, just think about it."

"I'll do that, matey," Agreen promised. "I'll do just that. I'll *think* about it."

"I can't ask for more. Please tell Lizzy how much I appreciated the coffee and cakes. And give her my love." He smirked. "Since you won't allow me to do that myself." Richard donned his tricorne hat and departed.

~ ~

The Boston Harbor Islands had long exerted a strong pull on Richard Cutler. From an early age he and his brother Will had taken great pleasure in exploring the islands' delightful copses and beaches, and in unearthing Indian artifacts for their collections and clams for their supper. Here, too, they had discovered young love, each on his own, together with a young lady happy to defy the social conventions against sailing alone with a young man to a deserted island. Grape, Peddocks, Spectacle, Little Brewster—these and others in the string of jewels protecting Boston and its southern shores held blissful memories for Richard, many of them involving the mind, body, and spirit of Katherine.

Today, as the single-masted Cutler & Sons packet conveyed Richard from Hingham to Boston, just as it had many times in years gone by, he let his mind wander neither to the past glory of such memories nor to hopes for the future. Since the death of his wife, Richard had given scant thought to either the present or the future unless the issue at hand involved a member of his family, particularly one of his two sons or his daughter. This, he had come to realize, was why he had repelled for so long any threat to the walls of his heart's defenses. Today he no longer had either the will or the resolve to resist an assault. Nor did he any longer see the point of hiding behind the walls. His heart yearned instead to welcome the warm and beckoning winds of change.

Once the larboard side of the packet boat had bumped up against Long Wharf and the helmsman had secured her bow and stern to a bollard with a buntline hitch, Richard stepped up onto the pier. "Well done, Jim," he said. "Have a safe return to Hingham. I'll be returning tomorrow at four bells in the afternoon watch. If you need anything before you cast off, or when you return, you know to ask Mr. Hunt."

James Matthew Parnell touched his hat. "I do know that, Captain. Thank ye kindly. I hope ye have a most pleasant evening and a good night."

"I intend to, Jim. Please convey my kind regards to Carol."

"I shall do that, Captain. She will be most pleased that you remembered her."

"She's a hard woman to forget, Jim. You have been blessed in marriage."

After a quick word with George Hunt at the offices of Cutler & Sons, Richard walked purposefully through Faneuil Hall toward State Street and Boston Common. It was a favorite route of his regardless of his destination. Given to the city as a gift in 1736 by Peter Faneuil, who financed its construction from profits earned in the slave trade, Boston's commercial hub was designed in the style of an English country market. Following a fire in 1766, Faneuil Hall was largely rebuilt along its original lines. In 1806 it had doubled in size under the architectural genius of Charles Bulfinch.

The hustle and bustle of The Hall, as it was widely referred to, had always fascinated Richard. Yet today he walked through it with his eyes set dead ahead.

At the junction of Park and Tremont Streets, Richard crossed over into Boston Common, a fifty-acre park that in 1634 had been set aside as a cow pasture for all citizens of Boston to use. Its northern edge abutted Beacon Hill, home to the fashionable set of Boston society, many of whom were proprietors of shipping companies that competed against other cities and other nations for the riches of the Far East. One such family had been, in its heyday, the Endicotts, who resided at 14 Belknap Street. It was to this address that Richard felt himself irrevocably drawn this late afternoon.

His knock on the thick oaken door of the Georgian mansion was answered not by the butler, Charles Dawson, but by Adele Cutler. As was her custom whenever she encountered her father-in-law, she beamed with delight as she embraced him and planted a kiss on each of his cheeks.

"How wonderful to see you, Captain!" she greeted him. "Mother said you were coming here to dine with her tonight. She is most happy that you are." She gave his arms an extra squeeze. "I can assure you that we all are."

Richard stepped inside the grand hallway. Seeing no one to hand his coat and hat to, he held onto them. "I am hoping we shall have the pleasure of your company at supper, Adele," he said.

"Alas, I fear not," Adele said, barely hiding her smile. "Katherine and I have been invited to dine with Frances and Robert," referring to her sister and brother-in-law, Robert Pepperell, who lived nearby in Louisburg Square, the crown jewel of Beacon Hill. "Little Jacob misses his cousin, and I have not seen Frances in weeks. We will likely spend the night there as well," she added innocently. "I hope you don't mind."

"Not at all," Richard assured her. "I shall look forward to a future occasion. Jacob is doing well? And his parents?"

"All are well, thank you. Katherine and I must be off. I'm just waiting for Mother to—ah, here she comes now. What perfect timing."

Richard looked down the hall at the woman approaching from the kitchen. Anne-Marie Endicott was the older image of Adele, and as always she bore herself like the French marquise she once was. Age had robbed her of none of her innate beauty. Her purple velvet dress enhanced her coloring, and the modest but finely set jewels that adorned her wrists and earlobes sparkled in the light streaming in from a setting sun. The smile she was giving Richard was warm, intimate, inviting—the sort of smile one gives to a longtime friend, or a longtime lover.

She stepped up to Richard and brushed his lips with her own. "How lovely to see you, my dear. You had a pleasant voyage from Hingham?"

"Most pleasant. Thank you."

"I am glad. I shall endeavor to make your trip worthwhile and thereby add to your pleasure. First allow me to relieve you of your coat and hat, and then we shall retire to the library. I have set out the last good bottle of Madeira left in this humble establishment. I'm sure you will recall it. It was Jack's favorite."

"I do recall it," Richard replied, adding, "with great affection and admiration." They smiled at each other, their eyes locking.

"Goodbye, Captain," Adele ventured into the intimate quiet. "I shall look forward to hearing what you have to tell Mama about Will and Jamie, and I shall especially look forward to seeing you again. I love you, Mama." With that, she left for the nursery to collect little Katherine.

"I lit a fire to warm the room," Anne-Marie said when they were seated next to each other on a settee in the library. The room was sparsely decorated, but the leather-backed books of all descriptions that lined the walls gave it a cozy feel. It was Richard's favorite room in the four-story townhome. "When the sun goes down this time of year it can get rather chilly."

"As it has this evening." Richard made a show of glancing into the hallway. "Where is Charles? I expected to see him when I walked in. You haven't let him go, have you?"

"Heavens, no," Anne-Marie said with a laugh. "I merely gave him and the cook the day off. I would be lost without them, and besides, things aren't *that* bad. I manage quite well. Mind you, I can afford few luxuries. Except, of course, the great luxury of being entirely alone with you this evening." She lifted her glass. "Cheers to you, my dear friend."

They clinked glasses.

"Delectable," Richard commented as the smooth, dry Portuguese wine coursed down his throat. "Just as I remember it."

"Is everything just as you remember it, my dear?"

Again their eyes locked. "Yes," Richard confessed softly. "Everything."

When Richard offered nothing further, Anne-Marie said, "I am reminded of something, Richard. Do you remember the day I took you to see *The Barber of Seville* in Paris? We rode in a carriage from my home in Passy to the Tuileries Palace."

"Of course I remember that day," Richard said. "It was my eighteenth birthday. January 19, 1778."

"Do you remember what you said to me when you thanked me for the gift I had given you? I had said, 'You're welcome. I hope you enjoy the play.'"

"Yes. I said, 'I will,' but I wasn't referring to the play. I was referring to the gift of your company."

She reached for his hand, took it in hers. "That's it exactly. You really do remember that evening, then."

He put his free hand over hers. "Of course I remember it, Anne-Marie. I remember it all."

"All? Including what happened afterward?"

He nodded. "Especially that. We never did see the play," he laughed. "Even when we were there in that theater box! And we left after the first act."

"Yes. We did. I'm afraid I could not control myself."

Her light laughter was cut short when Richard said, quite seriously, "Nor, as it turned out, could I. Nor can I now."

She sighed inadvertently and looked deep within him. "I want you to know something, Richard. I want you to know that that night was the happiest of my entire life." Her voice had assumed an earthy quality. "I mean that. I mean it with all my heart and soul. Thank God we had a few more nights together after that first one. The memories have sustained me all these years."

He squeezed her hand. "I'm sorry things didn't work out the way you wanted them to, Anne-Marie. I had already met Katherine and I—"

"Hush now." Anne-Marie pressed a finger gently against his lips. "Let us not talk of that, Richard. It serves no purpose. Life works out the way it is supposed to work out. It is not for us to gainsay what God has ordained. Let us be grateful that we have gone through life as friends and that we have each other now. It is enough. It *has* to be enough. It's all we have."

Richard brought Anne-Marie's hand to his lips, turned it over, and dabbed at the palm with his tongue. Then, pressing her hand to his heart, he looked into her eyes and saw glints of tears there. Suddenly doubting, he said, "Do you still want me, Anne-Marie? Do you still want me the way you did back then?"

"No, my dearest Richard," she said to him with equal urgency. "Not as I did back then. I want you the way I want you right at this very moment."

In one motion they reached for each other and blended into a hard embrace. When he moved, her lips came to his and opened to allow him entry with his tongue. Then, ever so gently, she moved her lips to his ear.

"Come upstairs with me, my dearest Richard," she whispered. "Come to my room. Come to my bed. Thirty-five years of unrequited desire await you there."

CHAPTER TEN

Alexandria, Virginia

August 18, 1814

"BLOODY HELL!"

Lt. Seth Cutler swore quietly as he supervised the agonizingly slow evolutions of freeing HMS *Seahorse* from the clutches of Kettle Bottom Shoals. She had run aground yet again on these seemingly endless and shifting shoals at the approaches to the mouth of the Potomac River. Getting her off the shoal posed no great logistical challenge. It was simply a matter of lugging her fourteen 18-pounder guns—along with her smaller 9-pounder bow chasers and just about everything else movable and weighty—from the forward half of the ship to her stern quarters. With most of her 270-man crew following suit, the bow of the *Artois*-class Royal Navy fifth-rate would also lift off the sand in which she was embedded. She could then be towed sternward by her full complement of ship's boats into deeper water. No, the details were not challenging, but it all took time. Too much bloody time! And this was the third such incident in the last two days, notwithstanding the best efforts of her seasoned crew to sound the water's depth by casting a lead line. So, too, had HMS *Euryalus*, the other frigate in the squadron, and the three bomb vessels run afoul, as had HMS *Erebus*, the 108-foot vessel carrying an array of Congreve rockets, and HMS *Manly*, a gunboat sporting ten 18-pounder carronades. It was, in the words of Commo. Sir James Alexander Gordon, "a bloody nightmare!"

"I say, someone's head is going to roll for this," said a dapper sea officer who walked up beside Seth Cutler. "As it jolly well should." He spoke out of earshot of the sailors and Marines toiling on deck, and his tone conveyed the polish and pedigree expected of one born to command in the Royal Navy. "This channel should have been far better marked. Those buoys out there are all but useless. We have followed them to the tee, and look where it has gotten us. Captain Gordon is none too pleased, I can tell you!"

"Indeed he is not, William, and I don't need reminding of that," Seth grumbled. "I have just come from his cabin. He blames me for every hour of every delay we have incurred. I understand his frustration, of course. *He* is the one who will be held responsible if we fail to support Admiral Cockburn and General Ross and provide a distraction for the Johnnies. Woe to us all if we put the admiral and general in jeopardy by failing to clear a way for their escape from Washington. And that we cannot do if we are stuck on these godforsaken shoals."

"How far do you figure we are from the river's mouth?" William Shirley asked amiably. He and Seth had become fast friends during their time together as fellow officers in *Seahorse*. "It can't be far, if you believe the charts."

"For once, I do believe the charts. The entrance is just ahead. See that headland yonder?" Seth pointed up past oyster-laden inlets to a modest headland on the bay's western shore. Thirty miles across lay its eastern shore. "The water is deep there, and the river is five miles wide. And the wind, praise the Lord, holds in our favor. I pray it remains so."

Their discussion was interrupted by a shout of alarm when a wave of consequence crested against the side of the frigate's hull, causing a sailor to lose his footing and let go of a breeching rope. The carriage of the six-foot-long gun he was dragging behind him broke free momentarily before being reined in by the exertions of three other sailors servicing the three-thousand-pound mass of black iron.

Seth watched the potential disaster in the making. "God's eyes," he breathed, keenly aware that a mounted gun careening out of control could reduce a human bone to dust in a matter of seconds. "If we are to die, let us die honorably in battle, not crushed to death aground on some bloody wedge of sand three thousand miles from home."

"We'll get there, Seth," Shirley consoled. "We'll get there. And when we do, those Yankee Doodle Dandies will be singing a different tune. They will have hell to pay. *That* I can promise you!"

— · —

The news—at least what sense could be made of it—was becoming increasingly disturbing. It was bad enough that a potential disaster was brewing before their very eyes, but the lack of any credible communication made the situation intolerable. The British had landed at Benedict, a Maryland fishing village on the Patuxent thirty-five miles southeast of the nation's capital, and were marching north toward Upper Marlboro in the sweltering heat. That much, at least, seemed certain. And then there was the reputation of the British commander. Maj. Gen. Robert Ross was a veteran of Wellington's Peninsular Campaign and a British Army officer widely admired even in American military circles for his confidence, aggressiveness, and unique strategies and tactics as a campaigner. Together with Admiral Cockburn, Ross was leading a force of four thousand Napoleonic War veterans who had spent most of the last three months on transport ships crossing the Atlantic. They were now itching for a fight, or so it seemed to a public flirting with abject panic.

There was more bad news. To get to Benedict, Ross and Cockburn had to get past a gunboat flotilla on which the American officers had pinned their hopes. This the British had done, military dispatches reported, with shocking and depressing ease. Hardly a shot had been exchanged before Revolutionary War hero Joshua Barney, realizing the futility of his position, ordered the entire flotilla scuttled to keep it out of the hands of the enemy. Barney and his sailors had abandoned ship and joined a ragtag group of American soldiers, most of them raw militia recruits, hastily called into action to stop the British advance.

"So Washington *is* the target," fumed Stephen Decatur. He and Oliver Hazard Perry had recently arrived in Washington—Perry by order of the War Department, Decatur because he thought his military expertise might prove to be of value there, despite his having to leave Philadelphia and the fitting out of his new command, USS *Guerrière*. The two naval captains were conferring with Capt. James Cutler and Navy Secretary William Jones in the secretary's office at the Washington Navy Yard.

Decatur slammed his fist on the table. "I knew it. I *knew* it!" he ranted. "I tried to convince Armstrong, but he refused to even listen. The man is a blundering idiot! So, for that matter, is William Winder. What a sorry excuse for a general *he* has turned out to be! Lord Christ in Heaven, how could two such seemingly intelligent men be so naive and misguided?"

In response to the perceived threat to the mid-Atlantic, Secretary of War John Armstrong had created the U.S. Army's Tenth Military District encompassing the area extending from Washington to Baltimore. Armstrong, however, downplayed the threat to Washington and continued to insist that the British were planning to attack the plunder-rich port of Baltimore. To compound his errors, at least in the opinion of many military leaders, he had promoted Col. William Winder to the rank of brigadier general and put him in charge of defending District Ten. Winder was by trade a lawyer from Baltimore who possessed no meaningful military credentials. To date, he had passed his time as brigadier general visiting unimportant outlying posts while doing precious little to beef up the Tenth's defenses or requisition additional troops, fortifications, and artillery pieces. This despite vigorous urgings and protestations from more qualified military strategists, most of whom served in the Navy, and three of whom were seated in this very room. A fourth, Capt. John Rodgers, was reported to be making all due haste to Washington, as was Capt. David Porter.

When Decatur had settled down from that uncharacteristic outburst, Jones coughed discreetly into a fist, a clear signal that he was uncomfortable with such chastisement of both a fellow cabinet member and a duly appointed senior Army officer. "Winder will stop Ross, you'll see, Captain Decatur," he said without much conviction. "He wields in his command more than double the number of soldiers and artillery pieces as the British. Plus, he fields 350 head of cavalry."

"You're dreaming, William," Perry interjected disgustedly. "I agree with Stephen. Armstrong refuses to call up the regulars. He's relying strictly on the Maryland and District militia. Because he is, so is Winder. Winder is incapable of thinking for himself, and they both think we're back in the revolution with the Minutemen of Massachusetts ready, willing, and able to meet the call to arms." He closed his eyes for a moment as if to regain his composure. "But enough of that. The issue before us is not Winder's competence. The issue is what we can do to defend the capital. Is there *anything* we *can* do?" He looked at Jamie. "Any thoughts on that, Mr. Cutler? On Lake Erie I learned to rely on your brother's opinions. He not once let me down. May we presume to rely equally on your judgment and experience?"

Jamie opened his mouth to answer but closed it again at the sound of a horse being reined in hard outside the building. A hard rap on the front door was followed by the rapid clip of footsteps hurrying up the hall and a second set of raps on the office door.

"Enter," Jones called out.

An orderly opened the door and saluted the assembled officers, then walked straightaway to Jones and handed him a dispatch. After another salute he turned and left the chamber.

The eyes of the three naval officers remained riveted on Secretary Jones. As he read the dispatch, they noticed the skin of his face paling and his eyes widening. His fingers trembled slightly as he read through what appeared to the sea officers to be a chronicle of catastrophe.

"What is it, William?" Perry asked warily.

The look Jones gave him was one Perry would not soon forget. "We have met the British at Bladensburg."

"Yes? And?"

Jones placed the dispatch gently on the table. When he spoke, he spoke to it, not to the three officers. "It was a rout, I am sorry to say, a complete and utter rout. Our boys fled the field at the first British volley. The only line to hold was that commanded by Commodore Barney and his sailors. But that line, too, collapsed eventually." He looked devastated, much like a man who had just learned of the sudden death of one dearly beloved. His lips trembled. "There is more, I'm afraid," he went on after patting his brow with a handkerchief. "The British are apparently not stopping despite the heat. They're again on the march. And as if matters aren't bad enough, a Royal Navy squadron has been sighted entering the Potomac."

After a moment of stunned silence, Jamie said, "Bladensburg? That's only five or six miles away, isn't it?"

Decatur leapt to his feet. "Gentlemen," he said briskly, "we have work to do!"

———

The youthful midshipman from Kent collapsed his long glass and tucked it securely under his right armpit. With a brisk stride—careful not to appear too eager in front of the men—he picked his way along the frigate's larboard gangway leading aft toward the quarterdeck. As he approached the mizzenmast he spied the ship's boatswain, Carl Wilson, standing by on sharp alert, as was the entire ship's complement. The midshipman motioned Wilson to follow him. When he climbed the four steps to the quarterdeck, Wilson remained on the main deck. As a warrant officer he was not permitted on that platform of privilege unless invited by his captain.

At the railing the midshipman snapped a crisp salute. "Fort Washington in sight, sir," he announced.

"Very good, Mr. Kendrick," the silver-haired, finely proportioned, and superbly uniformed sea officer airily responded. The midshipman might as well have reported sighting a gaggle of geese on the distant shore. Nothing in the captain's tone suggested that his squadron had failed in its primary mission to support Rear Admiral Cockburn and Major General Ross in their attack on Washington. He was already too late for that. The distant fires of the previous night had made that all too clear. Now, if Ross needed a quick exit back to the fleet via the Potomac—or if he required an escape route by water—there was none to be had. Unless he had decided to remain in Washington, he would have no choice but to plod his way back to Benedict as best he could. And *that*, Captain Gordon surmised, could be an extremely dangerous course of action, given where the British army was, deep in enemy territory.

Delays be damned, Gordon was determined to carry out his orders to clear the Potomac River of enemy resistance. Here was his opportunity to fulfill at least that part of his mission. And perhaps, he speculated optimistically, Cockburn and Ross *were* waiting upriver for him after all. He turned to his first lieutenant and gave him a slight nod.

Seth Cutler squeezed the front end of his fore-and-aft officer's hat in response and then removed a speaking trumpet from its becket attached to the helm. At the quarterdeck railing, he raised the trumpet to his mouth. *"Beat to quarters!"* he shouted. *"Clear for action!"*

Immediately the call was transmitted through the shriek of the silver bosun's whistles carried by Wilson and his three mates. Young Marine drummers on the gun deck launched into a staccato tattoo that relayed the captain's orders throughout the ship, sending sailors and Marines scurrying through the evolutions of preparing a ship for battle. The six other vessels of the squadron echoed the call to arms, and the Potomac suddenly came alive with all the extravaganza of a military parade. At the rear of the squadron, detached from it, sailed the sixty-foot brig *Anna-Marie*, a Royal Navy dispatch vessel.

Seth raised his long glass to his eye and peered at an impressive stone edifice perched on a bluff ahead. It had three levels of cannon, presumably an array of 32-pounders on the top tier and 18-pounders on the bottom two tiers. What little he knew about Fort Washington had been transmitted by British intelligence before the squadron left for the Potomac on August 17. The fort was built on White House Landing, six miles downriver from Washington City. Of special note because it was the only seaward fortress of note protecting the nation's capital, it was manned by a mere fifty or so Army personnel. Although Seth realized his imagination might be playing tricks on him, he thought he detected lingering wisps of smoke in the air above and beyond the fort, remnants of a fierce fire that on the previous night had lit up the sky for several hours before finally being doused by a torrential rainstorm.

As the squadron approached within range of the fort, Seth and his shipmates passed several tense moments waiting for the first salvo of belching fire. But none was forthcoming. To all appearances the fort was abandoned. The British would not take that for granted, however.

Because the waters at this stage of the river had narrowed somewhat, the two frigates could not maneuver sufficiently to present a full broadside. Nonetheless, as *Seahorse* veered to the river's western bank and *Euryalus* to its eastern bank, the frigates fired their forward guns as a distraction while the bomb vessels *Aetna*, *Devastation*, and *Meteor* passed between them. These smaller vessels would sail up close to the fort, line up three abreast, and lob twenty-seven-inch mortar shells down onto the exposed enemy positions below.

Explosion after explosion resounded before a single cannon on the fort's top tier returned fire. The shot was so poorly aimed that it flew over the entire British squadron, including the dispatch vessel bringing up the rear. Then, in no sequence or organized fashion, several other cannon from the two lower tiers belched orange flame and white ash, sending plumes of water towering up from the surface waters but causing no damage to the ships. Their only victims were schools of fish floating dead upon the surface, killed by underwater concussions.

"Seems rather haphazard, doesn't it, sir?" commented Midn. Oliver Kendrick. Since reporting the sighting of the fort, he had been standing at ease waiting for further instructions, his hands clasped firmly behind his back in timeless quarterdeck fashion, his eyes set dead ahead. "The gunnery, I mean. They have yet to score a hit of any sort. 'Twould seem the Johnnies are ill prepared for battle."

Seth did not immediately respond, although he too was surprised by the Americans' desultory response to an assault that was clearly causing massive destruction to the walls and roundhouse of a strategically vital fort. *Erebus* entered the fray with an onslaught of thirty-two-pound Congreve rockets. The rockets, a recent addition to the British arsenal, had been designed by the Mysoreans of India and used effectively against the British Army, which enthusiastically adopted them. They were fired in rapid and deadly succession from a ladder-like structure and proved to be as effective on the Potomac as they had been on the battlefield at Bladensburg. It was not so much the three-foot-long explosive attached to a fifteen-foot stick that inflicted terror and horror on the recipients. It was the sight of the projectiles approaching at breakneck speed, one after another, trailing a tail of fire. Many of the rockets exploded before reaching their target; others screamed over the parapets and slammed into whatever was in their deadly path.

As Seth was struggling to make sense of what appeared to be extreme American apathy, suddenly there came a blinding light immediately followed by an explosion of such authority that both land and water trembled. A volcanic mass of stone, iron shards, and other bits of debris spewed high above White House Landing and the British squadron before plunging down on what was once an imposing fortress and was now a pile of rubble. In *Seahorse*, commissioned and warrant officers—in company with every ordinary seaman and Marine on the upper deck—dived for what cover they could find until the volcanic spew was spent and Fort Washington was no more.

"Blimey!" Midshipman Kendrick rasped, momentarily ignoring naval protocol and discipline, and clinging hard to the mizzenmast. "Do you think a mortar shell struck her magazine, sir?"

Seth rose to his feet and brushed himself off. He looked quickly about the quarterdeck, his first concern for his captain. When he saw him and others in his company safe and sound, he said, in a tone of stunned disbelief, "I seriously doubt it, Mr. Kendrick. An explosion of that magnitude had to be self-induced. The Jonathans, it appears, have decided to blow up their own fort and save us the trouble!"

⌐⌐

Reports that were once dire had now turned hopeless. Official dispatches from the front lines were no longer necessary—or practical, since there was no field officer secure enough to write one and nowhere to send it even if he could. The few citizens left in the District of Columbia were now living in a surreal world. Hardly a soul walked the streets. No sound cut into the quiet dread that spread ripples of gloom and doom within the buildings of government and private enterprise. Since early afternoon, when word of the disaster at Bladensburg had been widely disseminated, the eight thousand residents of Washington had scattered to the winds, fleeing in concert with the fragments of a ravaged army seeking refuge somewhere, anywhere.

"The British have entered the city," Stephen Decatur announced somberly, although unnecessarily, to his fellow naval officers gathered in the main building of the Washington Navy Yard. Although they all held the rank of captain, and John Rodgers, just arrived in the capital, held seniority over the others in length of service at that rank, even he had deferred to Decatur's vast experience and successes at sea and in government circles. "We haven't much time. On my way here just now, I saw what I believe to be the last carriage to leave Washington. It bore the presidential seal."

"Madison?" David Porter inquired.

Decatur nodded. "Yes, but not the president. He left Washington hours ago to exhort the troops. I believe it was Mrs. Madison."

"Dolly?" Perry asked rhetorically. "Fitting that she was among the last to leave the capital. She's quite a woman. Sleeps with her rouge on her bedside table and a sword under her bed. Or so says the rumor mill."

"The rumor mill is probably correct," Rodgers said. "Mrs. Madison is a formidable woman. She had a reason to remain here as long as she did, although God knows what it was."

Decatur waved away the conversation and gazed hard at his colleagues. "Gentlemen, you know what we have to do. See to your duty and then get away from this city as fast as you are able. In two days' time we shall reconvene at the locations we have specified. Bring as many men and supplies and guns as you can muster. I have already ensured that the two brigs are in place out of sight and properly prepared. Mr. Cutler, in the meanwhile, you are to return to your wife and home, as I intend to do. We will all understand if circumstances prevent your timely arrival."

"I'll be there," Jamie vowed.

When John Rodgers stood up, the other four officers followed suit. "Good luck, gentlemen," he said. "May God watch over you, your families, and our country in this time of peril."

After that benediction the five naval captains shook hands and went their separate ways. Jamie, stone-faced, walked straightway to USS *Truxtun*, moored to the dockyard wharf a few feet away. First Lt. Robert Manning met him on deck after Jamie had walked up the gangplank and passed through the larboard entry port. Dusk was settling rapidly over a ghost town that just twenty-four hours earlier had been a bustling center of government.

"Is everything ready as ordered?" Jamie asked his first officer.

"It is, sir," Manning replied. He hesitated. When he spoke again, despair clogged his voice. "Sir, are you quite certain there is no other option?"

"Quite certain," Jamie snapped at him. "Do your duty, Lieutenant. And then abandon ship. Handsomely, now!"

Manning saluted, turned on his heel, and disappeared down the forward hatchway to meet the skeleton crew he had picked for the task at hand. Jamie remained on the upper deck until he heard the faint crackle of a fire emanating from below and breathed in the first wisps of smoke drifting up through all three open hatchways and gun ports. Only then did he retrace his steps down the gangplank to the wharf, where he glanced through the windows of the office building he had just vacated and noted yellow flames licking up from the highly combustible materials piled high within the spacious rooms of the first floor. Satisfied that the fires had taken, he glanced one last time at his ship, now ablaze, before turning to salute two Marines on guard duty and descend a ladder leading down to a small boat bobbing on the river. Settling himself in the stern sheets, he hunched his shoulders forward and sank deep within himself as the oarsmen cast off and started pulling across a glassy mile-wide stretch of water that reflected the glow of his ship and her sisters in the throes of death.

— ~ —

By the time Jamie's boat pulled up alongside the docks of Alexandria, the flames he and his fellow officers had set in the Navy Yard seemed to be consuming the entire city. By the time he reached his home on Queen Street and burst through the front door, it looked as though the universe itself was on fire.

"Jamie!" Mindy cried out when she heard the door open and her husband calling out to her. She raced down the stairs and into his arms. For several poignant moments they held each other tightly. "Jamie! Jamie!"

she cried at length, still clinging to him as if for dear life. "The British are burning Washington!"

"Yes, I know," he said.

She stepped back a pace. "Why?" she demanded to know. "Why would they do such a monstrous thing?" Both her tone and her eyes had a wild edge to them.

"Revenge."

"Revenge? For what?"

"For burning their parliament building in York. And most of the other government buildings there. Back in April of last year, remember?"

She nodded thoughtfully. "I do remember that. But it was a necessary act of war, was it not?"

"Necessary? No," Jamie said bitterly. "It was a senseless desecration of the capital of Upper Canada. Pike"—referring to Brig. Gen. Zebulon Pike, the American army commander at the Battle of York—"had won the battle. He had the British on the run. But instead of chasing down the enemy, he chose to torch the city and imperil innocent civilians. What you see across the river is the price America is now paying for Pike's reckless abandon. As a result, I have lost my ship tonight, and America has lost her capital."

She pressed her face into his neck, breathing in the aroma of acrid smoke mixed with perspiration that clung to his clothing. "I am so sorry, my darling. I am truly sorry. But I thank God that you are here with me, safe and in one piece. The British will not attack Alexandria."

"I tend to agree with you. But we must take precautions nonetheless. A British squadron is on its way here."

"So I have heard, Jamie."

Jamie went on glumly, "The only thing standing in its way is Fort Washington. But I doubt it can hold. Capt. Samuel Dyson took command of the fort just a week ago. And many of the guns are reported to be of poor quality and in poor repair." He snorted in disgust. "In any case, our army seems incapable of stopping *anything* these days!"

"It doesn't matter whether they stop them or not. The British won't attack Alexandria," she said flatly.

It was not what Mindy said but the certainty with which she said it that made Jamie take note. He held her at arm's length. "What do you mean, it doesn't matter?"

She touched his cheek with the palm of her hand and heaved a heartfelt sigh of regret. "Sit down, Jamie. You need to be sitting down to hear this."

"No. I need to be standing. Right here, right now. What is it, Mindy? Tell me."

She dropped both her gaze and her tone of voice. "Not long before you came home I went to visit Abigail Simms. I know you told me not to leave the house under any circumstances, and I was not keen to disobey you," she said hastily. "And Lord knows I would do nothing to jeopardize our baby. But Abigail is my dear friend, and she lives just down the street. I had to speak to *someone*, Jamie. Besides, I thought she might have news. Her husband is the mayor's brother, you know."

"I am well aware of that." Jamie's lack of outer reaction belied his inner turmoil. "Go on."

She looked up. "Earlier this evening Mayor Simms sent a delegation to Admiral Cockburn in Washington."

Jamie's lips tightened, but he remained stone-faced. "For what possible purpose?"

Mindy swallowed hard. "He is offering to surrender Alexandria to the British if they will spare the city."

⁓

The craft approaching HMS *Seahorse* two days later was nothing out of the ordinary. Clinker-built, it might have been a fishing dory or a workboat used along the solid oaken wharves of dockside Alexandria. Four men pulled on the two sets of oars, one pair each the starboard and larboard sides. Two other men sat in the stern, each dressed Quaker style in somber black trousers, white ruffled shirt, light black cotton coat, and black round-top hat. Behind them, its base inserted in a stern socket, fluttered a large white flag. In the bow, a seventh man sat facing forward, there presumably to help fend off the fifteen-foot boat from the frigate's hull.

The midshipman on deck duty cupped his hands at his mouth. "Boat, ahoy!" he called out, then lowered his hands waiting for the reply.

"They're landsmen, Mr. Roper," Seth said to the youth in mild reproach. "They do not understand naval protocol. I shall do them the courtesy of meeting them at the entry port and escorting them to the captain's cabin. He is the man to whom these two gentlemen undoubtedly wish to speak. Pray go below and inform the captain that he has visitors."

The midshipman snapped a salute, "Yes, sir!"

When they reached the entrance to Captain Gordon's after cabin the two Americans hesitated before entering, uncertain what they might face inside. It was inglorious enough to have had to balance themselves upright in the wobbly dory and then, cursing out loud despite themselves, climb the steep steps built into the frigate's tumble home. Desperately had they gripped the two stretches of rope running down the sides of the steps as they fought to maintain their dignity during the strenuous climb and not fall backward into the boat or, worse, into the river. And then, after finally negotiating the last step and maneuvering gratefully through the larboard entry port, they were met by an officer clad in the impeccable blue, gold, and white of a Royal Navy dress uniform standing in front of a ship's company eyeing the two men with what must have been more than a splash of mirth despite their steely expressions.

But now, in the splendor of a post captain's day cabin, the twists and turns and stabs of inadequacy they had experienced during the past few minutes seemed to be magnified a hundredfold. The cabin's artwork and bookcases, the exquisite wingback chairs set upon a decorative black-and-white checkerboard canvas carpet, seemed more in keeping with a library in a grand Georgetown manor than a captain's cubby. And the man seated behind the splendid teakwood desk personified a combination of ease, elegance, and erudition that one rarely saw in Alexandria. As the Marine on sentry duty withdrew from the cabin and closed the door behind him, Lt. Seth Cutler introduced the two Americans to Captain Gordon.

"Captain," he said, as the two visitors removed their hats, "I have the honor of introducing you to Mr. Charles Simms," indicating the taller of the two men. "Mr. Simms is the mayor of Alexandria. This other gentleman is Mr. Peter Davenport. He heads the city's Common Council."

When Gordon gave the mayor a questioning look, Simms quickly explained, "The Common Council is an advisory committee of sorts."

Gordon nodded his understanding. "Good day, gentlemen. Welcome on board His Majesty's Ship *Seahorse*. I am Sir James Alexander Gordon, captain of this vessel and commodore of this squadron. This gentleman at my side is my first officer, Lt. Seth Cutler. Pray tell us how we may be of service to you this fine morning."

Simms cleared his throat. "Captain, we realize you are a busy man. So by your leave we shall come straight to the point. Are you aware that Mr. Davenport paid a visit to Admiral Cockburn on the evening of the twenty-fourth? To discuss the terms of surrender of our fair city?"

Gordon's expression of polite interest did not change. "I am not aware of that, Mr. Simms. What did the admiral propose?"

"He proposed naught, Your Grace," Simms replied, using an inappropriate form of address. Seth attributed his lack of proper etiquette to a combination of ignorance and arse-kissing. "But he was most anxious to learn of your whereabouts."

"I see. And what did you tell the admiral?"

"I told him that you were believed to be somewhere on the Potomac, but that you had not yet arrived in Alexandria."

"I see," Gordon said a second time. Still his expression did not change. "So, am I to understand that Admiral Cockburn has deferred to me to discuss terms?"

"He has, Your Grace."

"And the admiral has departed Washington?"

Simms waved a hand at the charred ruins of the Washington Navy Yard visible through an open gun port. Beyond lay the charred ruins of other government buildings, including the President's House. "Not much point in remaining here, is there, Captain?" he said with an ingratiating smile.

Gordon looked away, said nothing. In the interlude Simms chanced a glance at Davenport and then began fidgeting with the narrow brim of his hat as Gordon sat quietly, drumming his fingers on the table while seemingly searching for an answer in the deckhead above. Then, in a voice of resolve: "Mr. Simms, Mr. Davenport, here are my terms of surrender: By our count there are twenty-two merchant vessels moored between here and Georgetown. Those vessels are hereby forfeited to the Royal Navy as spoils of war. Judging by their low freeboard, most of these vessels are heavily laden. Is that assumption correct?"

"That is correct, Your Grace," Simms assured him, adding helpfully, "These ships contain produce of all kinds and descriptions, including wines and cigars of high quality. To entertain you and your officers on your return voyage, you see."

"Very well, then. Have these ships prepared to set sail with the tide this Thursday, September first. In addition, you will create documents in which you attest that the city of Alexandria, Virginia, has surrendered to His Majesty's government, a copy of which you shall deliver to me. I shall require no further terms from you, and in consideration for your surrender I pledge that no harm shall come to either Alexandria or Georgetown. Such terms are acceptable to you?"

"Quite acceptable, Your Grace," Simms replied, unable to conceal the relief in his voice.

"It is done, then. Lieutenant Cutler will see you out. Good day to you, gentlemen."

On the following Thursday HMS *Seahorse* and the warships in her squadron departed Alexandria and began the one-hundred-mile voyage to Admiral Cochrane's fleet in the Chesapeake. Behind the squadron sailed the twenty-two merchant brigs, schooners, and snows that Gordon had appropriated as the terms of Alexandria's surrender to the Crown. *Anna-Marie*, the dispatch vessel, had been sent ahead several days earlier to inform Cochrane of developments.

Gordon was taking no chances. He had informed his officers that until the squadron reached the Chesapeake, every man jack would remain on high alert for shoals, floating debris, and areas ripe for ambush among the thickets and bluffs clustered along the banks of the Potomac. He expected the occasional sniper to take potshots from shore, and his fears were warranted. A quartermaster's mate had already been struck down, and several bullets had ricocheted off a mast or railing, tearing out a chunk of pine in the process.

"I am particularly concerned about that plantation we passed on our voyage upriver," he confided to three of his commissioned officers late the following evening as they relaxed in his cabin following a perfunctory meal of biscuit, salted meat, potatoes, and gravy. Progress had been slow that day due to fluky winds and the need to wait for the slower merchant vessels to catch up. Tonight the squadron was anchored in mid-river, and after they finished their meal the officers took tea rather than the customary glass of wine or port. Precious little sleep awaited any of them that night, and while the larders were full and the merchant ships replete with luxuries of one kind or another, Gordon was loath to allow himself or his officers to imbibe anything that might induce sleep or momentary sloppiness. "If I were the Americans and I desired to lie in wait to surprise my enemy, I would set up shop there. Questions? Concerns? You have permission to speak freely."

"I know the bluff in question, Captain, and I quite agree with you," Seth ventured. Protocol allowed him, as first officer, the opportunity to speak first. "It's called Belvoir Plantation. According to the charts it's about fifteen miles downriver from White House Landing, and so about ten miles from where we are at the moment."

"I know it as well," asserted 2nd Lt. William Shirley. It will be a challenge to dislodge a battery placed on that bluff. It's perhaps the highest point of land between here and the Chesapeake."

Gordon had anticipated that remark. He was about to comment on what he had in mind to elevate the guns should such action be required when an alarm sounded above. The stomping of bare feet running on the main deck above them was followed by the clomp of boots coming down the aft companionway. Following the hail of a Marine on guard duty outside, the door clicked open, allowing entry to a young midshipman.

"Sorry to disturb you, Captain," the midshipman fairly exploded, "but there are two fireships approaching. Mr. Keating," referring to the fourth lieutenant and the current senior officer on the deck, "requests your presence at once!"

All four officers were up in an instant and making for the door and companionway in order of rank. On deck, it demanded but a moment to absorb the dire threat. Two vessels—both brigs by the look of them, although it was difficult to distinguish rigging and spars, so consumed were the two vessels in towering yellow flames—were coming at the squadron, one on a collision course with *Seahorse*, the other on a course to collide with the frigate *Euryalus*.

"Get the boats over!" Gordon commanded. "Man the oars and grappling hooks! Sailors, take position with repelling poles!"

As boat crews worked quicktime to get the ship's boats over the side and manned with oarsmen, other sailors took position shoulder to shoulder along the starboard railing. Each sailor clutched a ten-foot oaken pole to try to ward off the fireship if all else failed. As the boat crews rowed furiously toward the lead vessel, grappling hooks held at the ready, Seth spied three shadowy figures on the deck of the lead fireship diving into the Potomac.

"Sergeant Gregory!" he barked at a Marine sergeant standing by to help wherever he was needed.

"Sah!"

Seth jabbed a finger ahead. "Position a squad of Marines at the bow. You see the splashes in the water? Three men are making for shore. Stop them!"

"Sah!"

Gregory called four Marines to the frigate's bow and pointed at the white splashes fast approaching the Potomac's western shore. The splashes were barely visible, even with a night glass, despite the ample light thrown off by a harvest moon and the blazing inferno bearing down on them. "Take aim, take aim, steady now. *Fire!*" he bellowed. Five shots rang out, one of them from Seth Cutler's pistol. "Reload!" Gregory shouted as tiny plumes of water shot up where bullets pinched the surface of the river. The splashes kept going.

"Take aim, take aim. *Fire!*"

This time, Seth noted with satisfaction that one bullet at least had found its mark. Near shore he saw a swirl of water, as though a large fish had suddenly been snagged and was thrashing about. In the next instant a number of ghostly black figures came running out of the bush to wade into the brackish water and pull someone out onto the shore.

"Stand down!" Seth Cutler ordered, seeing the futility of further volleys. A quick glance to his right confirmed that the threat posed by the fireships had been thwarted. Both were under tow to the eastern bank of the river, there to run aground and burn themselves to ashes.

On the river's west bank, behind a protective slab of granite rock not far inland, Stephen Decatur and David Porter dropped to a knee beside Jamie Cutler. With a small gesture Decatur dismissed two other men who were tending to the young Navy captain. Drawing out his knife from a side pocket, he cut away Jamie's cotton shirt, its left side drenched in blood. Quickly Decatur removed his own shirt, cut off its two sleeves, and together with David Porter tied one sleeve around Jamie's wounded left shoulder and used the other to fashion a makeshift figure-eight sling.

Dazed and in shock, Jamie watched the proceedings as best he could. "Captain?" he wheezed at Decatur.

"What is it, James?" Neither Decatur nor Porter raised their eyes from the task at hand.

"Did Mark and David make it?" Jamie asked, referring to the two other crew members of USS *Truxtun* who had volunteered to sail with him on the fireship. "And did our plan work?"

"They did," Decatur assured him. "But I'm afraid the answer to your second question is no. The British used grappling hooks to latch on to the fireships and tow them away. I have to give them credit. They carried that out smartly. Damned if I know anyone else who could have done it as well. Present company included."

When Jamie tried to lift his head, a jolt of pain coursed through him. He slumped back down. "I'm sorry, Stephen. It's my fault. I should have remained aboard longer."

"Belay that, Captain. You're talking nonsense. You could not have stayed longer. You have burns all over your body as it is. Had you remained aboard any longer you would have been cooked! What's more, the wind gave out on you."

"Not to worry, James," Porter soothed, trying to sound lighthearted and encouraging in the face of adversity. "Rodgers and Perry will put things to right at Belvoir. The bleeding seems to be in check here. And that figure-eight sling reminds me of the time in Saint Kitts when I tended to your father. He was a lieutenant in *Constellation*, and I was a snot-nosed young midshipman. I was also the one responsible for a spar falling on him and breaking his clavicle. I'm sure he has told you that tale," Porter laughed.

"Yes, he has." Jamie closed his eyes and gritted his teeth as yet another stab of pain besieged him. When he opened them again, he looked hard at his two colleagues. "How bad is it?" he wheezed. "Tell me truly. I want to know the truth!"

Porter deferred to Decatur, who, finished with his work, looked at Jamie and said, "The truth is, I don't know. You've lost a lot of blood and the humerus is shattered. That bullet must have hit it smack on. Our chief worry now is infection. We need to get you into the care of a surgeon. A wagon will be here shortly to take you back to Alexandria. I shall accompany you and see to the details. It's the least I can do."

Chapter Eleven

Plattsburgh, New York

September 11, 1814

DAWN WILL BREAK FAIR, THE THIRTY-TWO-YEAR-OLD LIEUTENANT SUR-mised as he came on deck buttoning up his uniform coat, *and the winds have shifted. Today is the day.*

Although the sun was not yet above the horizon, the stars were fading and the first indications of night's end were detectable in the eastern sky above the southern tip of Grand Isle, at thirty-one square miles the larg-est island in Lake Champlain. Already the light northeasterly breeze—a fair-weather breeze in this month of September in New England—was stirring the telltales high on the mizzen shrouds.

Rubbing his hands against the morning chill, he began walking forward along the sixty-five-foot length of his command. Although USS *Preble* was the smallest vessel in the American naval squadron—not counting the six oar-powered gunboats—and her armament consisted of but seven 12-pounder long guns and two 18-pounders, her naval ensign flew grandly from its place on the mizzen halyard. Launched several weeks earlier after being built in backbreaking record time by Noah and Adam Brown, she had been christened in honor of Capt. Edward Preble, a naval commander of international acclaim and impeccable cre-dentials. That she had then been given to Will Cutler to command was a singular honor for the young lieutenant and a source of immeasurable pride. Because his father had served with distinction under Commodore Preble during the war with Tripoli, Richard Cutler was counted as one of "Preble's Boys," the most sought-after epithet in the U.S. Navy. Now, following in his father's footsteps, Will was yearning for equal glory as a naval officer.

At the foremast, Will paused to gaze out upon the looming scene of a battle that, if American military intelligence and Commodore Macdonough were correct, was now only a few hours away. There, to the north, the squadron was arrayed in defensive formation in a line running north to south across a bay flanked on its northern shoreline by Cumberland Head, a large bluff jutting out into Lake Champlain, and on its southern shoreline by the town of Plattsburgh, New York. *Eagle*, *Saratoga*, and then *Ticonderoga* were anchored, as was *Preble*, at both bow and stern to keep them steady in the water, their starboard guns run out and trained southeastward toward the entrance to Plattsburgh Bay. Each vessel had a spring line attached to the capstan amidships leading forward to the anchor cable at the bow, a device that allowed the vessel to be moved and her guns properly trained without having to weigh anchor or go through any of the other evolutions of naval gunnery.

Behind them, tucked in close to the bay's northeastern shore, bobbed six highly maneuverable gunboats, also at anchor, the single 24-pounder long gun of each mounted in the bow ready to be deployed wherever Fate or necessity might require it during the heat of battle. Beyond them and stretching down the western bank stood the church, mills, mercantiles, and other outbuildings of Plattsburgh, a town that was quickly deserted when its three thousand residents received word on the first of the month that a British army was marching southeast from Lower Canada. Four miles beyond Plattsburgh, to the south, Will could just see Valcour Island, where in 1776 a naval squadron under the command of Benedict Arnold had delivered a hammer blow to a considerably larger Royal Navy squadron. Arnold's victory ended the immediate threat of a British invasion of the fledgling Republic of Canada, an invasion that, if successful, would have isolated the four New England states and effectively taken them out of the rebellion. Today, Will realized—as did every member of the American squadron, whatever his rank or rating—that the stakes were just as high.

At precisely 5 a.m. a chorus of ship's bells clanged pleasantly from the four American warships anchored in the bay, two bells from each ship. At that moment Will was mulling over the previous evening's discussion in the after cabin of *Saratoga*, the squadron's flagship. In the lull following the bells' peals Will heard footsteps approaching him from behind.

"Good morning, sir," a cheerful voice greeted him.

Will recognized the voice as that of Daniel Clive Mayes, an affable and self-effacing man of twenty-five years who nonetheless was a fierce taskmaster commanding deference and obedience from even the most recalcitrant sailors. Will credited Mayes with instilling, in a remarkably short span of time, the rough discipline and efficiency demanded of a navy ship's crew both in the rigging and at the guns. He felt most fortunate that Commodore Macdonough had assigned Mayes to *Preble* as her first officer. Since arriving from Lake Erie several months earlier in the company of the Brown brothers, Will had had precious little opportunity to come to know the character and skills of the officers currently available for duty. Fortune had smiled on him, aided by a good word put forth on his behalf by his father to Navy Secretary Jones, then relayed from Jones in Washington to Commo. Isaac Chauncey at the American naval base at Sackets Harbor on Lake Ontario.

"Good morning, Mr. Mayes," Will replied, using the formal address in deference to a team of sailors on their knees nearby holystoning the wooden planks of the ship's deck to a bleached white. "You slept well, I trust?"

"I did, sir. Like a babe in arms. And you?"

"I did, what little sleep I was able to snatch, helped along by the commodore's generosity with his port—so generous, in fact, that I feared I might pitch overboard during the return row to *Preble*. That would hardly have done in front of the men. Those on first watch would have spread word of it about the ship like a wildfire."

"I daresay they would have, sir," Mayes said with a chuckle. "And I must agree, it was a delicious port, a fine-tasting spirit with no aftereffects this morning. Odd in a way, isn't it, the commodore's propensity for alcohol, given his staunch religious beliefs."

"Not odd at all, Mr. Mayes," Will countered, careful to keep his voice low. "Episcopalians enjoy their alcohol as much as any man. Have you ever known an Episcopal priest to abstain, however devout his character and intentions? Or for that matter, any shepherd of any faith?"

Mayes paused to consider that. "Now that you mention it, sir, no, I have not."

"There, you see? They enjoy their spirits as much in a bottle as out. It's the way of the world, and either way it's heavenly."

The officers laughed softly together, then fell silent as each contemplated the slowly spreading dawn, felt the first feeble stabs of warmth in the air, heard the sounds of a ship coming to life in a freshening breeze, and remembered the words of warning and exhortation spoken the previous evening. At length Daniel Mayes said, "The commodore is right, you know. All *Confiance* has to do is stand off and on at the entrance to the bay and blast us. Our carronades would be useless at that distance, and our long guns are no match for hers. We'd have no choice but to cut our cables and attack."

HMS *Confiance*, the flagship of the Royal Navy squadron, was a fifth-rate frigate, the largest naval vessel ever to sail on Lake Champlain. Her thirty 24-pounder long guns, fifteen to a side, were far superior in number to the eight long guns of *Saratoga*, the sloop-of-war serving as flagship to the American squadron. The weight of the British frigate's broadside exceeded that of the entire American squadron, not even counting her numerous carronades, which were effective only in close-quarter engagements.

Will glanced over his shoulder. The sailors on deck duty had moved on, and no other ship's personnel were in sight except for Neil Stricher, the vessel's sole midshipman, who was currently serving as deck officer. Will returned his salute, then, when the midshipman had moved on, gave his vest pocket watch a quick glance. Coming on to 5:30. In thirty minutes, at four bells in the morning watch, the men would be roused for breakfast and battle.

"Macdonough is correct on that point, Dan," Will agreed, resting his forearms on the starboard railing and again gazing out to where the British squadron—a frigate, a brig, two sloops-of-war, and twelve gunboats—would soon make their presence known. American military personnel had closely followed the squadron's progress from the Royal Navy base on Ile aux Noix, an island on the Richelieu River in Lower Canada thirty-eight miles to the north.

"Macdonough is also correct," Will went on, "in believing that Downie will not fight a defensive action." Capt. George Downie, the acting commodore of the British squadron, was well known for his aggressiveness. "He won't be able to resist an enemy that to his mind is lined up for the kill. No, he'll come straight at us."

"In the tradition of Admiral Nelson."

"Exactly so. We saw this on Lake Erie, and I'd wager all I have that we'll see it here, too. To do otherwise would be viewed as dishonorable in the eyes of the Admiralty and in the eyes of Downie's commanding officer, Commodore Yeo. And when the British do attack, we can only hope that our spies are correct in believing that because *Confiance* was so hastily built—and in fact was still in the hands of carpenters and riggers as she was being towed away from Ile aux Noix—she is not yet ready to go up against any enemy. Our intelligence confirms that her crew is composed of more army recruits than navy. Prévost has been in such a hurry to get his invasion of New York under way that he has likely overlooked key elements of sound planning and preparation. His inattention to detail in this instance could be his undoing as commander-in-chief today and an army officer tomorrow. Should the British fail here today, he will be the one blamed, not Downie. Hell, reports have it that Downie joined the squadron only two days ago."

"So you agree that the British army's attack at Plattsburgh will coincide with the Royal Navy's attack here in the bay?"

Will glanced up at Cumberland Head and then across the bay to a knoll on Crab Island. Commodore Macdonough had ordered a gun battery erected on both spots. The one on Crab Island was manned by hospitalized soldiers and sailors too debilitated to fight in the field or on deck but strong enough to yank a lanyard on a 6-pounder cannon. In his deployment of artillery, he had coordinated efforts with Brig. Gen. Alexander Macomb, the thirty-year-old Army officer now in charge of challenging the British on land after the former commanding officer, on orders from Washington, departed for Sackets Harbor with four thousand regulars. Macomb would have to make do with a handful of regulars and 1,500 militia from Vermont and New York, the vast majority of whom had no desire to fight, and most of whom were either invalids or raw recruits. Thus far, Macomb had waged a brilliant rearguard campaign against the nine thousand seasoned British soldiers marching against him. Making full use of roadblocks, sniper fire, false roads leading to cul-de-sacs and ambush, and other delaying tactics, Macomb had bought valuable time to bolster his defenses on the ridge of the south bank of the Saranac River.

"Yes, of course," Will replied. "To do otherwise would make no sense."

For no reason a vivid image of Adele and his daughter, Katherine, flashed into his mind. He closed his eyes, willing the image to linger. It didn't, but another memory did, this one of the previous evening during the meeting with the squadron's officers in Commodore Macdonough's cabin. After a detailed review of battle strategy and tactics to be followed the next morning, Macdonough had turned to the flagship's senior midshipman. "So, Mr. Abbott," he had inquired, "are you now prepared to die for your country?"

"Certainly, sir," the stoic nineteen-year-old from Westford, Massachusetts, had replied without hesitation. "That is what I came into the service to do."

Will opened his eyes and said softly, "God forbid the British overrun Macomb's redoubts and seize those shore batteries. Were they to turn their firepower on us, we'd be hard-pressed."

"Yes, sir," Mayes agreed. He checked his watch. "It's time, Captain. I'll have the bosun rouse the men."

"Do that, Lieutenant."

❧

"There, Captain. It's the signal."

Will looked to where Mayes was pointing. Amid the highest peaks on Cumberland Head a stack of white birch logs had been set ablaze. It was the prearranged signal to the American squadron—and to Macomb's regulars and militia dug in along the Saranac River—that the Royal Navy squadron had been sighted and was approaching.

"Clear for action, Mr. Mayes," Will said quietly. "Beat to quarters."

Mayes picked up a speaking trumpet. "Beat to quarters," he shouted through it, his call immediately taken up by a single Marine drummer beating in time with young Marine drummers in *Eagle*, *Saratoga*, and *Ticonderoga*. There was no need beyond protocol for the dramatic display. Since finishing breakfast more than an hour earlier, every sailor and Marine in the American squadron had been standing by his assigned battle station.

At 9 a.m. the British squadron rounded Cumberland Head on a close haul in line abreast. Peering through a long glass, Will instantly recognized the wisdom of Macdonough's preparations. The British were without doubt as aware of the composition and disposition of the American squadron as the Americans were of the British squadron. A string of lookouts placed from the mouth of the Richelieu River down the northwestern shoreline of Lake Champlain to Plattsburgh had kept the American commanders apprised of enemy movements. Macdonough knew what was coming at him and when it was coming. He had in fact predicted that the battle would take place yesterday, but the strong headwinds of the morning discouraged the British from sailing south.

Will also had no doubt that the British battle plan had been well rehearsed, at least on paper. They knew exactly what they were about. Commodore Downie might have joined the squadron just a couple of days earlier, yet he had to have either devised or approved of—or simply been informed of—a naval deployment that Sir James Lucas Yeo, commander of British naval forces on the Great Lakes, believed would vanquish the last line of defense of a supply line vital to General Prévost's successful invasion of America through New York. Downie was a respected Royal Navy officer, else he would not be in command of this squadron, and his expertise was a major obstacle for the Americans to overcome. Then again, Will reasoned, Thomas Macdonough possessed his own stellar credentials as a naval commander, and he too represented a major obstacle for the British to overcome. Since the ice on Lake

Champlain had melted in April, the thirty-year-old Navy veteran from Middletown, Delaware, had been harassing the British ships with whatever he could find to float, and he had done so with such efficiency that Commodore Yeo had replaced the former commander, Daniel Ping, with Capt. George Downie and had ordered *Confiance* built and made ready with all due haste.

"Starboard guns primed and ready, Captain," reported Stephen Beckwith, *Preble*'s boatswain, doing double duty as chief gunnery officer. He had learned both trades while serving with Midshipman Macdonough in USS *Ganges* during the Quasi-War with France, and later while serving under Lieutenant Macdonough and Capt. Stephen Decatur in the 12-gun sloop USS *Enterprise* during the war with Tripoli. Macdonough had not forgotten Beckwith's dedication to his craft and his country, and he had been quick to sign on the native of Stonington, Connecticut, the instant he learned of Beckwith's availability for duty.

"Thank you, Beckwith," Will replied crisply. "At my command."

"On your command, sir." Beckwith saluted his captain and turned on his heel.

Events unfolded almost exactly as Macdonough had predicted the previous evening: four British sailing vessels and ten gunboats coming straight on against four American sailing vessels and six gunboats. Even the rigs of the opposing vessels were similar, with the notable exception of HMS *Confiance*, which dwarfed the other vessels in the bay, looking almost Brobdingnagian to Will.

Confiance suddenly veered to larboard and opened up with her fifteen starboard long guns in a rolling sequence of flame and ash. *Saratoga*, her target, took the full brunt of the broadside before returning fire, although the number of her guns and the decibels they produced seemed anemic compared with the thunderous output of the British flagship. Nevertheless, to Will's immense satisfaction, *Saratoga* seemed to suffer minimal damage while delivering a knockout blow to one of *Confiance*'s long guns, judging from the harsh *clang* that resounded about the bay.

Will swept the arena of battle with his long glass. Sailing ahead of *Confiance*, Ping's 16-gun brig *Linnet* and the 10-gun sloop *Chub* were making for USS *Eagle*, the vessel anchored on the northern extreme of the American defensive line. Their combined broadside was twice what *Eagle*'s eight long guns could offer in reply unless her captain could lure in his adversaries close enough to bring her twelve 32-pounder carronades to bear—which was unlikely, Will concluded, unless Henley cut his anchor cables and sent *Eagle* on the attack.

Closer to Will, the schooner *Ticonderoga* was already exchanging fire with the British gunboats, which had lunged forward like a pack of wolves smelling blood to savage their prey. *Ticonderoga* was taking hits—as were *Saratoga* and *Eagle*—but thus far the integrity of the stout wooden frames of the American warships had not been compromised. All four sailing vessels in the American squadron had been built quickly but expertly by Noah and Adam Brown, and what they built was built to last, even in battle.

"*Finch* is coming at us, sir," Daniel Mayes said to Will in a voice quivering with excitement.

"As we all assumed she would," Will replied, fairly shouting over the din of ship's guns that were turning the once placid bay into a swirling bowl of stinking, acrid smoke punctuated by the violent and deadly roar of ships' guns. "Is the reception committee in place?"

"It is, Captain," Mayes assured him. "It awaits your pleasure."

The two American officers knew the provenance of the adversary now bearing down on them. HMS *Finch* had been built in Vergennes, Vermont, as a merchant sloop before being refitted for naval service. In June of the previous year she had been captured by the British and commandeered into the Royal Navy. When in American hands she had carried ten guns, and at sixty-four feet she was similar in length to *Preble*. It made sense that the British would put her up against *Preble*.

A quick glance ashore to the town and the bluffs revealed no enemy action on land as of yet. Surprised, Will shifted his glass southeastward to *Finch* a few hundred yards distant, her sails close-hauled and taut, her bow throwing off spray. "Not yet," he murmured, more to himself than anyone else. "Not just yet. Wait. Wait. A little longer. A little longer. Wait until she turns." When at last she did begin her turn, he cried out, "*Now, by God! Now, Mr. Mayes! Fire!*"

Lieutenant Mayes repeated the order, and the five long guns on *Preble*'s starboard side belched orange flame and white sparks. Four of the five shots slammed into the little three-masted frigate, one against *Finch*'s hull and the other three in her rigging. One shot sprung a stay on her foremast, causing it to teeter in the aftermath of that first shock of broadside. Yet she fought on undeterred, supported by a squadron of British gunboats, pumping one broadside after another into *Preble*. Sailors on *Preble*'s deck threw themselves flat on the sloop's deck or crouched low behind the railing, and it was all Will and his lieutenant could do to remain standing in the face of the brutal onslaught.

For another quarter hour the two vessels exchanged fire without major consequence to either hull, although *Finch*'s halyards and stays and shrouds were taking a vicious beating. Then two things happened almost at once. A round shot from *Finch* struck the *Preble*'s aft railing, sending a volley of spear-like wooden shards through the air as though hurled by a squad of Spartan warriors. One shard struck Daniel Mayes in the right thigh, impaling him several inches deep. As though what had happened was nothing out of the ordinary, he grabbed hold of its outer end with both hands and slowly but steadily extracted it from his muscle and flesh before tossing it over the side. A stream of blood flowed freely from the ugly gash to form a pool of red liquid on the afterdeck.

Before Will could react, a second shot, this one from one of the other American vessels, slammed into *Finch*'s mainmast. The shot punched through the mast a few feet above the deck, leaving jagged edges of white pine exposed, and the rest of the mast crashed down on deck and rolled overboard into the lake. As the mast plunged downward, it took with it much of the rigging supporting the foremast and mizzen. Will glanced to his left. At the helm of *Ticonderoga*, Capt. Stephen Cassin lifted his bicorne hat in salute. With the support of the American gunboats he had beaten back the British gunboats and then, having a better angle than *Preble*, had administered the *coup de grace* to HMS *Finch*.

Will lifted his hat in reply, then bowed slightly in tribute. As *Ticonderoga* repositioned her starboard guns to take aim at *Confiance*, now anchored a good four hundred yards from *Saratoga*, Will peeled off his uniform jacket and cotton shirt, ripped off a sleeve with a knife, and wound the material tourniquet style around the open wound in Mayes's thigh.

"Don't worry about me, sir, I'm fine," Mayes protested, struggling to stand.

"Stay where you are, Lieutenant," Will admonished. "You've lost a lot of blood and I shan't see you losing more." Gently he settled Mayes against the starboard aft bulwark. "Now sit there and sit still. That's an order!"

Will, bare-chested, rose to his feet and related to Mayes what he was seeing. *Finch* was drifting helplessly toward Crab Island. There was nothing her captain could do. She was in irons with no one able to come to her rescue by land or water. As she reached the shallow depths of the island, the 6-pounder battery Macdonough had positioned there outside the hospital opened fire. After the second volley, *Finch* struck her colors.

"One down," Mayes exulted when Will told him.

"Rather more than that, I believe," Will replied. "From the look of where those British gunboats are now positioned, they won't be causing us further worry. Rather un–Royal Navy of them to run away from a fight."

"It is, sir," Mayes said weakly in reply. "Perhaps that's because they're manned by local Canadian militia units."

"More than likely." Will picked up the speaking trumpet that Mayes had dropped on deck. "Mr. Beckwith!"

"Sir!" the boatswain replied, running up.

"Mr. Mayes has been injured, so I am relying on you. I shall have the anchor cables cut and the jib and tops'l raised. We shall go to the aid of the others."

"We've suffered damage to our top-hamper, sir," Beckwith cautioned. "And we have five dead and a number of wounded."

"I regret that, but my order stands. Our hull is intact and our sails are untouched, and were it just you and me left alive, we would still render assistance. Understood?"

"Understood, Captain."

As *Preble* got under way, Will Cutler took stock of the ferocious battle being waged fifty yards ahead. Like two adversaries late in the rounds of a grueling boxing match, the two flagships were continuing to slug it out, *Confiance* relying on the sheer weight of her hammer blows—which were becoming increasingly erratic—while *Saratoga* relied on her fighting skills. By this time most of *Saratoga's* starboard battery had been upended and was lying impotently on deck—which was why, Will noted with satisfaction, Macdonough had ordered her bow anchor cut loose and the kedge anchors laid out on her starboard quarter hauled in. Slowly, ever so slowly, the American flagship turned around until her fresh larboard battery was brought to bear.

The pounding continued on both sides. As *Saratoga* turned, Downie had the opportunity to rake her exposed stern. But to Will's surprise he failed to capitalize on that opportunity. He had allowed the American flagship to pass through the evolution unmolested and then to wreak havoc upon his own ship. Why? Will had no clue.

Linnet, meanwhile, had blasted her way to the American line and was pounding *Eagle* mercilessly. *Eagle* had focused her guns initially on *Chub* in an effort to knock her out of the fight before responding to *Linnet*. *Chub* had struck her colors, but *Linnet* remained very much on the offensive. It was as though her commanding officer, Daniel Ping, deposed from squadron command, was taking out his frustration on the American sloop, hoping to regain the respect he had lost and the glory he had once envisioned.

Will pointed. "Steer for *Linnet*," he ordered Beckwith. Through a speaking trumpet to the gun crews on deck: "Larboard battery, make ready! Starboard battery, stand by!"

As *Preble* surged toward the enemy brig with all the speed she could muster, Will heard a throaty cheer erupt from the deck of *Saratoga*. A moment later he surmised why. In attempting to mirror the American flagship's maneuver, *Confiance* had faltered, exposing her own stern to a raking fire from *Saratoga's* fresh larboard guns. With her rigging chewed up beyond effective use, her rudder splintered, and her guns askew, her captain had ordered her ensign taken down. *Confiance* was surrendering!

With her surrender and the surrender of two other vessels in the British squadron—and with the British gunboats now staying well clear of the heat of the engagement—*Linnet* had no options left, regardless of her captain's desire to fight on. Before *Preble* could unleash a single shot at her, she too struck her colors.

With the fall of *Linnet*'s flag, the battle for control of Lake Champlain was over—as was the battle for control of all the Great Lakes. The threat of a British invasion from Canada was over as well.

As an eerie silence settled over the bay and the town of Plattsburgh, Will knelt down beside Mayes and checked the bandage. "Right. Let's get you and the rest of our wounded ashore to that hospital. From the looks of it, Dan, you'll come through just fine."

Mayes gritted his teeth against the pain and nodded. "Yes, sir, I shall," he said softly. "Thank you, sir."

CHAPTER TWELVE

Hingham, Massachusetts

September 11, 1814

THE VISTA THAT STRETCHED OUT BEFORE RICHARD CUTLER WAS AT once dreamlike and firmly real. He was standing at water's edge on an unfamiliar beach of squeaky golden sand that glistened under a cloudless sky. The sun blazing above him cast a treasure trove of jewels upon a wind-swept, white-capped turquoise sea. The air temperature was ideal— neither too hot nor too cool—and a refreshing northwesterly breeze tousled his long blond hair. He lifted his face to the sun and felt it warm his skin beneath the blue-and-white dress uniform of a U.S. Navy captain.

None of this seemed out of place to him. He had enjoyed the pleasures of many similar beaches on the coasts of America, Europe, and West Indian islands, and what he was seeing and sensing today he had experienced many times in those places. Except for two things. Here, the color of the sea and the sky and the beach, and even his clothes, was shockingly vivid. This could not be a dream, because his dreams were always composed in obscure, dullish grays.

And yet how to explain the presence of his former command, the frigate USS *Portsmouth*? She was hove to no more than fifty yards offshore under all plain sail to royals. Although he could not be sure—the distance was too great to make out fine detail with the naked eye—he thought he recognized old shipmates on her: Lt. Eric Meyers, Able Seaman Harvey Cole, Sailing Master Josiah Smythe, Boatswain Peter Weeks, and other men he had come to know and respect while in the

Navy or as shipmates in a Cutler & Sons merchant vessel. They were all there together. How odd. Then he saw that the ship's cutter was being lowered on its tackle into the water. After it splashed onto the sea, a regal figure bedecked in the grandeur of a Royal Navy post captain's dress uniform clambered down into it. What a British sea officer was doing aboard a U.S. Navy frigate off this beach was a mystery to him, but not one he felt he had to unravel. Everything seemed to be as it was meant to be.

Once ensconced in the little boat, the Englishman stood with one hand braced against the frigate's wooden hull while offering his other to help another figure step down. This other figure, clearly a woman, was dressed entirely in white, from the shawl covering much of her head to the long white gown draping her slender body. How the woman was able to keep her balance, and keep her attire looking so crisp and clean, were further mysteries to Richard, as was the identity of the naval officer who gallantly settled her into the stern sheets before taking a seat on a center thwart and fitting a pair of oars into their thole pins. Why the officer was going it alone without the services of a coxswain and boat crew was yet another baffling mystery.

The officer pushed off from the frigate's hull and then spun the cutter's bow toward the beach by backing on one oar while pulling on the other. With the comfortable strokes of one born to the sea he started rowing the cutter toward shore. Even as the boat neared the beach there were no sounds: no creaking of the oars, no splash of water dripping off the blades of the oars, no screech erupting from the gulls he could plainly see wheeling overhead. Nor was there any scent: no aroma of salt air, no ammonia-like smell of washed-up seaweed or kelp, no stench of dead and rotting crustaceans on the beach sand. All seemed at peace, perfectly in place, exactly as it should be.

Now something very strange happened. Not only did *Portsmouth's* crew suddenly break out in loud applause, but others walking on the beach toward him did as well. Richard glanced about. To his utter stupefaction he recognized many of those people. To his right, his father, Thomas Cutler, and his mother, Elizabeth, were in step with his brother Will and his uncle William. On his left, to his continued stupefaction, he saw a man bearing an uncanny resemblance to John Paul Jones, the captain under whom Richard had served as a midshipman in the Continental sloop-of-war *Ranger*. Walking with him were others with whom Richard had served in the Continental Navy and, later, in the U.S. Navy. All of them were applauding as if in appreciation of—or anticipation of—some memorable performance.

Despite the sudden appearance of so many people dear to his heart, Richard's eyes were drawn back to the cutter, now nearing the spot where he was standing. Still he could not make out the identity of either of its passengers. The man had his back to Richard, and the woman sat huddled in her linen gown. Only after the bow had hissed onto the sand and Richard had grabbed hold of the bight of its bowline to help haul it up onto the beach did the British officer face him.

"Hugh?" he gasped. "Hugh! Can that really be you?" Not daring to believe what his eyes were telling him, Richard waded into the water to stand alongside the officer seated in the boat. "Hugh?" he repeated a third time, his tone soft and incredulous.

"Ahoy, old boy," the officer said, smiling. "It's been awhile, hasn't it." He placed a hand on Richard's arm. "It does me good to see you. I bring you glad tidings and someone very special to you. Behold my beloved sister," he added, sweeping his right hand toward the cutter's stern. "I believe you are well acquainted with her."

As if on cue the woman removed her shawl, revealing a vision of youthful beauty, the memory of which had long been the stuff of his dreams. Her curly chestnut hair came tumbling down onto her shoulders and the delicate swell of her breasts, and her hazel eyes locked on the blue of his.

"Dear God," he choked. "My lady, my darling, how is this possible? Can it truly be you?"

"Yes, my love," Katherine said, her eyes glistening with unshed tears. "I have missed you so. But know that I am waiting for you. It won't be long now, my darling."

Richard was flooded with certainty that this was a promise. He *would* see Katherine again. Without another word he scooped her up in his arms and held her tightly against him. As the applause on shore reached a crescendo, he closed his eyes, and the world began swirling around him. "I love you so, my dearest," he whispered over and over again, "I love you so."

—⁓—

"I love you, too, Richard. I have always loved you. From that first moment we met. You know that, don't you?"

Richard opened his eyes to see not Katherine but another woman in his arms. For a moment he did not know where he was or who she was. It was barely light in the room despite the curtains and windows left open to admit the cool night air. He was not standing on a beach; he was lying in a bedroom on the second floor of a spacious house on Ship Street that he had come to frequent on a regular basis. The house belonged to his son Will and Will's wife, Adele, and at the moment he was naked in bed next to his daughter-in-law's mother.

"Of course I know that, Anne-Marie," he murmured. As she nestled closer to him and laid her head on his chest, he began gently kneading the firm muscles of her back. "Why do you ask?"

Her hand in turn caressed the weathered flesh of his chest and stomach. "I ask because you sounded so earnest, as though you needed to convince me. But you know I don't need convincing, don't you, my love?"

"I do know that. Of course. I must have been talking in my sleep."

She laughed softly and caressed his chest. "Just when I thought you were professing your undying love for me, you were merely talking in your sleep! Likely dreaming of some wanton woman of your acquaintance. Some buxom hussy you enjoy entertaining whilst I am sitting forlorn and neglected in my home in Boston."

"That's it. You have me pegged," he agreed solemnly. "I am gutted to be found out in such a way."

"As you should be," she laughed. "Because the truth always does win out." When her gentle ministrations on his stomach dipped lower, he again felt long-dormant stirrings in his loins.

Despite a lingering disorientation, Richard could not gainsay the intense pleasure of her touch. He longed for it. He craved it. "Now tell me," he said to lighten the mood, "exactly what do you put in that witches' brew you served me last night?"

She smiled knowingly. "I will tell you only what I have already told you: It's a family secret passed down from woman to woman since my ancestors first settled in Switzerland. Today, only my daughters and I are privy to the formula."

"Which explains their exceptional charm to men, and men's exceptional happiness around them."

"Yes indeed. And yours as well. And mine, by the way."

Despite himself, Richard laughed out loud at the mental image of her late husband standing naked by the marital bed and drinking the potion. Jack Endicott had rarely imbibed anything beyond coffee, whiskey, and Madeira, and he had rarely smiled except when consummating a business deal—which, according to what Anne-Marie had often told him, was about the only thing her husband had any interest in consummating.

"You thought that amusing, did you?" Anne-Marie said. "Well, then, you'll really like this." She slid down her hand and seized hold of him, squeezing and stroking him with such a depth of passion, skill, and carnal knowledge that she quickly had him writhing and moaning with desire.

An hour later, in the aftermath of sweet lovemaking, he awoke with a start. A glance at his pocket watch on the bedside table confirmed a time of 8:30. As he tossed the sheet and blanket aside, he felt her stir beside him and mumble a sleepy protest.

"Time to rise and shine," he whispered. "We'll soon have company."

He slipped out of bed, pulled on a shirt and pants, and padded out of the room and down the back stairway into the kitchen. He set four small white birch logs on live ashes within the wood-burning stove and waited for the agreeable sound of a fire crackling and popping to life. After adding more logs to build up the fire and heat the chamber, he placed a linen bag of ground coffee beans into a copper utensil filled with water and sugar and secured the utensil over the flames. He stood watching and waiting beside the stove, careful not to allow the water to boil and thus compromise the exquisite flavor of the beans. At just the proper moment he removed the copper vessel from the heat and poured the dark, aromatic liquid into a proper coffee pot, keeping it warm over the stove as he awaited the knock on the front door, which came at precisely nine o'clock.

"Come in, Caleb," he called out.

The door opened and Caleb Cutler entered the front hallway. "Good morning, Richard," he called back.

"Make yourself at home in the parlor, Caleb. I'll just take a cup of coffee up to Anne-Marie, and then I'll bring a cup in for you."

Several minutes later Richard handed his brother a mug of steaming black coffee and sat down across from him in the matching brown leather chair. He lifted his mug in salutation. "Cheers," he said, before taking a sip and sighing contentedly.

"I must say," Caleb remarked after a short spell, "you have become shockingly domesticated, my brother. And that worries me. Not only do you brew the finest spot of coffee to be found in Hingham, you serve it to your lady in bed—which is where I presume she is at the moment. My God, sir, you keep on doing that and you'll make life very difficult for the rest of us poor men!"

Richard smiled. "You are hardly one to talk. As I recall, you had a flock of young ladies fawning all over you in your earlier life, especially on Barbados. You went to great lengths to please them, and they to please you."

Caleb returned the smile. "That was different. I was pleasuring them, yes, and they were pleasuring me. But I can assure you that what I was serving them in bed was not coffee or tea!"

"Point taken," Richard said, laughing. "And, may I add, admired." Then: "Must you return to Boston today? Having you here in Hingham brings back many happy memories."

"It's the same for me, Richard," Caleb avowed with feeling. "If I had my druthers, I would spend more time in Hingham than in Boston. I much prefer the quiet and serenity of Hingham, especially now that Cutler & Sons has only limited business. The British blockade has cut deeply into our profits. Case in point? I'd wager the sugar I just stirred into my coffee did not arrive on a C & S vessel. Am I right?"

"I'm afraid you are. As for our profits, I reviewed the numbers last week with George Hunt, and they did look rather bleak. George is quite concerned—as am I, and you as well, I am sure. Your contact with British officials is wearing thin, I presume?"

"That's an understatement. Unfortunately, Britain no longer regards New England as a 'favored nation.' Even those of us who remain adamant in our opposition to Washington and the war are ignored these days. There's not much more I can do. We just have to sit here and wait it out while our cargoes rot and our profits dwindle to nothing. If this war continues much longer, we'll be in peril of going under, as impossible as that would have seemed not so long ago. Other shipping families of our acquaintance are experiencing similar difficulties. It's abominable. Utterly abominable."

"Something is bound to happen soon. Our intelligence indicates that Britain is about to play her hand in the Chesapeake and on Lake Champlain. She may already be doing that. When it comes, Will and Jamie will be right in the thick of the fighting. And then, of course, there is Spanish West Florida and Louisiana. General Jackson defeated the Red Sticks at Horseshoe Bend, but now that the British no longer have the Creeks to fight their battles for them in the South, they'll do their own fighting."

Andrew Jackson's Tennessee militia had defeated the Muscogee Creeks at Horseshoe Bend the previous March, further dampening the Native Americans' Tecumseh-inspired rebellion, but no one believed the war was over. The Indians had been little more than a nuisance compared with the British Army.

"It hasn't happened yet because of the wretched weather down there and this being the hurricane season," Richard added. "We believe the British will lean on their Spanish former allies to let them use Pensacola as a naval base. You know the Spanish will let them because they're desperate to hang on in Florida. They haven't got much else in this hemisphere beyond Cuba and Puerto Rico. Then, of course, there's Mobile and the richest prize of them all: New Orleans. That's why we need all the allies in Louisiana we can get."

"With Jean Lafitte at the top of the list, I suppose?"

Richard nodded. "Of course."

"I doubt he'll make much of an ally," Caleb said dismissively.

"Perhaps not. But I'd far rather have Lafitte as an unreliable ally that an outright enemy. His empire is impressive. Both sides are courting Lafitte, and if he throws in his lot with the British, General Jackson would be hard-pressed to stop them."

"And what terms are we offering Lafitte to prevent him from allying himself with the British?"

Richard shrugged. "Nothing specific at this stage. Monroe has given me wide latitude to negotiate. My orders are to do whatever is necessary to get him to throw in with us. Or, at the very least, to ensure his neutrality."

"That's a tall order," Caleb remarked. "I wish you good luck, brother."

"Thanks. I suspect I'll need it. I should say *we'll* need it. I have finally persuaded Agee to accompany me."

"I am certainly pleased to hear that. He has saved your skin more than once already."

"He has. As he often takes pleasure in reminding me."

After an interlude of silence Richard changed tack. "You're still planning to attend that convention in Connecticut in December?" Highly placed Federalists from the five New England states were planning to meet in Hartford on December 15 to address their grievances against the government in Washington and to debate possible forms of redress.

"Yes. I have pledged that I would, and I will, whatever the consequences. But I doubt there will be any consequences. Because nothing will be resolved. The fire has gone out of the belly of the beast, so to speak. No one will suggest anything brash. We'll talk and we'll talk and we'll talk some more. But that's all we'll do: talk. We may even talk of secession, but it won't amount to anything. So you needn't worry about me—or any of us—in Hartford. Think of us as a group of old business colleagues coming together to gripe and complain and dream of what might have been."

Richard slowly shook his head. "That may not be how the government sees it. So again I say, be careful. And there is this, Caleb. I received a dispatch from Secretary Jones in which he informs me that Gallatin has already departed for Ghent to meet with Colburn. So who knows? By December 15 the war may be over."

Albert Gallatin, a former senator and ambassador, was now serving President Madison as secretary of the treasury and plenipotentiary minister to the kingdom of the Netherlands. His mission in Ghent was to initiate peace talks with Henry Colburn, the British secretary of state for war and the colonies. The British government was open to holding such discussions as long as certain conditions were met. Such conditions, which involved Britain retaining possession of captured territory at the time the treaty was signed, were anathema to President Madison and his cabinet.

"I know all about that," Caleb allowed. "It's no secret to anyone. It's yet another reason why the convention in Hartford—assuming it takes place at all—will accomplish nothing. After all, why stir the stew when the pot's off the stove?" He lifted his mug to his mouth and drained it. "I reckon both sides are sick to death of this war," he said as he placed the cup down. "God knows I am. Which is why I prefer Hingham to Boston these days. Life here is more sane and meaningful—perhaps, as you say, because of the memories. I can only imagine what our father would make of this mess."

Richard shrugged. "He wouldn't think much of it. Nor would he think much of you sticking your neck out and putting yourself and your family at risk. Now is not the time for that. As *you* say, both sides are tired of this war. It was a tragic mistake when it started, and it's a tragic mistake today. Don't make it worse by putting yourself at odds with Washington and becoming more deeply involved in a fight you cannot win. That's a no-win proposition if ever there was one. And it could land you in prison."

"I doubt it," Caleb scoffed, then added with a grin, "Besides, if I get tossed into the brig, you will come to my rescue. What official could gainsay a war hero, and a U.S. Navy captain to boot, running to the aid of this poor and helpless representative of the people?"

Richard sighed. "You're hardly poor and you're hardly helpless, Caleb, else you wouldn't have been invited by our governor to go to Hartford. Just don't push your luck. That's all I ask."

He got up to refill their mugs from the kitchen. When he returned, the conversation drifted inevitably to other family members: Will and

Jamie, of course; young Thomas Sprague, born to Diana and her husband, Peter, on March third; their sisters, Anne and Lavinia; their cousins John and Robin Cutler in Barbados, with whom they had learned the ways of the sea and the glorious allure of sugar cane, molasses, and rum in global markets; and Edna Stowe, the family's loyal housekeeper since 1783, who was finally losing her heroic battle against the afflictions of advancing age. The reminder of that prognosis cast a pall of sadness upon both Cutler brothers, especially Richard. Katherine had held Edna in great esteem and affection and had often chastised her husband for his merciless teasing of their fastidious housekeeper.

When Richard remained silent, his eyes staring into his mug, Caleb said, to spark the moment, "Cheers to Rebecca and Abigail, eh? Were Monroe to promote them both to the rank of brigadier general, we actually might make some progress in this war."

Three days previously, the two young daughters of Scituate Lighthouse keeper Simeon Bates had been left at home alone with their mother while the rest of the family visited friends in nearby Hingham. The girls had watched aghast as a British warship anchored off the entrance to Scituate Harbor and launched two longboats armed with Royal Marines, who were clearly on their way to burn the town's wharves. Abigail and Rebecca, realizing it was too late to warn local citizens of the invasion, took up fife and drum and began playing their hearts out. The British Marines, apparently thinking that the martial music trumpeted the approach of the town militia, turned their boats around and beat a hasty retreat back to their ship, which soon weighed anchor and sailed away.

"Agreed," Richard said in a more chipper tone. "And God bless them both. At this stage, the United States will take a victory however and wherever it comes!"

Footsteps coming down the front stairway into the front hall heralded the approach of Anne-Marie Endicott, who walked in wearing a fashionable blue damask dress with a pure white cotton shawl draped across her shoulders. A pair of the low-heeled, lace-up leather shoes that had become all the rage peeped out from beneath her skirts. The smile she wore was infectious, and her bright blue eyes shone with affection.

"Good morning, Caleb," she said cheerily. "Richard said you would be dropping by. I hope we shall have the pleasure of your company for dinner today?"

"Good morning, Anne-Marie," Caleb said, standing up. "You look ravishing, as always." He shook his head in bewilderment. "What you see in my sorry brother is beyond my ability to grasp. But I suppose there is no accounting for taste, is there? As to my staying for dinner, I'm afraid I shall have to defer your kind invitation. Business and my wife are summoning me back to Boston."

He walked over to Anne-Marie, gave her a warm kiss on her cheek, and said, quite seriously, "Be well, my sister. I hope you don't mind me calling you that. During the past few months I have come to think of you *as* my sister and have often wished it were so."

Anne-Marie blinked. "Thank you for saying that, Caleb," she half-whispered. "It means more to me than I can say."

"Good. I am glad." As Caleb gathered his tricorne hat and his coat, he cast his brother a final glance. "You're sailing for New Orleans in two weeks?"

Richard nodded. "Yes, Agee and I are sailing on the twenty-fifth from Long Wharf. I would prefer to sail on an earlier date. Time is growing short. But hurricane season is upon us, and we can't risk running into one. Besides, the emissary we have sent ahead to Grande Terre will have informed Lafitte of our expected date of arrival and made all the necessary arrangements. Be that as it may, Anne-Marie and I want you and Joan to join us for supper at Belknap Street the night before we sail."

"It will be a celebratory affair," Anne-Marie explained. "To wish us all good fortune in the months ahead. We shall break out the best Madeira I can find and raise our glasses to success and victory. And to a quick end of this war."

"I shall happily drink to that," Caleb said with conviction. He waved a final goodbye before walking out of the parlor, down the hallway, and out the front door, careful to close it gently behind him.

CHAPTER THIRTEEN

North Point, Maryland

September 12, 1814

THE DELAY WAS BECOMING INTOLERABLE, AND IN THE OPINION OF SOME of the officers, perilous. True, only a week had passed since the burning of Washington and the British force's withdrawal from the Potomac to the boats waiting at Benedict, Maryland. From there they had rowed down the Patuxent River to the ships in the Chesapeake and sailed on to Tangier Island. As a Royal Navy lieutenant, Seth Cutler was accustomed to waiting much longer than ten days for something material to happen. But as a military officer he also knew the inherent dangers often linked to a decision to delay action, whatever the perceived risks. In this instance the risks did not seem very great. After all, the delay had nothing to do with what the enemy was doing or planning, but rather with the current phase of the moon and the tides influenced by the moon.

"I wager we'll cast off soon enough," William Shirley declared to Seth and their mutual friend and fellow commissioned officer Geoffrey Sayres. They were sharing a pot of tea and a platter of cakes at one of the few retail establishments open on Tangier following the British occupation of the island. At tables nearby, other navy and army officers were similarly engaged in quiet conversations. "As the saying goes, we need to strike while the embers are hot. Every hour of every day we delay gives the Jonathans that much more time to shore up their morale—and more important, their defenses."

Outside, on the island's picturesque fields, glens, beaches, and nearly every other spot where a man could pitch a tent were bivouacked 1,200 of the 4,200 troops under the overall command of Maj. Gen. Robert Ross. Many of them were Colonial Marines, a corps comprising former slaves who had been promised freedom in exchange for a year's service to the Crown. The veterans among the soldiers—those who had fought in Spain and had marched against Washington—were now earmarked to march against Baltimore in company with six hundred sailors and Royal Marines from the ships. These men were under the nominal command of Rear Adm. Sir George Cockburn and three of his officers.

"As if there ever was a valid reason for this delay," Sayres groused under his breath. "Does Cochrane honestly believe that water levels could ever get so low as to endanger a frigate? God's eyes, our ships have been sailing in these waters for how many years now?"

"Belay that, Geoffrey," Seth cautioned. "We've already discussed it. It's not that the water level is too low at low tide; the shoals have shifted, making our charts even more unreliable than they already were. Have you forgotten the mess we got into as we approached the Potomac last month? I didn't think so. I know you're frustrated. So are we all. But I respect the admiral for wanting to ensure that no ship goes aground or is damaged in any way, and that is less likely to happen on a neap tide. And that, my lad, is only a few days away. So be of good cheer."

"I grant you all that," Sayres said, "but I still maintain that each day that passes gives Yankee Doodle an advantage. We may come up against it when we finally land, assuming we ever do. And there is no glory in sitting idle."

William Shirley dismissed that last remark with a wave of his hand. "No need to get all fired up, Geoffrey," he said. "The Yankee Doodles are no match for us. That battle at Bladensburg—if you can even call it a battle—was a bloody cakewalk. The Doodles ran so fast from us they raced right through Washington and out the other side, leaving their own capital defenseless and open to plunder and pillage. Their national capital, by God! What army does such a thing? So fret not, my friend. When we do land—and we will in the very near future—there will be plenty of glory to go around. We'll blow Baltimore sky high, and we'll destroy that bloody lair of privateers. For every ship of ours they have seized and for every cargo of ours they have appropriated, we shall extract tenfold in revenge. Mark my words!"

"Right, then." Seth rose to his feet. "Time to shove off to the flagship. We have a briefing at six bells, in case you have forgotten. Perhaps we'll learn our fate then."

The date was September 7, 1814.

The briefing was held in the day cabin of Sir Thomas Cochrane in HMS *Tonnant*, an 80-gun ship of the line and former French third-rate that Admiral Lord Nelson had captured in Aboukir Bay during the Battle of the Nile. The cabin was a spacious and exquisitely appointed apartment befitting the 10th earl of Dundonald and a naval officer so renowned for his courage and leadership in European waters that Napoleon had nicknamed him "the sea wolf." Every furnishing, every oil painting, every Wedgewood teacup and cut-glass decanter stood as a testament to good breeding, good fortune, and good taste. The four freshly painted 24-pounder long guns bowsed up tight against the bulwarks, two to a side, added to the cabin's martial grandeur. As a young midshipman up from his cramped and squalid quarters on the orlop deck, Seth had once remarked to his shipmates that entering this vast, elegant space must be akin to entering the great hall of a royal palace.

Those attending the briefing constituted the brain trust of the Royal Navy fleet in the Chesapeake: Admiral Cochrane himself, of course, and his second-in-command, Rear Adm. Sir George Cockburn, each clad in a dark blue frock coat embroidered with twin gold epaulets, gold facings, and gold buttons; Maj. Gen. Sir Robert Ross, wearing the elegant red coat and white trousers of high rank in the British Army; his second-in-command, Col. Sir Arthur Brooke, in command of the 4th Regiment of Foot, along with another colonel and a lieutenant colonel in command of the other two regiments of one thousand soldiers each; plus the captain of each of the nineteen capital ships in the fleet and three of the fleet's executive officers selected for shore duty. These naval officers wore the blue-and-white uniform of commissioned rank but with less gold finery than their seniors and only one epaulet for the lieutenants. So spacious was the cabin that each of the officers present was seated comfortably on a sofa, a wingback chair, or a Chippendale chair transferred from the admiral's dining alcove on the starboard quarter at the stern of the ship.

As liveried servants bustled about serving beverages, the officers listened intently to the battle plan that was being laid out for them by Flag Capt. Charles Kerr, a beefy, officious man with a generous nose and square jaw whose skin, to Seth's mind, seemed too smooth and unworried to belong to a career Navy officer hardened at sea on a quarterdeck.

"So there you have it, gentlemen," Kerr concluded. "As you will doubtless agree, the plan I have described is as inspired in design as it is straightforward in execution. In sum, we intend to squeeze our enemy between a two-pronged assault on Baltimore—one prong coming by land and the other by water. Our ultimate objective is the destruction of Fort McHenry guarding the entrance to the harbor. We have no intention of entering that harbor. Indeed we cannot. The enemy has sunk the local merchant fleet across the entrance so that no vessel can enter or leave. But no matter. Our mortars and rockets will make short work of the fort's defenses. Fort McHenry will fall, and when it does, General Ross will be on hand to accept the sword of surrender from this fellow Armstead." Kerr's contempt for Maj. Gen. George Armstead, the American officer commanding the one thousand militia and regular Army troops inside the fort, was obvious. "General Ross's presence will be most fortuitous because he will have just added to his personal arsenal the sword of Mr. Smith." Maj. Gen. Samuel Smith, the militia officer in charge of erecting and defending Baltimore's inner defenses, was likewise considered incompetent.

Although Kerr's voice and demeanor had remained professional, his last jape sparked a round of tittering across the cabin, which General Ross ended with a rough clearing of his throat. "So, gentlemen," Kerr closed his remarks, "if you have questions, now is the time to ask them."

A scattering of questions followed, the majority relating to the strength of the city's and fort's defenses. Kerr acknowledged that he did not know the actual size of the enemy force in and around Baltimore, although he did assert that while several units of Army regulars were entrenched within Fort McHenry, he had been informed that the forces that would likely be opposing Major General Ross on Patapsco Neck were militia units mostly from Maryland, with a few units from Virginia and Pennsylvania thrown in for good measure.

"Militia units!" he spat contemptuously. "We saw the fighting spirit of those chaps at Bladensburg, did we not?"

Many of the officers nodded and smiled, but no one offered a comment.

"Sir," Seth ventured into the ensuing lull, "with respect, is it true that the fortifications at Hamstead Hill are anchored by Captain Rodgers and the sailors of his squadron?" Hamstead Hill was the three-mile-long system of earthworks and redoubts that formed the centerpiece of the city's inner defenses.

The look Kerr gave the young lieutenant suggested that he found the question unnecessary, if not impertinent. "I believe that is correct," he allowed. "What of it? And what do you mean to imply? Do you happen to know this officer?"

"No, sir," Seth replied. "I know of him, however, and I know some of his acquaintances. I daresay there is not a man in this cabin who does not hold Captain Rodgers in high regard. If I am to lead men against such an officer, I should like to know as much as possible about his preparations."

"Yes, well, well," Kerr spluttered, apparently unsure how to respond. He looked as though he might be about to broach the subject of Lieutenant Cutler's heritage and loyalty to Britain. Cutler was, after all, a colonist and not an Englishman born. Other senior officers had raised the issue in the past. But if that were the case, Kerr clearly thought better of it. Cutler's current commanding officer was Admiral Cochrane's son, and for a reason Kerr did not understand but nonetheless had to respect, Captain Thomas Cochrane thought highly of Cutler, as did the captain who had preceded him in command of *Seahorse*.

"You have raised a valid point, Lieutenant," Robert Ross interjected. Although he spoke to Seth, it was clear to all that his words were intended for Kerr. "It is an issue I have myself raised in recent days. Great Britain is not in the habit of sending her officers on a fool's errand. Be assured that within the five days we have until we launch our assault we shall garner whatever information we require. Now, unless you have something further to say, Captain Kerr, and if there are no further questions, Admiral Cochrane and I declare this meeting adjourned."

The offloading began at six bells in the second watch on Monday, September 12. The fleet had sailed from Tangier Island on the eleventh and was now anchored in fourteen fathoms of water several hundred yards off the extreme end of a five-mile-long peninsula extending east–southeast into Chesapeake Bay from the city center of Baltimore. The choice of North Point as the launch point for an assault on Baltimore was obvious. The relatively flat terrain of Patapsco Neck was sufficiently narrow to allow for a concentration of forces, yet wide enough at the eastern approaches to Baltimore to accommodate a coordinated attack from several different directions. At the same time, the British flanks would be protected throughout the short march westward by the Back River to the north and the Patapsco River to the south.

In fact, North Point was so obvious a choice for an invasion by land that the American forces had had their muskets and cannon trained on Patapsco Neck for several days before the British landed. The British expected the Americans to be lying in wait for them, of course, but most of the senior officers who had witnessed the debacle in Bladensburg considered that an advantage. Battle could be joined swiftly and the defeat of the Americans accomplished without wasting the time necessary to hunt them down.

By six bells in the morning watch, all 4,200 soldiers, Marines, and sailors—along with supplies, fieldpieces, horses, munitions, and a company of Royal Sappers—had been ferried from ship to shore in a flotilla of longboats, gigs, barges, pinnaces, launches, and jollyboats. Doing so under the mantle of night had proven an unnecessary precaution. For whatever reason the enemy had done nothing to harass the landing at North Point. Perhaps, Seth brooded, it was because they had prepared a reception for the British once they were ashore and out of range of the fleet's long guns.

The morning was fair and pleasantly cool as Major General Ross set out on North Point Road, having sent scouts ahead to scour the countryside for any hint of enemy activity. With him rode members of his staff and his personal bodyguard. Behind that group rode the two colonels and the lieutenant colonel in command of the three regiments of footsoldiers wearing regimental red coats, white cotton shirts and white crossbelts, light gray trousers, and, in place of the traditional white-trimmed tricorne hat, regimental shakos.

Behind them rode Rear Admiral Cockburn and his naval officers; a battalion of scarlet-coated Marines marching four abreast, some with white skin, some with black; and a brigade of three hundred ordinary and able-rated seamen selected for their infighting skills with pistols, tomahawks, knives, belaying pins, and fists. Seth felt a strong affinity toward these sailors. He had come to know many men like them as a young man serving before the mast in the Cutler family's merchant fleet. They did not possess the elegance and erudition of the officer corps, but when push came to shove in a barroom brawl or in fierce hand-to-hand combat, it was their hands in which he wanted to place his trust and his life. Years ago at his home in Barbados, Seth's uncle Richard Cutler had taught him that the chain of command in a naval or merchant vessel involves respect going down as well as up. It was a lesson that had stood Seth in good stead over the years, and he was grateful to his uncle for teaching him that lesson.

Near the tail end of the column rumbled an array of military supply wagons, two of which were oversized and pulled by two horses each. The sides of these two wagons were hinged and could be let down to reveal a platform on which was secured a ten-foot-tall, multi-slotted battery for launching thirty-two-pound Congreve rockets. Twenty-five soldiers of the Royal Marine Artillery commanded by Lt. John Lawrence marched beside and behind the wagons.

Their initial route took them northward along a well-maintained road up a gentle rise. At its crest, on a farm a signpost identified as Todd's Inheritance, the British were afforded a sweeping vista of Chesapeake

Bay. As each crested the hill, British soldiers and sailors paused briefly to gaze down upon the fleet sailing away from them en route to Baltimore. *Tonnant* led the way, the flagship's large naval ensign with the cross of St. George fluttering majestically high on her halyard on the mizzen. Sailing with her were the frigate *Seahorse*—Seth's ship—and others with whom he had sailed on the Potomac: the bomb vessels *Terror*, *Volcano*, *Meteor*, *Devastation*, and *Aetna*; the rocket ship *Erebus*; and sloops-of-war, brigs-of-war, and other warships of the Royal Navy strike force.

"A marvelous sight," Lieutenant Shirley, marching alongside Seth, commented. He too had paused to admire the majesty and ponder the significance of the flotilla. "I shall always remember this moment, Seth, and this sight. Those ships will see us victorious on the morrow."

"God willing," Seth confided.

"He is certainly willing," Shirley said, "or so our Captain Kerr ardently believes. Weren't you listening to him yesterday?"

"I was listening, William. Just not with my full concentration."

Shirley chuckled. "Quite the windbag, isn't he? He did go on rather more than necessary."

As they marched on, the road turned left to hug the peninsula's northern coast along the Back River, a tidal estuary of Chesapeake Bay. Along the way, to no one's surprise, they passed a number of recently dug trenches and other shallow earthworks that the Americans had erected and then abandoned. Well, Seth mused, the Jonathans couldn't run forever. The road and the estuary led directly to Baltimore, and there they would have to turn and face their pursuers. They had marched two miles when Ross called a halt. It was approaching the noon hour, he was apparently hungry, and they had come upon a stately farmhouse that would do nicely for a spot of lunch with Admiral Cockburn and Colonel Brooke. The owner of the property, a farmer by the name of Gorsuch, had little choice but to accommodate the senior British officers. He invited them inside to dine, although he regretted that he had little to offer them. The other officers were also invited inside, but to less congenial quarters. The rank and file sat down outside in what shade they could find and ate from the provisions they carried on them and water drawn from a trough and the farm's two wells.

Halfway through dinner the tranquil early September afternoon was shattered by the sudden pop of musket fire emanating from perhaps a half mile down the road. The officers inside the farmhouse jumped to their feet, and those on the outside instinctively reached for their weapons. General Ross was first out the door, calling for his horse and personal guard.

"General," Seth heard George Cockburn call out, "do not go out there on your own ahead of us. You don't know who or what awaits you. Pray wait until we have the men properly arrayed."

"Nonsense, Admiral," Ross called back over his shoulder. "I know precisely what awaits me out there. Those are my men under fire, and I *shall* know what is happening." With that, he put boot to stirrup and swung himself up onto his saddle. With a squeeze of his legs and a flick of the reins he was off, leading the twelve men of his personal guard in the direction of the skirmish that was continuing to flare.

Brooke, Cockburn, and the other officers went about ordering the men into formation and were about to follow their commanding officer down the road when a shocking sight brought them up short. Seth saw it first: a riderless horse in the distance galloping toward them. Even as he sounded the alarm, all eyes became transfixed on that horse, which, as it neared the assembled force-at-arms, was clearly General Ross's horse.

There was more.

"Unless my eyes deceive me," William Shirley said to Seth, "I see blood on the horse's saddle."

Seth wiped his brow with the sleeve of his blue uniform coat and then peered through a small spyglass he carried in the coat's pocket. "Your eyes do not deceive you, William," he murmured after a moment. "There *is* blood on the saddle, and there is blood on the horse's flank. That blood must belong to General Ross. There can be no other source."

He and William watched in mounting despair as the drama's disastrous denouement played out before them. Details of what had happened began filtering through the ranks. Within the half hour, when the last of the twelve soldiers in the general's personal guard had returned, most of the pieces of the puzzle had been fitted together. The skirmish, a member of the general's staff reported to Colonel Brooke and Admiral Cockburn, had been a setup. The Americans had dispatched a small unit of cavalry to attack the defensive perimeter Ross had put in place, but their true mission was to draw the British officers away from the relative safety of the farmhouse. Ross had hardly left the camp when sharpshooters hidden in trees opened fire on the general and the captain of his bodyguard. Ross had been hit in the arm and chest and had collapsed off his horse onto the ground.

"We requisitioned a cart from a farm," Seth overheard a corporal report to Brooke, "but by the time we were able to place the general in it, he had died. We have recovered his body and that of Captain Howard, and we have seen to the wounded."

"Very well, Corporal," Brooke replied. "Signal the fleet to send back a boat. See that the bodies of the officers are returned to *Tonnant* along with those who require the services of Dr. Herrick, her surgeon. The other dead we shall bury here."

"Yes, sir." The corporal saluted and wheeled his horse around.

William Shirley had listened to this conversation with growing wrath. "Bloody savages," he cursed under his breath as the corporal hurried off. "Targeting officers violates every rule of war. Savages, that's what these American bastards are. Bloody *savages* I say!"

"There *are* no rules of war, William," Seth said. "We have done the same or worse to them, and you know it. Forget about that. All such hatred does is cloud your mind."

—◦—

The sun had passed its zenith and was on its downward arc when the British forces resumed their advance toward Baltimore. Colonel Brooke, now in command, was a respected officer who had fought with distinction in Spain during the Napoleonic Wars; he had, in fact, led many of these same Redcoats in the campaigns in Europe. But he was no General Ross. The loss of their beloved general took the very heart from his men. When news of Ross's death first filtered through the British camp, Brooke had seemed as dazed and confused as everyone else. But in a short span of time born of necessity, his life experience and his life mission had taken hold, and with the help of Admiral Cockburn and the three naval officers he was able to seize control of himself and the situation.

Not long afterward, with another mile under their belts, the British came upon what they had all along sensed was waiting ahead. Facing them across North Point Road, from perhaps three hundred yards away, they beheld an enemy force drawn up in three lines, one in back of the other. At right angles to the road on both sides stretched a chest-high wooden fence extending out from the road for about fifty yards. A quick survey of the terrain confirmed that here was the narrowest point of land the British had yet encountered on Patapsco Neck. To the right, on the north side, the Back River remained clearly visible, its placid blue waters ruffled hardly at all by the southeasterly breeze. Further protecting the American left flank was a creek winding its way from behind the third American line to curve northward into the Back River.

To the south, on the left side of the British advance, a tidal estuary knifed northward from the Patapsco River to almost meet the Back River, thereby splitting the peninsula nearly in two. All around them the Maryland Tidewater landscape was graced by a cover of lush green grass, copses of white oak and southern red pine, and, in the distance beyond the American lines, gently rolling hills interspersed with patchwork fields of yellow-husked corn. Overhead, puffs of white cumulus clouds drifted lazily within an otherwise flawless late-summer sky.

Smart, Seth thought to himself as he surveyed the enemy lines. The American commander, whoever he was, knew his business. To reach Hamstead Hill and penetrate the city's defenses the British would have to push past this defensive position. It would be no easy matter, even though the British appeared to have a considerable advantage in numbers.

Brooke held up his hand, and the long line halted. After a brief consultation with Cockburn and the two regimental commanders, he sent out word for the Redcoats to fan out on both sides of the road and ordered the naval officers to keep the Marines and sailors where they were.

The senior officers retired to the rear and dismounted, and the British began their advance. At first they marched unimpeded while their foes waited in silence. Both sides needed to close the gap between them to a hundred yards, the maximum effective distance for a smoothbore musket or an army rifle.

Seth, William, and Geoffrey led their force of seamen forward at a slow but steady pace as British soldiers spread out to the right and left of them in disciplined files of red and white, their muskets at full cock and held level at the waist.

Suddenly Seth spied six cannon, three at each end of the American front line. The muzzles of all six were trained inward at the Marines and sailors on the road.

"*Down!*" Seth cried out, his call echoed by other field commanders. "*Everyone down!*"

The columns dropped flat as the six cannon belched fire and iron. Some men failed to react quickly enough; a combination of round shot and canister shot ripped through the British ranks, pulverizing flesh and bone into a mangled mass of blood and gore. Wounded men screamed in agony; others simply fell where they stood, killed instantly when vital organs were struck by a streaking four-pound iron fist.

As the seamen regrouped from that first shock, they heard, first from behind their front line and then above them, the unmistakable *swoosh* followed by the equally unmistakable high-pitched shriek and whine of Congreve rockets. The rockets were weapons of terror that either burst in midair in soul-wrenching explosions or screeched over the fence directly onto enemy positions.

Cheering madly, British soldiers leapt to their feet or knelt on one knee, took aim, and fired. Bits of fence, struck by a hail of bullets, flew up into the air as the first line of Americans retreated and the second line moved up to take their places and unleash a volley of fresh hot metal.

For more than an hour the battle raged blow for blow, both sides taking hits as the Americans constantly interchanged lines to maintain a constant rate of fire. In the heat of it all, a burly boatswain's mate acting as a messenger for Admiral Cockburn came forward to Seth's position behind a slender pine tree not fifty yards from the fence. Bullets zinged in the air around the petty officer, forcing him to crawl the last twenty yards to the lieutenant on his stomach.

"Sir," he said when at last he reached the tree. He was covered in sweat and grime, and his eyes had a wild look as he glared up at his superior officer. Before he could say more he dropped his head and threw up his arms to protect it as another hail of bullets punched the ground around him, sending clumps of soil and grass into the air. "The admiral's compliments, sir," he gasped, "and he requests that you please be ready to move out!"

"When?" Seth demanded.

"At six bells, sir." Again the boatswain ducked and crouched as another barrage peppered the ground around them.

Seth glanced at his watch. Zero hour was in ten minutes. "Have Mr. Sayres and Mr. Shirley been informed?"

"They have, sir," the boatswain replied, "and they await your lead."

"Then they shall have it. Stand by, Patten. You're with me now."

"Aye, aye, sir."

Ten minutes later, at precisely three o'clock, the entire left side of the British formation rose to their feet and, wildly cheering, sprinted as a single spearhead toward an open section of terrain between the northern reaches of the Patapsco River estuary and the end of the wooden fence. Seth immediately realized that this was the same tactic the British had used with devastating effect at Bladensburg. Colonel Brooke was banking on his infantry's ability to storm the Americans' right and outflank them, thus forcing a second battle line that the larger British force could quickly overrun. Overhead, another volley of Congreve rockets rent the air, their eerie screams drowning out the war cries of the attackers.

As anticipated, the American lines wheeled right to counter the attack. It was then that Seth jumped to his feet, raised his sword high, and pointed it down the road. "*To me, brave lads!*" he shouted and started running forward. To a man, the sailors and Marines followed close behind him, their ardor, as with the Redcoats, fueled by fierce anger at the cowardly assassination of their beloved General Ross.

The front line of defenders at the fence opened fire.

From the corner of his eye Seth saw a Marine stumble, stagger forward, and drop to the ground. Then another. And another. Still they kept moving forward, wasting not a shot even when they noted enemy cannon erupting in flame and smoke, hurling round shot and whatever else could be crammed down the muzzles: nails, broken bits of horseshoes, shards of metal. Seth felt something tear into his left arm; still he kept running.

Almost at the fence an American militiaman standing upright with the barrel of his rifle resting on the top of the fence was taking aim. In a single motion Seth yanked a pistol from his belt, drew back the frizzen to full cock, raised it, took aim, and fired. The bullet struck the militiaman in the chest. He lurched backward as though slugged in the jaw before collapsing in a dead heap. Seth threw the pistol away and drew out another one he had hooked onto his belt.

The intensity of the British barrage, both on the flank and straight on, was having its effect. Soldiers on the American third line, farthest back from the action, wavered and then turned and fled. On the American right, those defending the flank faltered in their resolve, having sustained heavy losses, before they too took off in flight. It became a rout when the Marines and sailors stormed over and through the fence and overwhelmed the enemy. Unable to withstand the ferocious attack, the American force began to retreat westward en masse toward Hamstead Hill two miles distant, although to Seth's surprise the retreat was fairly orderly, almost as though it had been orchestrated. The rearguard continued to stop, kneel, and fire even as they ran from the arena of battle, keeping the British at bay until those out in front were approaching the protection of the earthworks and redoubts of Baltimore's outer defenses.

"Cease fire!" Seth ordered those within earshot, seeing no point in perpetrating further carnage. Some men complied with the order; others did not, too engrossed in the exhilaration of battle and the thrill of victory to stop. Seth had little mind or heart to try to stop them. He was experiencing the same array of emotions, and he was feeling very, very tired and more than a tinge of sadness and dejection. Such had always been the way for him after spilling blood and witnessing death.

"Limey officer!"

Seth heard the harsh words spoken behind him, but it took him a moment to realize that they were meant for him. Turning around, he was astonished to see an American soldier—a regular Army infantryman judging by his more formal blue-and-white uniform—pointing a pistol at him. The soldier had been hit multiple times—Seth noted four splotches of red soiling his uniform—but there he stood, defying the odds, weaving on his feet, looking as though he might topple over at any moment. Too stunned to say or do anything, Seth just stood there mutely.

"Seth!" he heard William Shirley cry out.

Seth glanced to his right, to the sound of Shirley's voice, just as the American squeezed the trigger of his pistol, sending a bullet straight into Seth's heart. A salvo of British gunfire riddled the American, dropping him in his tracks as Seth collapsed onto his knees and then fell face down onto the grass.

CHAPTER FOURTEEN

Grand Terre, Louisiana

November 1814

RICHARD HAD MADE EXACTLY THIS VOYAGE EIGHT YEARS EARLIER, except in reverse. As on the previous voyage he had followed the eastern seaboard, and when within sight of land had seen the same landmarks, most of them guides or warnings to mariners: the shining beacon of Cape Cod Light in Truro on Cape Cod; the 110-foot-tall Montauk Light at the eastern extremity of Long Island; and, farther south, after USS *Hampton* had sailed out well beyond the grasp of Royal Navy vessels on patrol and the fast-moving northerly flow of the Gulf Stream, the light-house on Tybee Island at the mouth of the Savannah River. From there it was south to what the Spanish referred to as Cayo Huesco at the end of the 130-mile chain of islands stretching southwestward from the main-land of Spanish Florida. Once *Hampton* was through the Florida Straits and into the Gulf of Mexico, the uninhabited Marquesas Keys and, thirty-eight miles farther west, Loggerhead Key and the other sparsely vegetated islets of the Dry Tortugas went by. In all, *Hampton* had sailed more than 2,500 miles, and even with mostly fair winds had consumed a good five weeks in the voyage.

Once past the Tortugas, a prearranged series of flags set high on *Hampton*'s signal halyard brought two vessels up to join her. One of them was *Dove*, a jaunty Baltimore clipper that Richard recognized immedi-ately. Jean Lafitte had appropriated it from Cutler & Sons during Rich-ard's return voyage from Barbados eight years earlier. Today, while sailing north by northwest on a broad reach, he kept his eyes on the distant horizon where the coastline of Louisiana would soon appear. What began as a fuzzy gray outline in his spyglass grew more distinct as the three vessels drew closer. The low, fragile barrier islands, which in his opinion served primarily as breeding grounds for malaria, yellow fever, and black vomit, and secondarily as a buffer to protect the mainland from the threat of hurricanes, seemed unchanged.

The low-lying islands formed a confusing morass of interlocking bays, bayous, streams, and brackish, insect-infested swamps. Grande Terre and Grand Isle, hidden within this complex on the western edge of the Mississippi River Delta, would have been difficult to find had the two vessels escorting *Hampton* on the current voyage—and *Dove* on the previous voyage—not led the way. Grande Terre was home port for these vessels, and for the men who sailed them, precisely because it was so difficult for a law or customs official to approach unseen. A veritable army of sentries and lookouts posted on the outer islands were concealed in small, shallow-draft *bateaux* within pungent-smelling swamp grass or in narrow, mosquito-infested inlets flanked by cypress trees draped with gray Spanish moss.

At length *Hampton* slipped between Grand Isle and Grand Terre into Lafitte's stronghold, Barataria Bay. Once they were in the lee of the barrier islands, the feeble breeze that had slightly mitigated the oppressive heat and humidity petered out altogether. As the sloop and her two escorts rounded up to douse sails and drop anchor, the remark of a man standing by the sloop's helm was similar to one Katherine Cutler had made eight years previously when she first espied these surroundings, albeit considerably less polite.

"Hells bells, Richard! Who in his right mind would choose to live in this godforsaken shithole?" He mopped his brow and chin with a damp handkerchief, and then slapped down hard on his forearm. "God *damn* these mosquitoes! It's *November*, for Christ's sake! Who has mosquitoes in November? They should have died *months* ago." He quickly began rolling down his sleeves to minimize the potential area of impact. "About the only things happy in this vomit hole are those fuckin' pelicans you see out there. And I'd wager that's because they have no sense of smell."

"Don't forget the alligators, Agee," Richard said. He smiled but kept his gaze fixed ashore on a long, narrow building of stone and wood capped with a steeply pitched roof covered by overlapping sheets of shiny metal that kept the interior dry. It had changed not a whit in eight years save for the quality of the metal on the roof.

Not much else had changed either. The fort was still there on the island's western top, a sturdy redbrick affair, the black muzzles of its cannon protruding out through embrasures in all directions, including landward. A few other single- and double-masted vessels lay at anchor within the horseshoe-shaped cove. Afore the warehouse a more substantial jetty had been constructed, presumably to permit more efficient loading and unloading of goods. There were a few new buildings as well, all of them dwarfed by the warehouse and another single-story dwelling that might be a barracks for the squads of armed men Richard could see walking about or standing watch.

As he took all this in, Richard marveled that the U.S. Army had been able to slip forty soldiers past those sentries to unleash a surprise attack on Grande Terre, neutralize the fort, confiscate a small fortune in stolen goods, and capture Jean Lafitte's brother, Pierre. Jean Lafitte had likely been caught napping, overconfident, with far fewer sentries posted. He would not make that mistake a second time, of that Richard was certain.

"There goes someone," Agreen remarked, his tone suddenly serious. He was pointing at an open ship's boat launched from the Baltimore clipper and bearing ashore a man clad in a simple pair of brown trousers and a gray-on-brown striped shirt. Judging from his position in the stern and from the red-and-white cluster of ribbons attached to the oversized red-checkered bandana he was wearing around his head, he was the ship's master. "He's on official business by the look of him."

Richard had also noticed the two oarsmen pushing the boat off from the clipper. "That would be my guess as well," he agreed. "It shouldn't be long now."

"I sure hope not. I need t' feel hard ground under my feet again. Captain Wallace did a fine job gettin' us here, and he has a good crew, but God knows I'm ready for dry land."

"Hardly the words of the seafarer I once admired," Richard dead-panned. "I fear retirement has made you soft, Lieutenant."

"I remind you I now hold the rank of captain," Agreen muttered. "As for anything about me goin' soft, you can ask Lizzy for her opinion. She'll set the record straight right quick."

"Point taken, Captain."

Thirty minutes later the same boat shoved off from the jetty with the same two oarsmen and the same passenger seated in the stern. When the boat settled against *Hampton*'s larboard hull, the man—a Cajun judging by his swarthy skin and black hair—cupped his hands at his mouth and called up at the array of faces peering down at him. "Capitaine Cutler?"

Richard Cutler raised his bicorne hat and held it above his head in a French-style greeting. "I am Captain Cutler," he called down.

The man motioned toward the steps built into the sloop's hull. "You come with me," he said in a tone that Richard deemed to be less than courteous.

Richard clapped a hand on Agreen's shoulder. "Let's go, Agee."

Captain Wallace stepped forward. "Good luck, Mr. Cutler," he said. "Be assured that we are standing by with guns loaded should you have need of them."

"Thank you, Captain," Richard said in reply. "Though I seriously doubt we shall require the guns or assistance. We shan't be long. Make ready to depart for Mobile on the ebb tide."

Wallace touched his hat in a salute to an officer equal in rank but superior in seniority. Richard returned the salute and, after saluting the quarterdeck, began clambering down the steps toward the boat. When Agreen made to follow him, the Cajun stood up and stepped forward to the middle of the boat, as if to block the route leading down into it. "*Non*," he protested loudly. "*Vous seulement, monsieur.* Only you."

"*Je regrette, monsieur*," Richard said as he stepped into the boat to claim the stern seat recently vacated by the Cajun, "but this man is coming with me."

"*Non, non*," the Frenchman insisted again, waving his hands back and forth as if trying to clear away a foul smell. "I do not know this man."

"Then allow me to introduce you to him. *Il s'appelle Agreen Crabtree.* He is my first officer and my friend. He is highly esteemed by my government, he is my brother-in-arms, and he is expected ashore," Richard said, adding, "We would not want to upset Monsieur Lafitte, would we?" He motioned for Agreen to sit beside him in the stern thwart.

The Cajun gave Richard a withering look but threw up his hands in bitter surrender. When they reached the beach, the Cajun led the way up a rough pathway to the front entrance of the warehouse. Richard noticed no sentry posted immediately outside the building—because, he figured, there was no reason to post one. Grand Terre resembled an armed camp these days; no one could advance this far toward its nerve center without being invited, detained, or destroyed.

Inside, in a space that served as the anteroom, the Cajun indicated that the two Americans should sit and wait. When they complied, he opened a side door and disappeared inside.

Richard and Agreen sat like two dutiful students waiting to be summoned into the headmaster's office. As they waited, both men kept their eyes fixed on the large double wooden doors that consumed much of the north-facing wall. Richard knew what lay behind those doors; he had caught several glimpses on his previous visit. Inside were the fruits of Pierre Lafitte's labor: goods and possessions of all descriptions that he or his men had seized at sea in the Gulf of Mexico, the West Indies, the open Atlantic, and just about anywhere else a merchant vessel laden with rich cargo might be sailing at its peril. The bulk of these goods, Richard knew from his earlier visit, was earmarked to be sold at a wholesale price to merchants from Louisiana to Jamaica grateful to Lafitte for securing for them merchandise to sell to their retail customers during the crippling American trade embargo. Some merchandise, Richard also knew, the Lafitte brothers reserved to sell in their own retail showroom in the French Quarter of New Orleans. Pierre Lafitte was thus responsible for procuring merchandise at sea that Jean Lafitte was then responsible for selling on land. The fact that the prices they charged to both their wholesale and retail customers were more than reasonable went a long way toward ingratiating the Lafitte brothers with the general populace, who either overlooked or did not care how the merchandise was procured.

The side door opened and the Americans were summoned inside. Jean Lafitte's office was more grandly appointed than Richard remembered it. Lafitte himself was much the same, however. Strikingly handsome, his shoulder-length hair was as dark and shiny as ever; his thin handlebar mustache and goatee were as well groomed as those of a French courtier, and his clothes as elegant as any fashioned by a Lyonnaise tailor. Only the noticeable bulge of his paunch when he stood to greet his guests suggested a lifestyle that permitted gastronomic indulgences.

"*Capitaine Cutler!*" he exulted. "*On se revoit!*" He sat down behind his large mahogany desk. "*Comment allez-vous, mon ami?*"

"*Je vais bien, monsieur,*" Richard replied. "And yes, Fate has seen to it that we meet again." He glanced around the spacious room graced with oil paintings, lush sofas and chairs, and colorful Turkish carpets. "Business is good, I see."

"Very good, monsieur," Lafitte assured him. "Business is very, very good." He cast a questioning look at Agreen and nodded his understanding when Richard introduced him. "*Bonjour, monsieur,*" he said cordially. "Welcome to Grand Terre. You are finding everything to your liking?"

"Entirely," Agreen said.

Lafitte laughed. "*Bon.* I always enjoy a good liar. *Mais pas de quoi, mon ami.* It matters not. May I offer you a beverage? I am having bourbon," he said, pointing to a half-filled glass on the desk. "I freely admit that I have become addicted to it. But you may have whatever you wish."

Agreen smiled. "Bourbon, please. I, too, am addicted to it. And that, I can assure you, is no lie."

"*Bon.* I like you, monsieur. You are a man after my own heart. Capitaine? What is your pleasure?"

"Bourbon as well."

"A threesome then. *Toujours ma preference.*" Lafttle chuckled at his turn of phrase as he got up to pour the golden liquid into two glasses, refreshing his own in the process. "Before we discuss business, Capitaine," he said in a lighthearted tone, "I must ask: How fares your beautiful wife? Katherine, I believe her name is. *C'est ca?*"

A shadow passed across Richard's face. Lafitte studied him intently when he failed to respond. "What is it, *mon ami?* What did I say?"

"It's nothing you said," Richard said quietly.

"Mrs. Cutler died six years ago," Agreen said into the ensuing silence.

Lafitte set the decanter down on the side table. "*Mon Dieu!*" he breathed. "Monsieur," he added, his eyes and facial expression conveying deep sympathy, "I am truly sorry to hear this terrible news. Your beautiful wife, dead? It is a tragedy!"

"Katherine had a tumor in her chest that her doctors could not treat," Richard said.

Lafitte shook his head despondently. "I have known many women in my life, monsieur," he said as he handed out the two glasses. "Many, many women in many different places. Not one of them—not one!—was more beautiful than your dear wife. Nor more of a lady."

"Thank you for saying that, monsieur," Richard said. "Katherine liked you, and she respected you. She would be honored that you remember her."

"Remember her? Monsieur, I could never forget her!" He downed a healthy swig of bourbon and then sat down, inviting Richard and Agreen to sit across from him on a pair of wingback chairs. *Ainsi soit-il*. On to business. If you are up to it, Capitaine. You are able to conduct business at this time?"

"Of course."

"*Tres bien*. Where do you propose we start?"

"I propose we start with the reason Mr. Crabtree and I are here."

"*D'accord*." Lafitte made a small gesture as if to say: proceed.

Richard cleared his throat. "As you are doubtless aware, in recent months the British have made two attempts to invade the United States. One attempt was made from Canada across Lake Champlain, and the other in the Chesapeake against Washington and Baltimore. Both attempts were repelled. Now the British are planning a third, and perhaps their final, attempt. This one, we presume, will be against Mobile. You, monsieur, are well established in this area. Not only are you as familiar with the terrain as anyone alive, you command a sizable force of men and ships. Great Britain desires your alliance with them in this conflict. So does the United States. We are well aware that the British have made you an offer for your services. The United States of America would now like to make a counteroffer. I was chosen to deliver this offer to you because of our previous relationship. I am fully authorized to make this offer. As is Mr. Crabtree. We both serve as special emissaries of President Madison.

"So you now have a choice to make. You can side with Great Britain or you can side with the United States. Or you can choose to remain neutral and do nothing. Of course, if you were to choose that option, you would be reduced to praying for an outcome favorable to your interests. Knowing you as I do, I suspect you wish to shape your future rather than have it shaped for you. Am I correct?"

Lafitte poured himself another slug of bourbon. When he held the bottle up questioningly, both Americans politely declined. "Of course you are correct, monsieur," he said blithely. "Praying is something I do neither with great regularity nor great ease. Nor with great expectations. *Continuez, s'il vous plaît.*"

Richard nodded. "We have an offer in mind. But before I discuss this offer with you, I would like to know, if I may, the terms of the British offer."

"To tell you would be poor negotiating on my part, Capitaine, and I take pride in my negotiating skills. But in this one instance I am willing to make an exception. Why? Because in this instance I have nothing to lose and nothing to hide. The British have offered me British citizenship, a full pardon for me and my men for any perceived wrongdoings, and a personal estate in any British colony I desire in the Americas. In addition, there would be a sum of money paid to me on an annual basis, the amount as yet undetermined. *That* is their offer, monsieur. Nothing more, nothing less. It is a good offer, no?"

"Thank you for sharing those details with us. We appreciate it. Is it a good offer? That depends. It only has teeth if the British win this war. If they lose, you lose. And you also stand to lose everything."

"Perhaps. Perhaps not. The fact is, Capitaine Cutler, that while I believe that the British may not lose this war, I also believe that they cannot win it either. Which is why I have no interest in their offer to me. Ah. I see that you did not anticipate such an admission at this stage of our negotiations."

Richard and Agreen exchanged a glance. "How have you come to draw that conclusion?" Agreen asked Lafitte.

Lafitte stirred his bourbon thoughtfully with his forefinger. Then: "It is not a difficult conclusion to draw, Monsieur Crabtree; not difficult at all. It was the same in your first war with England, *n'est-ce pas?* America is too big a land to conquer, and she has too many people and too many resources. More to the point, the British people have no heart for this war."

"Many Americans have no heart for it, either," Richard remarked. "Including my brother and others of my family's acquaintance. You have been honest with me, so now I am being honest with you."

"Yes, you are. And I thank you." Lafitte settled back in his chair. "You have heard what the British have offered me. Now we turn the tables, as you Americans like to say. What is your government prepared to offer me?"

"Amnesty," Richard replied.

"Amnesty? You mean, a pardon for my alleged transgressions?"

"That's one way to put it. A full pardon for you and those in your employ. On the condition that you give your word to henceforth pursue an honest living."

Lafitte smiled. "That is not much of an offer, monsieur. I do not require a pardon, because I am not a pirate. I am a privateer operating with letters of marque. We have been through this before, you and I."

"Yes, I know. But to my way of thinking, it *is* a good offer," Richard insisted. "You just said that the British cannot win this war. I agree. They can't. So, what are your choices? To continue as you are? Two years ago our military laid siege to Grande Terre. Many of your men were killed. You were forced to flee, and your brother was taken prisoner. We can attack again, should we wish to, and this time bring you and your men to justice. That is not an idle threat, monsieur. That is a fact. If the British cannot defeat us, you certainly cannot. Just six months ago Governor Claiborne," referring to the first elected governor of the state of Louisiana in 1812, "posted a bounty of $500 for your capture. So, yes, amnesty would be a great boon to you and your men. I urge you to consider this offer carefully, *mon ami.*"

Lafitte took another sip and held up his glass as if examining its contents. "What you say is partly true, monsieur," he said with a smile. "But you must believe me when I say that you *cannot* attack me again without suffering serious consequences. Never again will anyone catch me by surprise. As for your fearless governor, I am still here, am I not? Despite his bounty? Are you aware of how I answered his threat? You are not? *Ensuite*, let me tell you. The day after he posted his $500 bounty for my capture, I posted notices on every major road in New Orleans offering $600 for *his* capture and delivery to me."

Despite himself, Agreen burst out laughing. "Well, I'm knackered. You did that?"

Lafitte nodded.

"What happened?"

"Nothing happened. That is my point, do you not see? I am still here, as I said, and the governor hides under his desk in Baton Rouge. *That* is the power and influence I wield, monsieur. And *that* is what you seek to use against the British, *non*?"

"Yes," Richard had to agree. "It is."

"*Tres bien alors.* I have two conditions to add to your offer of amnesty. I am afraid that these two conditions are not negotiable."

"Name them."

Lafitte held up one finger. "My brother Pierre is released from prison. Immediately." He held up a second finger. "He and I keep everything we now have. In return, we pledge on our honor that henceforth whatever merchandise we sell, we sell honestly."

"And your men?"

"They will be dispersed as soon as the war is over and you have no further need of them. You have my word on that as well. Do I have your word? Can you promise me that your government will accept these two conditions?"

Richard allowed only a moment to elapse. "You have my promise."

"*Bon.* I trust you, Capitaine Cutler, and I trust you, Monsieur Crabtree. And because I do, I have information to share that I believe will be of great interest to your General Jackson. It will sweeten our deal, as you Americans like to say. As though a deal were a cup of coffee, yes?"

"I'm listening."

Lafitte drained his glass. "The British are not planning to attack Mobile, as least not straightaway. They are planning to first attack a more important city. More important to them, at least."

"Where is this attack to take place?"

"Right here," Lafitte stated with deadly earnestness. He pointed eastward. "New Orleans."

Richard and Agreen exchanged glances. "How did you come by this information?" Agreen asked.

Lafitte held up his empty glass as if in a toast. "Unless I am mistaken, it was your Dr. Franklin who once said, 'If you wish to know the mind of your enemy, bed his woman.' Did he not say that?"

"Something to that effect," Richard acknowledged. Then, as the implication of what Lafitte had just said sank in: "Surely you are not referring to Admiral Cochrane's wife?" Cochrane, Richard knew, had brought his wife, Maria, with him from England to Jamaica, the preferred hunting ground of the Lafitte brothers.

Lafitte feigned shock. "Monsieur, I am a gentleman! I am not in the habit of divulging that sort of information."

"Are you certain of this information, monsieur?" Richard demanded. "Absolutely, utterly certain? Much will depend on your answer, my neck included."

"I am quite certain, monsieur. You and General Jackson may rely on my words. We are allies now, *non*?"

CHAPTER FIFTEEN

New Orleans, Louisiana

December 1814–January 1815

THE NEXT MORNING USS *HAMPTON* WEIGHED ANCHOR AND SHAPED A course for Mobile Bay. The bay was a strategically vital parcel of land and water claimed by both the United States and Spanish West Florida, a colony of Britain's ally Spain. Although hotly contested, Mobile was currently under the control of Gen. Andrew Jackson and the Army regulars and militia units under his command. The general freely used the aphorism "might makes right" to justify the use of force to fulfill his nation's manifest destiny. His determination to occupy and annex this sparsely populated outpost of the Mississippi Territory was no exception. Plus, he had orders from Washington to do precisely that.

Captain Wallace carried with him two dispatches for General Jackson. One dispatch Richard Cutler had written the night before detailing his conversation with Jean Lafitte and his conviction that New Orleans, and not Mobile, was the initial target of the British invaders. Richard urged the general to leave posthaste for New Orleans and prepare for battle there. The second dispatch was one that Richard had carried with him since departing from Long Wharf in Boston. It was written, signed, and sealed by the hand of James Monroe, secretary of state and secretary of war, and it directed Jackson to act upon the counsel of Capt. Richard Cutler, USN, as though it came from the president himself.

"I sure as hell wish we were sailin' with them," Agreen grumbled as he and Richard watched the stern of the sloop-of-war disappear into a bank of ground fog lurking low over Barataria Bay. "We can't leave this miserable hellhole soon enough t' suit my taste."

Take heart, Captain," Richard encouraged. "Our time is coming. I promised General Jackson that I would personally deliver Lafitte to him in New Orleans, and you heard me promise Lafitte that I would see his brother released from prison there. I aim to make good on both promises. As soon as I do, we can sail for home."

"I do understand, Richard," Agreen said, "and I'm not tryin' t' hurry you. I've always admired your sense of duty. It's why I agreed to sign on with this little expedition. Well, that and the money. I don't regret my decision. But I'm missing home, I have t' admit."

"So am I, Agee. More than you might imagine."

"Anne-Marie, is it?"

"In part, yes," Richard allowed, adding thoughtfully and, to Agreen's ear, somewhat enigmatically, "but only in part."

The passage from Grand Terre to New Orleans was a relatively straightforward one, Jean Lafitte had claimed. He had made the trip dozens of times without incident, he said, and this trip should be no different. But it *was* different. A week after they set out, it became abundantly clear that a hundred-mile journey that should have taken four or five days was going to take considerably longer.

It came as a shock to Lafitte and his entourage when scouts reported sighting two British sloops-of-war and a brig-of-war patrolling the southern reaches of the Mississippi River. They had known the British were close, but not this close. Richard's first concern was the whereabouts and status of *Hampton*. Did she get through to Mobile before the British blockaded the entrance to its harbor? If she had been captured or otherwise detained, unable to deliver the dispatches to Jackson, Richard was on a fool's errand. Silently he cursed his decision not to send a second expedition to Mobile via an overland route instead of conceding when Lafitte insisted that such an expedition was imprudent, unnecessary, and fraught with risk. Any overland route would encroach upon the lands of the Red Stick tribes of the Creek Confederacy, the very tribes that Jackson had defeated at Horseshoe Bend earlier in the year. The Creeks thus had an ax to grind with General Jackson and anyone serving under his banner.

During the next several days, Richard, Agreen, and Jean Lafitte led eighty-seven heavily armed men through the boggy wetlands along the west bank of the Mississippi. Travel by boat on the river, however tempting and expedient it might have been, was avoided in deference to the British patrols. As they moved northward, however, they began to regret that decision because they spotted few boats of any description on the river. Only an occasional pelican swooping low in search of fish disturbed the placid water. Through the heavy brush they marched, pushing aside low-hanging branches and squelching through thick mud and leech-filled water. Though autumn had turned to winter, the heat lingered. Food, though plentiful, had to be scrounged from land and water, causing further delays. Sleep was fitful at best despite the cotton mosquito netting that was standard issue for every man. At the first sign of dawn each morning they broke camp and continued the agonizing plod along a virgin route rendered ever more miserable by frequent showers and summer-like thunderstorms that penetrated to the skin and made footing hazardous.

At last, at midmorning on Monday, December 29, they neared their destination. They heard it before they saw it. From ahead came the rasp of saws, the banging of hammers, and the crack of falling trees. The air became thick with the pungent aromas of freshly hewn timber and sawdust. Within the din they heard the exhortations of men in command and the grunts and shouts of men working in close quarters.

As they emerged through the mucky waters of a shallow swamp and a thicket of cypress trees, they saw a network of earthworks that formed an oblong battlement four or five feet tall, perhaps a hundred feet long, and fifty feet across. A number of cannon were mounted on what passed for parapets—one, at least, a massive 32-pounder. In the river, seemingly an extension of the fort's eastern defenses, lay a one-hundred-foot-long sloop-of-war, apparently aground. From atop the battlement flew the fifteen red and white stripes of the American flag, now boasting eighteen white stars within its navy-blue canton.

"Well, I'll be a horse's ass," Agreen remarked, stopping short and leaning on his musket. "We made it."

"Yes, *mon ami*," Lafitte agreed, his voice tired. "*Nous sommes arriveés. Finalement.*"

"*Bien fait, monsieur,*" Richard said to Lafitte. The sores, cuts, bruises, and insect bites plaguing his body underscored the mixed emotions and fatigue he too was experiencing. "Let's see what sort of reception committee awaits us."

The first officer they approached at the entrance to the fortification was, surprisingly, a naval officer who looked to be about the age of Will Cutler and looked remarkably like him. Surprised in turn to see two Navy personnel materializing from the swamps at the head of a band of bedraggled-looking misfits, the young man momentarily forgot protocol and stood gaping as the entourage approached him. Men wielding axes, hammers, and saws in the immediate vicinity likewise paused in their work to gape. When Agreen informed the officer of Richard's rank, the officer snapped to.

"Beg pardon, sir," he apologized, offering a passable salute. "My senses seem to have temporarily abandoned me. It won't happen again."

Richard returned the salute. "No apology is necessary," he said. "Be at your ease." He extended his hand. "I am Captain Richard Cutler, and I am here at the request of our government. This gentleman is my executive officer, Captain Agreen Crabtree, and this other gentleman is Mr. Jean Lafitte. Your name is?"

"Lieutenant J. D. Henley, sir," the officer replied. He took Richard's hand. "I have in fact heard of you, Captain. General Jackson mentioned your name just yesterday in a staff meeting. Yours and that of Mr. Lafitte. May I be the first to welcome you to New Orleans."

Richard released a long, silent sigh of relief. So Jackson was in New Orleans after all! "Are you attached to that vessel out there?" He pointed at the grounded sloop.

"The *Louisiana*?" Henley shook his head. "No, sir. I am the commanding officer of the schooner *Carolina*. She saw some action recently and is undergoing minor repairs in New Orleans. She should be back with us in a day or two."

"Who commands this battery?"

"Commodore Daniel Patterson, sir. He's in New Orleans at the moment. General Jackson has declared martial law in the city, and the commodore is seeing to the details."

"I see. I know Commodore Patterson. We served together in the Mediterranean and in the Indies." What Richard did not mention in Lafitte's presence was that it was Patterson and *Carolina* that had led the September raid against Lafitte's base on Grand Terre. If Lafitte recognized the name, he did not let on. "New Orleans is, what, five miles distant?"

"About that, sir."

Agreen asked, "Do we have other naval vessels in the area?"

Henley shook his head. "We do not, Mr. Crabtree. We had five gunboats on Lake Borgne"—referring to a forty-mile-wide lake due east between New Orleans and the Gulf of Mexico—"under the command of Lieutenant Thomas Catesby Jones. You may have heard of him as well. Unfortunately, the gunboats were all captured by the British two weeks back during an engagement on the lake."

"I see," Richard said. "Tell me, Lieutenant, is General Jackson in New Orleans at the moment?"

"No, sir. He is over there," Henley pointed across the river to beyond the east bank, "with the main army. His headquarters is behind what we call Line Jackson. You can see the western end of it just beyond the river. The Line is still under construction, as you will soon see for yourself. But we're making good progress. We should have it completed in a few days' time. Then we'll be ready for the British."

"Can you take us to the general?"

"Of course, sir. Right away. It will be my honor."

⌐⁓⌐

Andrew Jackson's reputation was well known to Richard Cutler and to many other informed Americans. Of humble Scots-Irish origins, he had been forced from an early age to fight his way to fame and fortune. At the age of thirteen he had enlisted in the Continental Army and had been taken prisoner by the British. Hardened by the experience, Jackson had studied law and subsequently represented his home state of Tennessee in both the House and the Senate. When he was appointed a colonel in the Tennessee militia, he added military rank to his expanding credentials. He already had a reputation for courage in the face of fire, having fought in numerous "affairs of honor" against men of substance, the most notorious of which had captured the imagination of a young nation. A newspaperman named Jack Dickinson had written an article in which he called Jackson "a worthless scoundrel, a poltroon, and a coward," in part because Jackson had defied the law and social mores by marrying a woman before her divorce from another man was finalized. Infuriated by the accusations and insults, Jackson called Dickinson out. At the appointed hour, having walked off the required ten paces back-to-back, each man turned to face the other. Jackson allowed Dickinson the first shot, which struck Jackson in the chest, missing his heart by less than an inch. Despite the serious wound, Jackson stood his ground, calmly raised his own pistol to eye level, and fired a slug through Dickinson's head, killing him instantly. When those in his party tried to put Jackson under the care of a surgeon, Jackson refused treatment, preferring to keep the bullet inside him as a memento joining a number of other slugs gained in similar engagements.

Richard was just as impressed by the general's softer side. After Jackson's victory over the Creeks at Horseshoe Bend, he took under his wing two young Indian children orphaned by the battle. He legally adopted them and took them to live at The Hermitage, the substantial plantation he owned near Nashville, Tennessee.

This morning, as Richard Cutler stood before the general, he understood why Jackson's renown was by now bordering on myth. The man had a presence few others possessed. They were in a mammoth military tent serving as Army headquarters. In attendance, in addition to Richard, Agreen, and Lafitte, were four officers—two colonels, a lieutenant colonel, and a major—presumably members of Jackson's general staff.

"Good morning, General," Richard said, saluting. "I am honored to meet you."

Jackson returned the salute and then offered his hand. Richard took it, feeling the coarse, weathered skin that was nonetheless warm and oddly comforting to the touch. When Jackson's steely blue eyes met the lighter blue of Richard's, his long, angular, almost gaunt face seemed to relax and brighten. "The honor is mine, Captain Cutler," he said earnestly. "Thank you for your dispatch. It was timely, to say the least. Without it we would have been caught somewhat unawares. Now, tell me, who are these two gentlemen with you?"

When Richard had made the introductions, Jackson said, with a zeal that seemed somewhat forced, "Pleased to meet you, Monsieur Lafitte. Welcome to our side. May I assume you brought a formidable party with you?"

"*Quatre-vingt-sept hommes*," Lafitte replied. "Eighty-seven men."

"I appreciate the translation," Jackson said gruffly. "Although I speak French, I much prefer my native tongue." He looked down his long nose at Lafitte. "Frankly, given your reputation, I had expected a considerably larger force."

Lafitte met his gaze. "Eighty-seven men is what I have, General. Good men, all."

"I can vouch for that, sir," Agreen put in.

"Then eighty-seven men will have to do," Jackson said. "Out there"— he motioned toward Line Jackson—"I have farmers, silversmiths, and blacksmiths in my command. So why not pirates? I will add them to the five hundred under Commodore Patterson on the west bank. We can use more men there.

"Now then, gentlemen, I mean no offense, but you look the worse for wear. I suggest you have a cleanup and a bite to eat. Beyond that I'm afraid we have no time to dilly-dally. Our scouts report a major British buildup on Lake Borgne and Lake Pontchartrain. We anticipate a major offensive very soon. Mr. Lafitte, may I assume that you and your men can advise us on British movements and how best to counter them on this terrain?"

"Of course, General," Lafitte assured him. "It is what we are here to do, *n'est-ce pas*? And it is why, today, you will release my brother from prison."

A shadow passed over Jackson's face. Again Lafitte did not flinch before the graveyard-cold stare. Seconds ticked by, then Jackson's face relaxed. "Yes, well, that is the arrangement, isn't it. I cannot promise his release today, as you would have it. But I can promise it will happen. Captain Cutler has given you his word on that, and you now have mine."

"*Quand, mon general? When* will it happen?"

"My God, sir, you are bordering on impudence!" Jackson snapped, his nostrils flaring. Then, in a more moderate tone: "By week's end. I will send word today to the authorities in New Orleans. You have my word on *that*, as well."

Lafitte nodded his understanding but offered no reply.

"All right, then. It's settled. Shall we meet back here in, say, an hour's time? I shall summon an orderly to take you where you may refresh yourselves. Oh, Captain Cutler," he added as if in an afterthought, "I am holding several letters for you. They are in a dispatch pouch sent to me from Mr. Jones." He rummaged through a stack of papers and leather pouches piled on a rectangular board that served as a desk. "Ah, here they are." He handed over the brown leather satchel.

Richard opened it and peered inside. He saw two envelopes sealed at the front fold with the blue wax and silver lettering of high office. One of them was clearly official in nature. But it was the other letter that caught his eye. It was written in the hand of his daughter-in-law Mindy.

Richard glanced up at Jackson. "If you will excuse me?"

"Of course, Captain. Please." Jackson motioned toward a nook in the tent that offered a semblance of privacy.

Richard went straightway to a Shaker-style wooden chair and sat down on it. He withdrew the envelope from the pouch, broke the wax seal, and unfolded the letter.

2 October 1814
14 Queen Street
Alexandria, Virginia

My Dear Papa:
I am writing this letter in haste, not knowing when or if it will reach you. I pray it does.

Jamie was injured several weeks ago in an action on the Potomac River. He was shot in the left shoulder, and while the injury at first did not seem

206

overly serious, infection set in and we feared for his life. Dr. Quigley saw no alternative to amputating the arm, a procedure that he performed yesterday at the hospital in the Washington Navy Yard.

The surgery was a success, as these things go. Jamie is clearly distraught by what has happened to him, yet he is determined to keep his spirits up for me and for the baby we are expecting in five months. Yes, dearest Papa, a baby! If it is a boy, we shall name him Richard. Another Richard Cutler! We can only hope that he will grow up to become a strong, kind, and steadfast man like his grandfather. Because there is already another young Katherine, a girl will be Anne Lavinia, both for your sisters and for the other Anne who has filled your last few years with happiness.

So the news is not all bad. When Jamie has regained his strength he will write to you himself. He remains weak and disoriented, but Dr. Quigley assures me that this is perfectly normal and not to worry. He promises me that Jamie will soon be his old self again. And happily, he has full use of his remaining arm. When we are able, we will move back to Hingham and live with my parents until we find a place of our own. Perhaps we will be neighbors! What joy that would bring us both—and your new grandson—because I am sure our baby will be a boy!

We send you endless love along with the hope and prayer that wherever Fate has taken you, you are safe and well. We talk of you often, and our pride in you and what you are doing gives Jamie much pleasure and comfort. You are forever in our hearts and forever in our thoughts.

God's blessings,
Mindy

With a heavy heart Richard contemplated Mindy's words, hurting for them both and yet heartened by her news of another grandchild—another Cutler to carry on the line and help make the nation strong, as he and his sons had tried to do. Images of Jamie as an infant, a boy, a young man with Katherine's coloring and hazel eyes flitted through his mind. Then he brought himself back to the present and reached into the pouch again.

The second letter was from Navy Secretary William Jones. In it he assured Richard that his son would continue to receive the best medical care possible. "Jamie is an American hero," Jones wrote, "and the pride of the Navy. His leadership and his sacrifices will never be forgotten." Jones went on to say that Richard's other son, Will, had served with equal distinction under both Captain Perry and Commodore Macdonough, and as a result had been granted an extended leave to visit his family in Boston. He concluded the letter by recognizing the considerable contributions and sacrifices the Cutler family had made to the cause, and passing on his hope and expectation that Richard would carry forward the family tradition by extending every assistance to Gen. Andrew Jackson and the Army of the South.

"What is it, Richard?" Agreen interjected when Richard sat stone still, staring down at the two letters. "Good news, I hope?"

In reply, Richard handed him Mindy's letter.

"We're not leaving," he said with grim resolve as Agreen read the letter. "We're staying, and we'll see this fight through to the end."

———

The next day, New Year's Eve morning, beneath lowering gray rain clouds, Jackson's and Lafitte's scouts returned to report a buildup of British infantry and supplies to the east of Line Jackson. They had seen such activity before, but back then, at the Battle of Lake Borgne, the entire British force had numbered about 1,500 Redcoats and Bullocks. Today they had seen a considerably larger force.

Later that same morning Richard was given a tour of Line Jackson by Lt. Col. David Cushing, a broad-shouldered, trim-waisted bull of a man who exuded a confidence that seemed born of wealth and privilege rather than accomplishments. He wondered if Cushing's optimism and dismissal of the enemy's capabilities might be misplaced. The British, after all, were reported to enjoy a three-to-one advantage in the number of ground troops, and most of their infantry and Marines had fought to victory on foreign soil against some of the finest soldiers in Europe. Indeed, Admiral Cochrane had at his disposal the elite of the British military machine, by all accounts the greatest fighting force the world had yet known. It was true that a handful of the 958 Army regulars under Jackson and many of the 3,000 soldiers in the militia units from Louisiana, Tennessee, Kentucky, and the Mississippi Territory—including two brigades of free blacks and a contingent of Choctaw Indians—had fought in wilderness campaigns against various Indian tribes allied with the British. But in those encounters they had employed frontier tactics incompatible with European-style tactics of concentrated musket and cannon fire— the very sort of situation they could expect to soon confront. Further, the hundred-odd Marines and sailors within the American ranks had limited experience fighting on land anywhere. Nonetheless, such was Jackson's regard for their fighting skills and spirit that he had placed them at the very center of the Line.

Although Line Jackson, as Lieutenant Henley had earlier acknowledged, was still a work in progress, Richard found it impressive. It faced eastward along a three-mile-long defensive position twenty miles west of Lake Borgne and Lake Pontchartrain. Its earthworks and breastworks were reinforced by massive wooden timbers and granite rocks hauled in from elsewhere. At irregular intervals, the muzzles of cannon of various calibers protruded through parapets heavily fortified with hemp bags packed solid with sand and soil. Complementing them was a series of eight redoubt-like batteries housing an array of cannon and mortars and snub-barreled howitzers. The northern end of the Line was protected by a seemingly impenetrable swamp, the southern end by a fast-flowing tributary of the Mississippi River. Directly in front of the Line, from its northern flank to its southern, bare-chested men worked steadily in a fifteen-foot-wide trench that Cushing called the Rodriguez Canal. Between the trench and Lake Borgne lay flat, open land interspersed here and there with cypress hammocks and other swamp vegetation.

"We had planned to increase the depth of the canal to eight feet and fill it with water from the swamp and the stream," Cushing explained, "but I doubt we'll have time to do that. The hour of reckoning is nigh upon us."

"So it would seem," Richard said. They were standing now at the center of the Line, and the sailors and Marines stationed there were clearly preparing themselves for battle. "What happened the night of the twenty-third, Colonel? I have heard snippets, but I would like to know more about it, if you are willing to tell me."

"Happily, Captain! It was a glorious affair. That night, Lieutenant Henley slipped down the Mississippi in *Carolina*, the schooner just returned from New Orleans. A British advance guard, you see, had managed to fight its way through to the river. But instead of capitalizing on their victory, their commanding officer—a chap named Keane, we believe—pitched camp on the grounds of the Lacoste Plantation! Waiting for reinforcements, if you want my opinion. Henley spotted their campfires and opened up with his carronades. At the same time, General Jackson and two thousand of our boys came out of hiding in the woods and attacked them." Cushing chuckled and rubbed his hands together gleefully. "We saw some damn intense fighting that night, let me tell you! I only wish I could have been there. But someone had to stay behind to watch over things. General Jackson sent Keane and his Redcoats packing, let me tell you!"

Richard nodded. "And now the enemy knows that this fight will not be an easy one."

"Damn right they do. So much for British arrogance, let me tell you."

"Thank you, Colonel, you just did." Richard made a show of studying the terrain to the east. "You're quite certain the British will come at us head-on?"

"I am," Cushing said firmly. "Really, they have no other choice. That's why we've gone to such lengths to fortify Line Jackson. If the British want to get to New Orleans, they must first come through us. And that," he said emphatically, "they will not do."

"I'm glad to know that. Is there really no other route of attack? Other than what we see here and up the east bank? I have to wonder. Why not go around Lake Pontchartrain and attack New Orleans from the north?"

"Can't," Cushing said dismissively. "The swamps up there are impenetrable. And have you ever run into quicksand? Your friend Lafitte has confirmed that an attack from the north is impossible. Soldiers would quickly become bogged down and become easy pickings for 'gators and bullets. Nevertheless, we have posted sentries there to sound the alarm just in case."

Richard continued to gaze out on an arena that he sensed would soon dictate the outcome of the war. "What about the Royal Navy? The river certainly is wide enough to accommodate sizable warships. What's to stop them?"

"Fort Saint Philip."

"Fort Saint Philip? Is that the fort we saw on the way here?"

"Has to be. It's all we have protecting the approaches to New Orleans from the Gulf."

"Not much of a fort, as I recall."

"It's strong enough to do the job, given the right commander," Cushing snapped, annoyed at Richard's apparent doubt. He glanced at his waistcoat watch. "Which reminds me. The general is expecting you in a few minutes."

———

Jackson lost no time in coming to the point. Barely allowing Richard time to take the chair he had offered, he said, "Captain Cutler, may I first say how very grateful I am that you and Mr. Crabtree have decided to remain here when it would have been entirely within your rights to leave. Bless you for that." Jackson ran a hand through thick reddish-blond hair that Richard noted was going prematurely gray. "Now, then, to the matter at hand: I had thought to ask a favor of you. But upon reflection I am not so sure if it is such a good notion after all."

"Ask it anyway, General, if you wish."

Jackson leaned forward in his chair, as if to speak confidentially. "You know of Fort Saint Philip?"

"I do. I saw it on the way north from Grande Terre. And just a few minutes ago, Colonel Cushing mentioned it. He made a reference to the fort serving its purpose assuming it has the right commander. Does that makes sense to you?"

"It makes perfect sense," Jackson said. "Colonel Cushing is quite correct. It is the reason for our discussion at this moment. The fort is under the command of a fellow named Walter Overton. He holds the rank of lieutenant colonel, but only as of last week. Overton is a politician, and apparently one of the few honest ones, but he has limited military experience. That fort is vital to our defenses. Were the Royal Navy to neutralize it and sail up here, my flank would be dangerously exposed. As a military man, you can well understand the dire implications of that."

Richard could indeed.

"That fort must be held at all costs," Jackson went on. "At all costs! I had thought to ask you to share command with Overton. However, in view of your extensive battle experience, I should prefer to have your services here more than there. You see my dilemma."

"I do see your dilemma, General, and I thank you for considering it a dilemma. I shall be happy to serve wherever you think me most useful. If that is here, and if you are amenable, may I propose a candidate for that other post?"

Jackson held up both hands, as if surrendering to the will of the gods. "Please do, Captain. I am all ears. Who is the commander you wish to propose?"

"Jean Lafitte."

"*That* scoundrel? Surely you jest!"

"I am quite serious, General. I met Lafitte some years ago, and I have come to know him again. He may seem foppish and arrogant, and his claim to be a privateer may be open to legal interpretation, but I can tell you from personal experience that he is a brave, intelligent, and, may I say it, honorable man who, like yourself, does not cower from a fight. He has a fort on Grand Terre, and he has defended it effectively against all comers, including the United States Navy. I can assure you that he would provide invaluable assistance to Colonel Overton."

"That is high praise, coming from you, Captain. I would be a fool to ignore it." Jackson thought a moment, then: "It may work out well after all. Sending Lafitte down there would separate him from Commodore Patterson up here. Not a bad idea, eh? There can't be much love lost between those two. And if Lafitte is as competent as you say he is . . ."

"He is, General."

Jackson nodded, his mind made up. "Right, then. It's settled. You will discuss this with Lafitte?" When Richard nodded, he said, "We can send him down there on *Enterprise*. She's due in tomorrow from Natchez with food and munitions after picking up Pierre Lafitte in New Orleans. Pierre can accompany his brother if he so chooses."

"How did *Enterprise* slip through the British blockade?"

"She didn't have to. She's coming down from Pittsburgh along the Ohio and Mississippi Rivers. You see," he explained, grinning at Richard's quizzical look. "*Enterprise* is not a sailing vessel. She is a steamboat. The dawn of a new age, eh, Captain Cutler?"

Early in the morning of Sunday, January 8, the few among the four thousand soldiers, sailors, and Marines stationed along Line Jackson who were sleeping were jerked awake by the roar of artillery fire and the cacophony of shells and rockets exploding into and above their positions. During the previous three days they had watched the British struggle to wheel up fieldpieces and Congreve rocket wagons from barges beached on the shores of Lake Borgne. When the activity on the flatlands ceased late Saturday afternoon, an eerie silence had settled over the looming arena of battle. That silence was now shattered.

"And so it begins," Agreen mumbled to Richard. The two of them, along with nearly everyone else on Line Jackson, were huddled with their backs against the earthworks.

"Apparently so," Richard commented dryly. "But with every new beginning there comes an end."

"Always the bloody optimist, aren't you?"

At the first lull in the barrage, Richard turned onto his knees and peered over the defensive barrier. He could not make out much beyond the billows of his own breath, made visible by an unusually cold daybreak in Louisiana. Rolling fog blanketed the land before him; all he could see of the enemy position were occasional flashes of orange fire flaring within the soupy gray mist.

Richard ducked as another round of cannon and rocket fire erupted, followed seconds later by the harsh *clang* of iron striking iron and a man's high-pitched scream. All eyes swung backward toward the cry of anguish and the horrific sight of a dying man. Whether his wound was inflicted by the round shot or by a shard of hot metal from the cannon it had shattered, a Marine private lay writhing in agony on the hard ground. His left leg had been blown off at the thigh, and his femoral artery was spurting blood with every beat of his heart.

"Jesus Christ Almighty!" a sailor cried out.

"Eyes front and center!" Richard shouted in an authoritative voice. "Corporal!" he demanded of a Marine noncom who seemed to have regained a semblance of composure, "Arrange a detail and get that man to a surgeon!"

"Aye, aye, sir," the corporal shouted back amid the riot of yet another British onslaught. Up and down the Line, plumes of dirt and sand and jagged shards of timber and stone spewed into the air as barrage after barrage rocked the makeshift barrier. Overhead, Congreve rockets shrieked and exploded, adding an air of confusion and terror and panic to the scene of battle.

"Hold the line, boys! *Hold the line!*"

Mounted on a gray horse, General Jackson was galloping up and down behind the Line waving his sword in the air, exhorting his men to take heart and stand firm.

Then the firing stopped. First one by one, then seemingly as one man, the soldiers, sailors, and Marines of Line Jackson knelt or cautiously stood, their gaze fixed eastward.

"Must have run out of munitions!" Richard heard someone down the Line remark.

No, Richard said to himself. Aloud, in the voice of command, he shouted, "*No!* Get ready, men!"

The command was echoed down the line, loudest of all by Jackson himself.

"Here they come!" someone warned. Then another and another took up the cry.

It was not what they saw, not at first. It was what they heard. From everywhere to eastward came the martial *rat-a-tat* of drums and, from the right, the harsh blare of bagpipes. Then, as the morning sun broke through the clouds, an army on the march loomed through the lifting fog: row after row after countless row of white trousers and red coats and cocked bonnets, muskets and rifles shouldered, expressions grim and determined, the military discipline drilled into them on the battlefields of Spain and Flanders propelling them onward in perfect rhythm, in perfect cadence, impervious to everything save the call to arms. They were here to deliver the full weight of the king's wrath and justice, however unsavory and perilous that might prove to be.

Beside them, to the south, marching in equally consummate ranks, trooped the 93rd Sutherland Highland Regiment, preceded by pipers clad in the regiment's blue-and-green plaid. Richard found the contrast between the splendid British soldiers and the Americans, many clad in frontier buckskin, almost ludicrous.

"*First line, make ready!*" Jackson cried out, his command repeated down the Line. The men assigned to that first line took position against the earthworks and raised their firearms to eye level. Gunners at the cannon and howitzers stood primed to yank lanyards.

"*First line! Fire!*"

A thousand rifles opened fire on the advancing British, supported by the thunderous applause of flame, ash, and round shot and grapeshot pouring from the array of cannon positioned along the Line. The effect was immediate and lethal. Redcoats and Highlanders either lurched forward and fell on their stomachs or were thrown backward by the impact of the hot shot, a mass of pulverized bone and gore, one behind another, as if knocked over in a gruesome game of lawn bowls.

The main body marched on toward Line Jackson undaunted, as if they had just been stung by nothing more than a swarm of pesky hornets.

"*Second line, make ready!*"

The first line stepped back to reload as a second line stepped forward to take their place at the earthworks. The third line took the former place of the second line in a well-rehearsed evolution that required but a few seconds to execute.

"*Second line! Fire!*"

Peering over the parapet through a small spyglass, Richard watched as another row of His Majesty's finest collapsed onto the ground. When an officer, a high-ranking one judging by his ornate uniform—perhaps General Pakenham himself—had his horse shot out from under him, he quickly remounted another, only to be immediately riddled by an onslaught of bullets and grapeshot. In a single fluid motion he slumped forward on his saddle and then slid off onto the ground. On the way, the heel of his left boot snagged in the stirrup, adding humiliation to misery as his body was dragged forward through the ranks of his dwindling command.

"*Third line, make ready!*"

Again the shift in lines. Again the onslaught of bullets, round shot, and, increasingly as the distance between the Line and the British decreased, the bark of grapeshot. Still the British marched on.

By now, the forward lines of the British were returning fire, and their aim was remarkably true despite the considerably smaller targets the Americans ensconced behind chest-high battlements presented. Yet the fighting remained decidedly one-sided. For every fallen American, ten British soldiers fell. In the narrowing distance, Richard saw another British officer fall from a horse, and then another. Why these officers persisted in offering such tantalizing fat targets confounded Richard, but something else far more puzzling was demanding his full attention. He nudged Agreen, standing next to him.

"What is it, Richard?" Agreen asked, pausing to reload his rifle. Around and above them came the shrieks, cries, and stench of war fought in close quarters.

Richard did not immediately respond, staring out in what seemed to be utter stupefaction. Richard dropped the skyglass from his eye before raising it again to sweep his gaze across the killing field. At length he muttered, "How do they expect to get here?"

"What?" Agreen edged closer. "What the hell are you talking about?"

Richard pointed ahead. "Look, Agee! Where are the fascines? Surely they have them. But where are they?" A well-trained army such as this one could not have forgotten to bring fascines, clumps of sticks or rods bound together that could be thrown into a ditch or canal to allow soldiers to cross it more easily. Could they? "And where are the ladders? How do they expect to scale this barricade without them? I say again: *How do they expect to get here?*"

"Damn if you're not right, Richard!" Agreen had no explanation to offer. He could only see what Richard saw: a once solid army now largely leaderless and dissolving into confusion and disarray. Here and there an officer led his men on a heroic but suicidal charge against Line Jackson. The bulk of them were shot dead or wounded before they reached the partially flooded canal. A few soldiers and a major managed to struggle across it but were gunned down as they tried to claw their way to the top of the earthworks. It was like shooting ducks in a barrel.

"Fire at will!"

Heartened beyond measure by what he too was witnessing, and smelling the blood of victory, General Jackson shouted the command to disregard drills and protocol and pump as much death into the enemy as circumstances and opportunity allowed. A great cheer went up as those positioned along the Line opened fire with a renewed vigor and vengeance. Soldiers in the rear eagerly pushed in to join in on what was fast becoming a bloodbath.

"It's a slaughter!" Agreen mumbled as he looked out on the horrific carnage. Hundreds of British soldiers lay dead or seriously wounded. A glance at his watch confirmed that it had taken a mere half hour to create such shocking devastation.

Richard stood mutely, shaking his head.

From the southern end of the Line a sudden great roar sounded. It was not the sound of the American defenders cheering. It came from men, legions of them, exhorting one another onward to victory for God, king, and country.

"The Royal Marines!" Richard exclaimed. "They're inside the Line. The west bank battery must have fallen!"

And so it had. A brigade of Royal Marines in company with the sailors of Cochrane's fleet had breached the western flank of Line Jackson and was storming in behind the defensive barrier. They had caught the militia units stationed there by surprise and had them either dead or on the run.

Richard slapped Agreen's shoulder. "Let's go, Agee!" To the American Marines and sailors at the center of the Line: "To us, boys! To us!"

Quickly the group joined a force led by General Jackson, who was determined to stem the tide by racing into the breach. The regulars and militiamen fleeing the breach paused and then, buoyed by the sight of their officers running past them in the opposite direction, toward the breach, turned around to rejoin the fray.

Like two shield walls at Agincourt the attackers and defenders crashed together—except that neither side had shields with which to protect themselves. It was sword to sword, pistol to pistol, knife to knife, and fist to fist. From point-blank range Richard fired his two pistols, then threw them at the Royal Marines closest to him. From a fallen Marine he snatched a sword and parried and thrust, parried and thrust, as he had learned to do many years ago on the decks of *Ranger* and then *Bonhomme Richard*. Two Marines went down, one gored in the chest, the other in the stomach. Nearby, a U.S. Army sergeant hurled himself at a Royal Navy sailor just as the sailor squeezed the trigger of a pistol. The discharge blew off half of the sergeant's face, leaving one side of a skull and broken teeth.

Reinforced by reserve units on Line Jackson, the Americans slowly pushed the British back. Some British Marines and sailors, demoralized by the clarion call of a general retreat clearly audible above the din, turned around and fled. Others laid down their arms and surrendered.

"Richard, look out!"

As Richard turned to his right toward Agreen's cry of warning, the sharp blade of a bayonet impaled him under his rib cage from the left. Through the sudden blinding stab of agony, Richard looked questioningly down at the wound and then up at the Royal Marine holding the rifle. The man was staring at him, through him, with a vacant yet sorrowful expression. As the Marine yanked back on his rifle to dislodge the blade, Agreen shot him in the side of his head.

Almost in tandem the Royal Marine and Richard slumped down onto their knees and then onto the ground. Richard felt for the wound and pressed a hand to it, astonished to find it smeared with blood when he lifted it to his eyes. He looked over at the Marine, whose eyes were now fixed on eternity, and then up at Agreen, whose stricken expression told him everything he needed to know.

"Jesus, Richard," Agreen choked out as he knelt down beside him. "Oh dear God, no!"

Richard grimaced. A deep, unrelenting pain was coursing through him, dulling his mind and senses. He was aware that death was claiming him, yet he felt no fear, no regret. Then, to his amazement, within the looming darkness there shone a light—a small one at first, a mere shaft, but expanding as if to consume the universe. It was a warm, soft, and oddly familiar light, providing immeasurable comfort in the seraphic image contained within it of one so familiar, so dearly beloved.

With all the strength he could muster, Richard gripped the arm of his lifelong friend and shipmate. "Take me home, Agee," he beseeched. "Take me home to Katherine."

The End

Historical Footnotes

The War of 1812 was a war that many historians and layper-sons maintain should never have been fought. To their minds the issues that divided the United States and Great Britain were not of sufficient import to warrant such a sacrifice of blood and treasure. Indeed, just prior to the United States declaring war, most of the key issues—impressment and sailors' rights chief among them—became moot when Great Britain rescinded the offensive Orders-in-Council and offered to make certain restitutions. Fighting for its very existence against Napoleon in Europe, Britain simply did not want to be bothered by what British politicians and war strategists viewed as a swarm of pesky mosquitoes buzzing around the lion's head.

But as is too often the case in human events, irreversible forces were already in play that made quick and painless resolution of issues nigh impossible. War Hawks in Congress and the president's cabinet were outraged that their country's honor had been impugned by the Royal Navy at sea and by British instigators stirring up trouble among Indian tribes along the frontier. The only possible resolution to such affronts, these individuals publicly remonstrated, was for the young republic to flex its muscles and prove to the world that Americans were prepared to stand up and fight for their principles, no matter the sacrifice. In more private, less vocal discourse, the same individuals rubbed their hands with delight at the prospect of invading Canada and annexing that vast territory to the United States, certain that the British were too occupied in Europe to stop them.

So war was declared, and war was waged.

With limited military resources in North America, British strategy from the onset of hostilities was to defend Canada and rely on the Royal Navy and Fate to facilitate an offensive. American strategy, by contrast, focused on invading Canada by land and fighting single-ship engagements with its handful of "superfrigates" at sea. Harassing British shipping was left to the armadas of privateers operating with letters of marque out of Baltimore and Boston and other East Coast ports.

In the two-year span of the war, a number of battles were fought as a result of these two strategies. As in most wars, some of these battles were significant and others were not. The purpose of this appendix is to provide background and historical context to certain of the lesser-known battles and events featured in this novel that nonetheless proved providential for the victor and disastrous for the loser.

— ‿ —

Whereas the battles on the Great Lakes, especially the Battle of Lake Erie (also known as the Battle of Put-In Bay), are well known to history, the ensuing Battle of the Thames (also known as the Battle of Morgantown) and the key role played in that land battle by Oliver Hazard Perry, one of this country's great naval heroes, are less known. American victories on Lake Erie and subsequently at the Thames River in Upper Canada (present-day Ontario) ended British hegemony on the Great Lakes and in the Northwest Territory. In addition, the death of Tecumseh landed a crushing blow to the Indian confederacy that the great chieftain had painstakingly and expertly forged in the years leading up to the outbreak of hostilities. After the Battle of the Thames, the Great Northwest and its base in Detroit remained quiet and secure in American hands for the duration of the war.

The Battle of Bladensburg and the subsequent burning and plunder of government buildings in Washington by the British in retaliation for the burning and plunder of their provincial capital of York (present-day Toronto) were certainly two low points of the war from the American perspective. Bladensburg was a debacle. For good reason has it been called "the greatest defeat ever dealt to American arms." The subsequent raid on, and surrender of, Alexandria, Virginia, was humiliating as well, but in this case the dark clouds contained a silver lining. Capt. James Gordon's delays in sailing his Royal Navy squadron up the Potomac and his dalliance in Alexandria bought the Americans valuable time to shore up their defenses in and around Baltimore, and led to Britain's withdrawal from the Chesapeake.

The battle for Baltimore is certainly one of the best-known engagements in the War of 1812. The heroism displayed by the soldiers, sailors, and Marines in defense of Fort McHenry is immortalized in our national anthem and is the stuff of legends. But it was the little-known Battle of North Point that set the stage for those heroics. The battlefield tactics executed by Brig. Gen. John Stricker and the Third Brigade of the Maryland State Militia gave the British a Pyrrhic victory but allowed the Americans at Hamstead Hill time to dig in and hold firm. So discouraged was Col. Arthur Brooke—the commander of the British landing force—following a sniper's assassination of the highly competent and much beloved Maj. Gen. Robert Ross that when he reached the well-fortified and heavily manned inner defenses of Baltimore, he ordered his troops back to the ships in the Chesapeake, leaving it to the vessels of Admiral Cochrane's fleet to somehow fashion a victory. As a consequence of the Battle of North Point, September 12 is today a Maryland state holiday known as Defenders Day—a holiday similar in scope and spirit to Patriots Day in Massachusetts.

The heroic action of Rebecca and Abigail Bates at Scituate Lighthouse is the stuff of legend, at least in Greater Boston. Today, a plaque erected at the lighthouse commemorates these two girls as the "American Army of Two" who dispatched a contingent of Royal Marines intent on doing harm to this coastal South Shore community.

A battle that is too often overlooked by both students and professors of history is the Battle of Plattsburgh, even though this battle is one of the most significant of the war. Commodore Macdonough's defeat of the Royal Navy squadron in Plattsburgh Bay ended once and for all the threat of a British invasion of the United States from Canada. With the Great Lakes and now Lake Champlain controlled by the Americans, the British were forever denied the lines of supply and communication essential to maintaining an army on the march. As a further footnote to this battle, the able British commander, Capt. George Downie, was killed midway through the engagement, dashing British expectations of a quick and easy victory. With his death, an American victory was nigh inevitable. Downie's flagship, HMS *Confiance*, was captured by the Americans, then taken into service by the U.S. Navy and placed in ordinary until 1820, when she was allowed to swing at her moorings. As a final footnote, the commander-in-chief of the invasion, Gen. Sir George Prévost, never admired for his aggressive tactics, failed to commit his sizable contingent of infantry and artillery to the battle, preferring instead to await the outcome on the lake. When that outcome became predictable, Prévost packed up his bags and brigades and hightailed it back to Canada.

Leaders of the Federalist Party met in Hartford, Connecticut, from December 15, 1814, to January 5, 1815. Historians are split on the role the critical issue of secession played at the convention. It is a fact that Governor Strong of Massachusetts had earlier contacted authorities in Canada to assess British interest in accepting an apologetic and separate New England back into the fold of the British Empire. And it is a fact that a number of delegates supported that initiative. But whether or not this was a serious inquiry or simply a ploy to get a rise out of Washington remains open to debate. Other suggestions were put forward in Hartford—such as petitioning Congress to expel the western states from the Union—but they quickly fizzled out. Madison and his Republican-Democratic Congress were too entrenched to seriously consider any of New England's proposals. In the end, after several weeks of intense yet ultimately fruitless discussions, the delegates returned empty-handed to their homes.

Because so much has been written about the Battle of New Orleans, not much can be added here. It was without question the most one-sided battle in the war. Glory for the overwhelming American victory rightly goes to Gen. Andrew Jackson, one of the few capable officers in the U.S. Army. However, criticism for the ignoble British defeat is heaped upon Lt. Col. Thomas Mullins, the hapless British Army officer responsible for procuring the fascines, ladders, and other siege equipment to cross the Rodriguez Canal and scale Line Jackson. The battle, however, did not end with the slaughter of thousands of Redcoats and the general call to retreat from the field. It continued for another week to the south of New Orleans at Fort Saint Philip. Despite numerous attempts to destroy the fort with mortar and rocket attacks from the same vessels that had earlier attacked Baltimore, the fort held. Unable to sail upriver, and unwilling to contemplate another frontal assault against Line Jackson without Royal Navy support, the British withdrew from America.

The whereabouts of Jean Lafitte and his brother Pierre during the Battle of New Orleans are unclear. Many historians speculate that he was at Fort Saint Philip and deserves credit for its successful defense. What history does not question is the bravery and fierce fighting that Lafitte's men exhibited during the engagement. Their material, logistical, and psychological contributions to the American cause are undeniable. And Lafitte kept his word to earn an honest living following the cessation of hostilities.

As a final footnote, what ultimately made both the Hartford Convention and the Battle of New Orleans superfluous was the signing of the Treaty of Ghent on December 24, 1814. The treaty—news of which took a month to cross the Atlantic—reestablished relations between the United States and Great Britain to *status quo ante bellum*—meaning, as they existed in June 1812. In other words, neither belligerent profited from the war. It can be argued, however, that the American victories at Plattsburgh and Baltimore dramatically affected the outcome of peace negotiations.

Moreover, it can be argued that as a result of American valor and resolve, displayed particularly by the officers and sailors of the U.S. Navy, the War of 1812 placed the fledgling United States squarely on the world stage, no longer a victim of playground bullying by other nations. France may have been defeated by the might of Great Britain, but the United States was not. Henceforth, when America took a position in world affairs, the world took careful note of that position.